PROMISE OF ZION

OTHER BOOKS/AUDIO BOOKS BY ANITA STANSFIELD:

First Love and Forever

First Love, Second Chances

Now and Forever

By Love and Grace

A Promise of Forever

When Forever Comes

For Love Alone

The Three Gifts of Christmas

Towers of Brierley

Where the Heart Leads

When Hearts Meet

Someone to Hold

Reflections: A Collection of Personal Essays

Gables of Legacy, Vol. 1: The Guardian

Gables of Legacy, Vol. 2: A Guiding Star

Gables of Legacy, Vol. 3: The Silver Linings

Gables of Legacy, Vol. 4: An Eternal Bond

Gables of Legacy, Vol. 5: The Miracle

Gables of Legacy, Vol. 6: Full Circle

Timeless Waltz

A Time to Dance

Dancing in the Light

A Dance to Remember

Barrington Family Saga Vol. 1: In Search of Heaven

Barrington Family Saga Vol. 2: A Quiet Promise

Barrington Family Saga Vol. 3: At Heaven's Door

Barrington Family Saga

VOLUME FOUR

PROMISE OF ZION

ANITA STANSFIELD

Covenant Communications, Inc.

Cover image *Hodgett Wagon Train at the Last Crossing of the North Platte* © A. D. Shaw. For more information go to www.adshaw.com.

Cover design by Jessica A. Warner, copyrighted 2008 by Covenant Communications, Inc.

Published by Covenant Communications, Inc.
American Fork, Utah

Printed in Canada
First Printing: January 2008

13 12 11 10 09 08 10 9 8 7 6 5 4 3 2 1

ISBN-13: 978-1-59811-516-1
ISBN-10: 1-59811-516-2

Acknowledgments

After thirty-something books, it seems appropriate to pause and publicly share the gratitude that continually fills me in my private life.

A special thank you to Kathryn Anderson, for making it so easy to go into the past through my journey with the Barrington family.

And to Suzanne, for giving me a retreat from my crazy life where I could find my muse.

And to my editors, Kathy and Shauna. You're the best!

Also, to everyone at Covenant, Deseret Book, and the ILDSBA, who has believed in my work and made it possible for me to share these stories with so many.

And, of course, to my wonderful family and my little army of friends—you know who you are—for standing by me and supporting me through the blessing and the burden of this remarkable gift; I know it's not always easy to be so close to the battleground, and I'm grateful for your encouragement.

Last, but never least, to my Heavenly Father and to my Savior, for Their love and sustenance, and to the Holy Ghost, for keeping me connected.

To the angels who push my handcart.

I know you're there, and without you,

these stories would never come to fruition.

We will meet again one day.

Prologue

Iowa City—1856

James Barrington walked swiftly toward where he'd left his horse tethered, then he consciously slowed his pace when an unmistakable constriction in his chest made it difficult to draw breath. By the time he got to his horse, he had to take hold of the saddle with both hands and will air into his lungs for a couple of minutes before he could find the strength to mount. Pushing away his concern over the unnerving symptoms, he paused to look back over the Mormon encampment before he headed home. The heat of late July had already dampened his clothes with sweat. His anxiety over his own health was completely overshadowed by a deep concern that weighed on his heart as he pondered the grueling process he'd seen unfold here over the past few months. Saints had arrived here from many places, already weary and bedraggled, having little or nothing to speak of, yet desperate to move on and travel another 1300 miles to the Salt Lake Valley. Their zeal and determination were admirable, even inspiring. However, the misery and hardship they had endured—and would inevitably yet endure—were difficult to observe. Many had been sleeping on the ground, with little or no shelter, frantically attempting to build their handcarts and gather supplies in preparation for the unprecedented walk to Zion. Most of them were not hearty people. They had not come from lives that had prepared them for this wilderness experience. Some had left behind fine homes and comfortable lives, giving up all they had to make this journey.

James thought of the belongings that had been discarded and left to rot, or sold for a pittance of their value in order to make room for necessary supplies in the tiny handcarts. He thought of the almost reckless preparations to set out, and he worried deeply that they would be ultimately insufficient to carry the people to their destination. He reminded himself that they had each done the best they could, given the circumstances. And their one common bond stood out boldly. Their goal of reaching Zion overrode all else because their undeniable testimonies burned in their souls. Every man, woman, and child knew beyond question that God the Father and His Son, Jesus Christ, were real and living and at the head of the Church that called to them from across continents and oceans. It was for Them that these people were willing to abandon all their worldly belongings, even their sensibility and reason, and keep traveling.

The most recent companies to set out consumed James's thoughts most of all. The people had already traveled 1700 miles before arriving in Iowa City. And the provisions to build their carts and fill them were not necessarily easy to come by. James and his family had worked hard to help these people, and he'd opened himself to the guidance of the Spirit in giving all that he could of his own financial resources. He had discreetly given a great deal, but no amount of money would purchase what wasn't available, and every ready hand working every waking hour had not been hasty enough to get the companies off any faster. But they had gone nevertheless, and James could only pray for their safe journey, while the names and faces of people he'd come to know through these weeks of preparation clung to his memory.

James rode more quickly, hoping speed would ease his troubled thoughts, but as he approached his home, his heart still felt heavy. He reminded himself that these people were in God's hands. He had done his best to do everything God required of him. Now he had to let go. And perhaps in a year's time he would once again see these people he'd come to know when they were all gathered in Zion. As for now, no more companies would be leaving until spring. It was simply too late to leave with any hope of arriving in the Salt Lake Valley before unfavorable weather set in.

Once home, James dismounted and led the horse into the barn, where he tossed some fresh straw into the animals' stalls and moved some bales of hay before he loosened the straps on the saddle and lifted it off. But his strength suddenly left him, and he felt lightheaded. He went to his knees, leaning heavily on the saddle that had gone to the ground with him. He resisted the temptation to curse aloud as a recently familiar sensation constricted his chest, as if some invisible vise surrounded his lungs, making it impossible for him to draw breath. It reminded him far too much of the experience of watching his son die of pneumonia, struggling to breathe and slowly suffocating. Except that James had no fever or infection, no coughing or pain. He simply had moments when he had trouble breathing, usually when he expended energy. The first few times it had happened, he'd brushed it off, crediting it to some sort of anomaly. The weather had been hot, and he'd been working hard. When it had continued to happen and became more difficult to ignore, he'd pondered whether or not he should discuss it with his wife. He didn't want to alarm her, but he'd just alarmed himself with it happening twice in less than an hour. Was there truly something wrong with him that would prevent him from lifting a saddle? The idea made him queasy, contributing to his lightheadedness while he slowly gathered his breath. He lowered his head farther and gripped the saddle more tightly, offering a silent prayer for strength and guidance. He had a family to care for and much work to do. And the very thought of taking his last breath without seeing Zion elicited an audible moan. It had been his only unfulfilled quest for more than a decade, and it would be many months, at the very soonest, before they could even begin their journey.

"What's wrong?" Eleanore asked, startling him. James turned to see his wife standing in the doorway, clearly distressed. The sun at her back illuminated her dark auburn hair but left her face in the shadows. It was far from the first time she'd been the answer to his prayers. She had been a source of strength and guidance in his life for as long as he'd known her. When he didn't answer, she was on her knees beside him, pressing her hands to his face. "What is it?" she asked.

James looked into her eyes and balanced his desire to keep her from worrying with his need to share his burdens. If she were struggling with something like this, he would certainly want to know about it. He finally managed to draw a deep breath and mutter hoarsely, "I'm all right now." "Now?" she echoed, her voice laced with panic.

James shifted from his knees to sit on the ground. Eleanore did the same, watching him with fear in her eyes. He put his head in her lap, certain that talking about this would be easier if he didn't have to look at her.

"Tell me what's wrong," Eleanore urged, and attempted to quell her pounding heart while she waited for him to speak. She pressed her fingers gently through his dark hair with a repetitiveness that betrayed her concern. She noted his obvious effort to take slow, steady breaths, which frightened her as much as his hesitance to say what he needed to say. He eased closer and wrapped one arm around her, as if he feared losing her.

"Tell me!" she insisted in a harsh whisper.

"Sometimes," he said, "I have trouble . . . breathing."

"Sometimes?" she asked, trying to remain calm and patient while her unexpressed thoughts were everything but. "How long has this been going on?"

"A few . . . weeks . . . maybe. I don't know. Until now . . . I really didn't think there was cause for concern. I didn't know that it was worth bringing up."

"And now?"

"Now I think there is cause for concern."

Eleanore eased gently away from him, then jumped to her feet. "You wait here. I'll get Frederick to harness the buggy. I'm taking you to a doctor *now.*"

"I'm not *that* bad off," James said, coming slowly to his feet. "Surely it can wait until—"

"We're going now," she insisted, and hurried out of the barn.

"I'll be right here," he said to no one but the animals while he brushed the dirt off his breeches.

During the drive into town, Eleanore was completely silent. James pondered a dozen different ways to open up a conversation. He finally just had to say, "Why won't you talk to me?" Still she didn't speak, and he added, "You can't be angry with me for this."

"Of course not. I'm just . . . angry."

"At who? What?"

"Nothing; no one—obviously. I realize that . . . whatever it is . . . it's just . . . one of those things that happens. But . . ." her voice cracked, "I'm scared."

"I'm scared too, but facts have to be faced."

"What facts? We don't know anything yet."

"I'm getting old, Eleanore."

"Old?" She sounded personally offended. "You're not *old.* Fifty-six is not *old.*"

He passed her a sidelong glare, then focused on the road ahead. "And you're thirty-four. Realistically, you will probably be left on your own far too long, because I'm not going to live forever."

"Not forever," she cried, and wiped her cheeks with her fingers, "but I'll not be making plans for widowhood just yet. We haven't even talked to the doctor. I'm probably getting upset for nothing."

"Probably," James said, and they both fell silent again.

This was their first visit to a doctor they'd never seen before, because the doctor who had attended them since their coming to Iowa had recently retired. He asked James many questions and did a thorough examination, listening to his heart and lungs through a stethoscope for what seemed like an hour. He finally declared, "It's difficult to know what it is, exactly. There's no way to make a conclusive diagnosis."

"Should I be concerned?" James asked.

"Not being able to breathe is certainly a concern, Mr. Barrington." His slightly condescending tone added to James's astonishment over such a statement.

"So, what *might* it be?" Eleanore asked, sounding barely patient.

"There are a number of possible illnesses that make breathing difficult, but he doesn't have the symptoms that go with those. Heart problems can make it hard to breathe, but his heart sounds fine. Truthfully, I'm not certain what it is. I would say just give it some time, and if it gets worse, perhaps we'll have more to go on."

"Just . . . give it time?" James asked, and the doctor nodded.

"Could it be fatal?" Eleanore asked.

"Not being able to breathe can certainly cause death, Mrs. Barrington," the doctor said with an edge of impatience that James had never before seen in a doctor.

Neither had he ever seen his wife turn almost visibly red with anger. He expected her to leave the room before she lost her temper. Instead she took a step closer to the doctor and snapped, "Your bedside manner is as deplorable as your inability to make an educated diagnosis. If you—"

James put a hand on her arm to quiet her. She glared at him but stopped talking.

"Doctor," James said, "is there anything I can do to keep this from getting worse?"

"If you have trouble breathing when you exert yourself, Mr. Barrington, then don't exert yourself."

His answer provoked a disgusted noise from Eleanore before she left the office, and James followed her out once he'd paid the fee. In the buggy she said, "What exactly did we pay him for?"

"I don't think I've ever seen you so angry."

"And why are you not?"

"Because getting angry would require exerting myself." He said it so calmly that it infuriated her further. "Eleanore." He shifted the reins to one hand and put his arm around her shoulders. "Listen to me. Unlike the last time my health was seriously threatened, I did not do anything irresponsible to bring this on. It just happened. And we must take it on as best we can and trust in God to guide us through this, as He has guided us through every trial we have faced. As I see it, if I'm careful and take care of myself, it could be years before it worsens enough to cause any serious trouble."

Eleanore sighed deeply. "I'm sure you're right; at least I hope you're right. But I would like the opinion of another doctor. I know there's at least one more in this city. And we won't be seeing *that one* again."

"Fair enough," James said, "but . . ."

"But what?"

"I don't want the children to know there's a problem."

"Do you think you can hide it from them?"

"Yes," he answered straightly.

"So . . . you're going to lie to your children and expect me to do the same?"

"No. If I don't exert myself, I won't have trouble, and therefore no one will notice. I don't want the children to be concerned, and I don't want anyone fussing or fretting over this—including you."

"Fair enough," Eleanore said the same way he'd said it a moment earlier. Nothing more was said throughout the drive home, but he knew she was worried. He was worried, too. But clearly there was nothing to be done about it beyond being careful.

When they returned home, a familiar horse was tethered near the house. Eleanore commented, "Oh, that nice young Brother Rollins must be here to see Iris again. I do believe he likes her very much."

"The question would be, does she like him?"

Eleanore just made a noise of agreement as she stepped down from the buggy. James went to unharness the horse, and she stopped him, saying gently, "Let Frederick do that." James scowled at her, but she added with firm tenderness, "When we lived in England, you were accustomed to having people do nearly *everything* for you. You're going to have to get used to letting people do the things that require any strain or lifting at all."

"I can unharness a horse and lead it into the barn," James growled. "I don't *want* to be the lord of the manor again, Ellie. I left that life behind a long time ago, and I much prefer this one."

"I'm not concerned about you lording over anyone, but Frederick works for you, and he's always happy to do anything you ask him. You don't have to tell the children, but I think you should tell Frederick. He's been your closest friend for years, and he can help see that you mind your health."

James exhaled slowly. She was right. He hated it, but he couldn't deny it.

"Also," she added, "the children are capable of doing a great deal. They don't need an explanation from their father in order to do a little more than you've asked of them in the past." She touched his face. "You mustn't be afraid to ask for help. Your health is the most important thing."

James nodded, nearly afraid he might cry. Already he hated this, but he *was* getting older; his life was changing, and he needed to accept it.

They were walking together toward the house when Iris's gentleman caller burst out of the door, clearly upset. James and Eleanore stopped and watched him untether his horse, then he saw them standing there. "Forgive me, sir," he said, "but your daughter is a shrew. I'll not be back." He mounted and rode away.

James and Eleanore exchanged a concerned glance and both sighed at the same time. "There goes another one," James said. "What on earth is she doing to upset these men so badly?"

"I've tried to talk to her." Eleanore sighed again. "She's quite adamant that all men—excluding her father, of course—are idiots, and she has no tolerance for their . . . how does she put it? 'Their archaic attitudes about women, and their mindless mentality.'"

"She may have a point, but I fear if she doesn't open her mind, she's going to end up a spinster and bitter for it."

"Still, she's a grown woman. We can't control her behavior."

James just sighed again and moved on toward the house, knowing he needed to find Frederick and tell him why they were going to trade off some of their regular tasks.

A few days later, James and Eleanore *did* see another doctor. He was more gracious and competent than the first doctor, and they determined that he would be the one they'd see from now on. He more or less gave them the same answers, except that he was apparently more educated when he had a name for the condition that perfectly matched James's symptoms. Asthma, he called it. The good news was that it wasn't contagious; the bad news was that there was no known treatment or cure. He gave James the same advice, to simply avoid exertion and take good care of himself. At least with two opinions they could more comfortably resign themselves to simply dealing with the matter the best that they could. Together they made it a serious matter of prayer and resolved to press forward, trusting in God, as they had always strived to do.

Chapter One

THE IMPEDIMENT

Casey Harrison guided his mare over the bridge and halted for a moment as the Barrington home came into view. Something imperceptibly warm tingled in his chest. He knew the feeling well. It had first come to him when he'd realized the missionaries harassing him actually knew what they were talking about, and he'd felt it again when he'd read the book they'd given him. He'd felt it when he'd come out of the waters of baptism, and it had come again when he'd arrived in Iowa City, where the Saints were gathering in preparation to move west.

He eased his horse forward, but slowly, taking in the two-story white house surrounded by some outbuildings as well as a thriving garden where he could see a man working. The man straightened his back and looked toward Casey as he approached and dismounted.

"May I help you?" the man asked, putting his hands on his hips. He had thick, dark hair, graying at the temples. He wore no hat, but wiped the sweat from his brow with a shirtsleeve. His accent was clearly British. They met eye to eye, which made him just over six feet tall.

"My name is Casey Harrison," he said and stepped forward to shake the man's hand. "But you can call me Case. I assume you're James Barrington."

"I am," he said.

"Brother Evans suggested I talk to you, Brother Barrington, and—"

"Please . . . call me James. I'm not fond of formality."

"Very well, sir. I—"

"Don't call me that either," James Barrington said. He was firm in his request, but not unkind.

"Right . . . James. I heard you were needing some help; that you have work available."

"There's always something that could stand to be done around here."

Case chuckled. "In other words, it's nothing urgent, but it's a great excuse to give poor souls like me the means to make some money and move on."

James Barrington tossed him an easy smirk and started pulling weeds again. Case stepped carefully over the thriving vegetables and started doing the same on a different row. "Clearly I can't hire every poor soul," James said. "Do you have family?"

"Just me."

"If Brother Evans sent you, I assume you're heading to Salt Lake."

"That's right."

James kept weeding and asked, "Where do you come from?"

"Texas, originally. I was visiting my brother on the East Coast when the missionaries found me." James glanced at him, and Casey added, "That *was* the next question, wasn't it?"

"It's on the list somewhere," James said. His eyes smiled before he focused again on his work. "Tell me about your family."

"My parents have both passed on. I have two brothers. Only one is still living. He's a big-city lawyer. He's married, got some kids. I admire him. He worked hard to get where he is. It's not easy to be a kid fighting to survive on a farm with a dad who drinks too much. But he earned his way through school, and he's doing great. I wasn't so noble, I'm afraid. I was a little too much like my dad until I found that amazing book."

Case wondered if this man would be put off by his confessions, but he wouldn't be anything less than honest with him. If he was going to work for him, he didn't want any secrets. He felt some relief when James said, "It *is* an amazing book, isn't it. You're clearly strong enough to do the things I'm getting too old to do. The job is yours if you want it. You can stay in the attic room of the extra house there." He nodded toward it, and Case took notice of the quaint structure just off the big house.

"I can sleep in the loft of the barn. I don't need such—"

"The attic apartment isn't much to speak of, but it's adequate, and it's sitting empty," James said. "You might as well use it; just keep it in order." He pointed to the saddlebags and bedroll on the horse. "Is that all you've got?"

"That's it. I travel light."

"If you need anything, let me know. You can probably figure out what needs to be done. If not, ask. You can join the family for meals if you can tolerate the noise, but I should warn you about my daughter."

Case chuckled again. "You're *warning* me?"

"I'll be frank with you, Case. She's brokenhearted and crusty. She's feisty, and she'll accuse me of hiring someone like you to try to get her married."

"And did you?"

James let out a quiet laugh. "If she'll have you, I'll kiss your feet."

A challenge. Case was liking this job more by the minute. James Barrington's daughter might never *have* him, but the quest could be very entertaining. He didn't feel nearly ready to be looking for a wife when he was still trying to catch up with his new way of living. But he was always up for a challenge.

"Is she pretty?" he asked, mostly in an attempt at humor while he continued to pull weeds.

"Far too pretty for her own good, in my opinion." James straightened his back and stretched it. "But she's got a good heart and a strong spirit." Case saw him nod and wave. He turned to look over his shoulder to see two women sitting on the side porch, who both waved back. One was dark, the other blonde, both clearly pretty. This job was getting better by the moment.

"So, which daughter should I be wary of?" he asked.

Case sensed astonishment from his new employer and turned to look at him. He saw a sparkle of humor in his eyes that contradicted the subtle growl in his voice. "The dark one is my wife. If you flirt with *her,* I'll have to give you a bloody nose." Case felt his eyes go wide and James Barrington added, "Yes, she's much closer to your age than mine, but she's very much taken. For some strange reason, she loves me."

"No worries, then," Case said, and James smiled, first at him, then at his wife. His daughter was looking elsewhere.

"Come along," James said and stepped carefully out of the garden. "We might as well get this over with."

Case followed James Barrington toward the house, unable to keep from watching this already renowned daughter as they approached. She was the most beautiful woman he'd ever seen. In fact, if she weren't moving, he might believe she was a doll in a store window. But a quick glance into her eyes had confirmed what her father had said. He wondered if it might be possible to break past her crusty, broken heart, then he wondered if it was best left to some other conqueror. Maybe he wasn't up to such a challenge, and maybe that was for the best.

As they stepped onto the porch, both women took him in inquisitively.

"Hello," Sister Barrington said, offering a friendly smile.

"Hello," Case replied. The daughter said nothing, and again turned her eyes away.

"This is Casey . . ." James hesitated and motioned toward him, apparently having forgotten the rest.

"Harrison," Case provided.

"Yes, Casey Harrison," he said.

"But call me Case."

"That's right," James said. "Case is going to be working here for a while."

"How nice," Sister Barrington said, but the daughter turned astonished eyes toward her father, then Case, then her father again. She was angry over what she'd just been told, and Case wondered what he might be stepping into.

"Case," James said, "this is my wife, Eleanore, and my daughter, Iris."

"A pleasure," Case said, nodding toward the mother, who smiled again, then the daughter, who boldly ignored him.

"Where do you come from, Case?" Eleanore asked, sounding genuinely interested. And her use of his given name made it evident she shared her husband's informal attitude.

"Back east," Case said, and gave her the same brief explanation he'd given her husband.

"He's going to stay in the attic room," James informed his wife.

"That's perfect," Eleanore said. Then she repeated her husband's offer when she added, "Now if you need anything—anything at all—you be sure to let us know." This provoked a glare from Iris toward her mother, although Case couldn't figure that this woman could literally be Iris's mother. He felt certain there was a unique story behind this family. He couldn't help wondering what it might be. While he had a desire to get to know James and Eleanore better, avoiding Iris seemed the best possible option; still, he had to admit being curious over the reasons for her overt lack of hospitality.

James said to his daughter, "Iris, why don't you get Lizzie and see that the attic room is tolerable to be occupied."

"Oh, that's not necessary," Case hurried to say, but Iris was already on her way into the house.

"It's not a problem," James insisted with a smile, but Case knew Iris disagreed. "Come along," he added, motioning toward the door. "We'll show you around, then you can get settled in."

"Thank you, sir," Case said, and James gave him a kindly scowl. "James," he corrected with a chuckle.

Case followed them toward the door, then hesitated. "Is something wrong?" Eleanore asked, looking back at him.

"I'm just . . . dirty from traveling, and—"

"Don't you worry about that," Eleanore said. "Just come in and make yourself at home."

"Thank you, ma'am," he said and stepped tentatively into the house, holding his hat in his hands. Eleanore and James *both* scowled at him and he corrected, "Eleanore."

James took hold of Case's arm, as if he sensed his resistance, and guided him into the kitchen where two women were chatting more than working. One was younger than the other, with red, curly hair. The other woman's hair was completely gray; they both wore it back in a bun. James introduced the older one as Stella, who greeted him kindly with an Irish accent. The other was Lizzie, who was clearly British. They were both very kind, and apparently they were pleased to have him there. Eleanore explained that Lizzie and her husband, Frederick, had come with them from England many years ago, and Stella had joined their household more recently. Stella had been hired mostly for her cooking skills. Lizzie just helped wherever she was needed. He learned that Lizzie and Frederick and their daughter, Mary Jane, lived in the little house beneath the apartment where he would be staying.

While they all chatted comfortably in the kitchen for a few minutes, Case took in James and Eleanore Barrington all over again. They were dressed so simply and behaved so humbly that he was startled to realize they were people with money. Not only did they have a fine home, but they had more hired help than most people, and throughout the conversation it became evident that James Barrington did no farming or any other manner of business that would produce an income. His respect for these people deepened, not because they were wealthy, but because they didn't act wealthy—at least not the way other wealthy people he'd known had acted.

As they headed out of the kitchen, Eleanore said to Case, "Now, don't be thinking you need to knock at the door if you need to come in to the house. The kitchen is always open to you, and you need to make yourself at home."

"That's really not necessary," Case said. "I'm more than happy with—"

"Don't argue with her, Case. As long as you clean up after yourself, she'll not have it any other way."

"Yes, ma'am . . . Eleanore," Case said.

He was briefly shown the parlor at the front of the house, and the library across the hall, where there were more books than he'd ever seen in one place. There was also a large desk and a couch, and he was told that he would often find James and Eleanore there, should he ever need to speak with them. They invited Case to sit down in the library and visit for a few minutes. Again he felt hesitant, and again Eleanore assured him that his dusty clothes were not a concern. They asked him many questions about himself, apparently more out of genuine interest than any kind of concern about his background. They were especially interested in his conversion to the gospel.

While they were sitting there, Case heard a door open in the distance, followed by a loud chorus of children talking and laughing.

"Oh, my," Eleanore said with a chuckle, "they're back from their walk. I knew the peace wouldn't last long."

"It never does," James said lightly just before three boys rushed into the room in search of their parents. Taking in the evidence that they'd been outdoors playing, Case felt a little better about his dusty clothes. He watched with amusement as the boys all tried to talk at once, reporting their adventures in the woods. Only when they'd told their tales did they notice a stranger present. James introduced Case to their three dark-haired sons, who all looked like James or Eleanore to some degree—and nothing like Iris. Jamie was eleven, Isaac nine, and Joseph seven. They were all handsome boys with a lot of energy. They reminded Case of himself and his brothers and the few good memories he had of his own childhood. He couldn't help but smile as he observed their antics before they ran off again to play.

Not a minute later, a young woman with red, curly hair appeared, and Case knew she belonged to Lizzie even before she was introduced as Frederick and Lizzie's daughter, Mary Jane, who was almost sixteen. In her arms was a little girl who looked sleepy. Mary Jane had apparently been in charge of listening for the baby while she'd been napping.

"And this is Mariah," James said, standing to take the child from Mary Jane. "She's two."

"And very attached to her father," Eleanore said as Mariah snuggled into James's shoulder. She had dark hair, but even at a glance, Case could see that she resembled Iris.

"Do you need anything else right now?" Mary Jane asked.

"No thank you, sweetie," Eleanore said. "Did you finish that book yet?"

"Not yet," Mary Jane said, "but almost."

"Then you'd best get back to it," James said. Mary Jane smiled and hurried away.

"Now you've met almost everyone," James said. Case took a silent tally, trying to recall everyone's names. He'd not yet seen Frederick, although his name had come up a few times. He wondered if there was anyone else. Already it felt overwhelming. But delightfully so.

They continued talking while Mariah got over her sleepiness and became as full of energy as her brothers. The conversation was finally halted when Eleanore said, "Oh, look at the time. Supper will be on in an hour. We should give you some time to settle in and freshen up."

"Just make yourself at home," James said, "and we'll see you in the kitchen in about an hour."

"Thank you . . . for everything," Case said and left the library, easily finding his way to the back door. As he considered the happenings of the last hour, he felt a little heady. It all seemed too good to be true.

* * * * *

Iris heard the back door close and moved to her bedroom window to see Casey Harrison leading his horse into the barn. He removed his hat just before he disappeared, exposing his sand-colored, wavy hair to the sun. She stood there stewing over this new impediment in her life until she saw him come out a few minutes later carrying a bedroll, with saddlebags over his shoulder, which apparently constituted everything he owned. She watched him go up the stairs to the attic apartment, then she hurried to find her parents in the library. She found them sitting close together on the sofa, holding hands, talking quietly, a scene that was highly common. She knocked on the open door, and they both turned toward her.

"Am I interrupting something important?"

"Of course not," Eleanore said. "Come in."

"What can we do for you, precious?" her father asked.

Iris got straight to the point. "Forgive me if I'm being blunt, but . . . you're doing it again, Papa."

"Doing what?" he asked, genuinely baffled, which infuriated her further. But she knew expressing anger to her parents would get her nowhere.

"You bring these . . . strangers . . . into our home . . . off the streets, and before you know anything about them, they're practically a part of the family . . . as if . . ."

"As if what?" her mother asked when she hesitated.

"As if you can just . . . trust them with nothing whatsoever to go on."

Iris saw her father lean forward, and his eyes took on a familiar intensity that came with concern. "Sit down, Iris," he said.

"I don't want to sit down. I—"

"Sit down, Iris," he repeated, and she knew he really meant to say, *Relax and stay calm.* Iris sat down across the room from them, and

James said, "I see no reason to mistrust someone until they give me cause to do so. And I—"

"But you know nothing about him, and—"

"I wasn't finished," he said with kind firmness, and she reminded herself to relax and stay calm, or she would only make a fool of herself—if she hadn't already. "He shares our religious beliefs, Iris, and I—"

"You can't automatically assume that he's a good man just because he's a Mormon. If he—"

"Iris!" James said in a stern voice he used rarely, but it certainly got her attention. "Is there a reason you won't let me finish a sentence?" Iris wrung her hands and looked away, searching for a suitable answer. Before she could come up with one, he added, "What's really going on here?"

Iris knew there was no skirting of issues with her parents. Honesty was the only option. "You're doing it again," she repeated.

"Doing *what?"* he asked again.

"It feels like you're . . . matchmaking, Papa."

James sighed and leaned back on the couch. She sensed that he wasn't completely surprised by her accusation, but he'd wanted her to admit to her feelings. "He came to me for a job, Iris. I didn't go hand-pick him because he has broad shoulders and a nice smile."

"Oh, he *does* have a smile," Eleanore said in a voice that was almost dreamy.

Iris saw her father toss his wife a comical scowl before he looked directly at her and said, "I have every reason to believe that Casey is a fine young man who is willing to work hard. Give me some credit for having a degree of discernment, Iris. If I'd felt any negative inclination toward him, I wouldn't have hired him. If he gives us any trouble, I'll let him go."

"And in the meantime?" Iris asked.

"In the meantime?" James echoed. "What does that mean? What do you think he'll do, Iris? Ransack the house and steal the silver?"

"Maybe," she said, knowing it sounded ridiculous.

"Then we'll buy more silver," James said. "There's little in this house that won't get left behind when we leave, anyway. Everything of real value is in the safe." James sighed again. "But that's not what's really bothering you, is it?"

Iris didn't comment, and Eleanore said gently, "What is it, Iris? You know you can talk to us about anything."

"I know," she murmured. "I just . . . well, I suppose I would just prefer that you hire people who are not single men of marriageable age. How can I not think that you have ulterior motives when marrying me off must surely be high on your list of priorities?"

Iris saw her father's eyes widen and felt sure he was angry. But his voice was even as he said, "My concern about your finding a proper husband in order to be happy could not remotely be described as 'marrying you off.' While I may joke about it occasionally, you should know me better than that."

Iris had to say, "Yes, I do. I'm sorry."

"Now, why don't you let us worry about Case, and you can worry about avoiding him as much as possible, if you so choose."

Iris left the room and hurried back upstairs while images of having him at the table for every meal came to mind. This was the fourth man of marriageable age that her father had hired and brought into their home since the Mormons had come to Iowa City. And there had been a number of others who had come and gone, doing odd jobs. The other three who had actually lived here for short periods of time had been nice enough, but they had all shown way too much interest in her, and she'd never felt comfortable around any of them. She knew these men had come to her father for work, and he was right when he said he didn't go hand-pick them as possible suitors. It just seemed like too much of a coincidence that all the men he hired were between the ages of twenty-five and forty—and single. She guessed that Casey Harrison was somewhere around thirty, and he *did* have broad shoulders and a nice smile. He also had riveting blue eyes that unnerved her just to think of them. It wouldn't be so bad to have hired hands around if her father didn't insist on their being a part of every family activity. She knew this newcomer would not only be present for every meal, he would also be there for family prayer, scripture reading, and anything they might do for fun. Avoiding him would be impossible, and ignoring him would be difficult. But she was determined to try. She considered him nothing more than an inconvenience in her life, and she wanted nothing to do with him. There was something in the way he'd looked at her that had left her uneasy, even if she couldn't explain it. She told herself that he would move on, as the others had done, but the last companies of the year had already set off for Salt Lake. No one would be leaving until spring, which meant that Casey Harrison would be here for many months—unless he did something to earn her father's disapproval. She could hope for *that.* Maybe if she were lucky, he *would* ransack the house and steal the silver.

* * * * *

Case entered the attic apartment and let out a spark of laughter. It *was* too good to be true. The furnishings were simple, but far more than he'd ever had in the whole of his life. Even when he'd been staying in his brother's home, there had been no room for him in the house, and he had slept in the loft of the stable. He couldn't remember the last time he'd slept on a real bed, and couldn't recall *ever* receiving such a warm welcome from anyone, anywhere. It was *definitely* too good to be true. But he was almost getting used to the growing list of blessings that were pouring into his life since he'd taken hold of the gospel and changed his ways. He laughed again as he put his few belongings into the empty dresser drawers, then he washed up with the ample supply of clean water that had been left for him. He put on his other set of clothes, grateful they were clean, since he'd laundered them just yesterday in the river. He didn't want to show up to dinner with this fine family, looking—or smelling—less than his very best. He concluded that once he was able to earn a little money, he needed to invest in some new clothes. It was nice to feel like they could be put to good use.

Case was buttoning his shirt when he heard a knock at the door. He pulled his suspenders up over his shoulders and answered it to see a young man, only slightly shorter than Case, but clearly lean and strong. He looked barely more than a boy, yet almost a man. And he looked nothing like anyone Case had met so far.

"Hi," he said with a kind smile and handed Case a stack of clean linens. He felt a little confused, since there had been clean towels in the room already, and he'd been told that the bed had been left with clean sheets.

"Hi," Case replied.

"My mother wanted to make sure you had plenty of what you need."

"Thank you," Case said and set the linens on the bed before he held out a hand. "Call me Case."

"Hello, Case," the boy said and returned his handshake firmly. "I'm Ben . . . Barrington." He added the last as if he sensed Case's curiosity over whether he belonged to the family, or if the mother who had sent him was among hired help. He then said, "And no, I don't look like the rest of them because I was adopted. I'm sure you're wondering, because everyone does." He said it with confidence and good nature, and Case immediately liked him.

Case couldn't help feeling curious over what circumstances brought Ben into this family, but he only said, "It's great to meet you, Ben."

"And you. Do you have what you need?"

"More than ample," Case assured him.

"I'll see you at supper, then," Ben said and left. Case closed the door and chuckled to himself. He wondered if there was anyone else he'd not met.

Case felt a little nervous as he approached the back door of the house. He felt tempted to knock, the same way he was continually tempted to be formal with these people who insisted on being informal. He recalled Eleanore's admonition *not* to knock, and he felt sure that everyone was far too busy to answer the door every time he needed to come in. He stepped inside and was quickly drawn to the source of many voices engaged in conversation and laughter. He stood in the doorway of the kitchen, completely unnoticed, while children and adults alike moved around the kitchen and in and out of the dining room next to it, all working together to put the meal on. Even James Barrington was in the midst of the bustle, when Case might have expected him to be seated at the table waiting for his supper. Instead, he was at the sink helping the little ones wash their hands; then he carried a platter of sliced bread into the dining room. Case took note of each person and was pleased to recall everyone's name, and he didn't see any faces he'd not already met. And only one that had been anything less than kind and gracious to him. Iris was holding Mariah on her hip while she told two of her brothers to go out to the summer kitchen and help Frederick and Stella bring the rest of the food into the house. Case realized then that there *was* a summer kitchen where the food had been cooked in order to keep the heat out of the house. As Jamie and Isaac passed by him to go outside, everyone was made aware of his presence.

"Oh, hello!" Eleanore said. "Do you have everything you need?"

"Very much so," he said, barely resisting the urge to call her ma'am. "Thank you."

Iris tossed him a cool glance and took her sister into the dining room.

"Come and sit down," James insisted.

"Can I help with something?" Case asked, not wanting to be waited on.

"It's all under control," James said, ushering him to the large dining table in the next room. "I assure you that you'll earn your keep, but I don't want you to keep the children from doing what's expected of them."

"Right," Case said, and took a seat when James did. Iris ignored him while she put Mariah into a high chair near their father. Within a minute, the entire meal appeared on the table, and the twelve chairs around it became occupied. The last to sit down was Frederick, and Case stood to shake his hand when he introduced himself. Frederick then sat beside Lizzie and pressed a kiss to her cheek the same moment that Eleanore reached across the corner of the table and took her husband's hand. James sat at one end of the long table, and Frederick the other, as if they were somehow equals in this unique household, although it was evident that Frederick worked for James. Case looked over the group once again. There was barely room for the twelve people seated around the table to eat comfortably. Twelve people plus a high chair, all a part of the same household, all living like family. And here he was in the midst of it, as if he'd been there forever. He glanced quickly at each face, and again he had to note that he felt nothing negative except from Iris, who just happened to be seated directly across from him.

Case was distracted from his thoughts when James asked Ben if he would offer the blessing on the food. Before the prayer began, they all took hands around the table. He found it difficult to remain composed as Lizzie took one of his hands, smiling at him as she did, and Ben took the other. He pondered his feelings during the course of the prayer, amazed at how prone to emotion he'd become since he'd discovered the Book of Mormon and all it represented. Before then he couldn't ever remember getting chills on his arms, or warmth in his spirit, or tears in his eyes. He'd not cried since some obscure day in his childhood when his father had hit him for doing so. But tears had come back to him as he'd read that most precious book, and now they came to him frequently. His presence at such an event as the blessing on the food among such a family stirred that tingling in his eyes; his efforts at keeping his emotions under control became especially difficult when Ben expressed gratitude for having Case with them, and prayed that he would be richly blessed in his life. Once the amen was spoken, Case hurriedly blinked back his tears and muttered a quiet thank you to Ben, who just shrugged and said quietly, "It's good to have you here." He leaned a little closer and added, "I think I can appreciate what it's like to be taken in by such good people." Case gave him an inquisitive gaze, wanting him to expound on that. Ben just smiled and said, "Some other time."

"So, Case," Frederick said while food was being passed systematically around the table, "I've been filled in a little about you. How long since you were baptized . . . if you don't mind my asking?"

"Not at all," Case said. "It's the greatest thing that's ever happened to me." He cleared his throat subtly. "Three weeks, and . . . four days."

Everyone was obviously amazed. Eleanore commented, "No wonder you're still practically glowing."

"Am I?" Case asked, not certain exactly what she meant.

"Oh, yes," Lizzie declared. "It shows in your eyes."

"So, what exactly have you been doing for the last three weeks and four days?" James asked.

"Traveling to Iowa," Case said, not certain he liked having so much attention on himself. "I was told this was where I would find people who shared my beliefs, and where I would also find the means to get to Salt Lake. So I set out. I just got here yesterday."

"Well, we're glad you're here," Eleanore said, and several voices agreed with her.

Inspired by their candor, Case had to admit, "I never imagined being so blessed." He happened to glance at Iris as he said it, but he saw something skeptical, perhaps disbelieving, in her eyes. He couldn't begin to imagine what she was thinking—and why she would be so cynical when everyone else was so gracious.

Case was relieved when the conversation veered away from him. While he enjoyed some of the best food he'd ever eaten, he was amused to hear every person at the table report the happenings of their day, accompanied by a great deal of gentle teasing and friendly banter. He was relieved to note that the family wasn't too serious, and they certainly weren't stuffy. Except for Iris. She hardly said a word. To look at her now, he could only think that she *was* serious and stuffy. He wondered how anyone could live this kind of a life and carry such an attitude. But he chose to ignore her and enjoy the other people at the table. The three younger boys were hilarious without trying to be, and Mariah was very entertaining with her funny words and her tendency to play in her food.

When supper was over, Case followed the example of the others and carried his dishes into the kitchen to wash them. Apparently everyone washed what they'd used, then each pitched in for another few minutes, and the majority of the meal was cleaned up very quickly. He was then invited to join them on the side porch, which was apparently common on summer evenings. While the children played in the yard, the adults visited comfortably—except for Iris, who was nowhere to be seen. When it began to get dark, they all went into the parlor where they read from the scriptures, and Iris showed up for that. Then the entire group knelt together for prayer, again joining hands in a circle. And again Case found it difficult not to start crying. He'd never imagined that a family such as this existed; or perhaps he'd imagined it, but had never really believed that it could be possible. This moment, in contrast to what he'd grown up with, made him wonder if he'd stumbled directly into heaven. He couldn't imagine why God would be so merciful as to lead *him* of all people to such a glorious second chance. Rather than trying to answer the question, he simply reveled in the experience and counted himself blessed.

Chapter Two
PRECIOUS IRIS

The following morning, Case rose from the best night's sleep he'd had in years—perhaps ever—and hurried out to the barn to get something accomplished that might meagerly contribute to being given such glorious boarding. The sun was barely peering over the horizon when Ben showed up to find Case already pitching fresh hay into the animals' stalls.

"Hey, that's my job," Ben said, trying to pretend he was angry.

"Beat you to it," Case replied, and they both chuckled.

Together they cared for the animals, milked the cows, gathered the eggs, and did some extra tidying in the barn. That's when Case realized there were four covered wagons lined up, side by side, in a section separate from where the animals were kept. He paused for just a moment, wondering if it meant what it seemed to mean. Ben read his mind when he said, "All packed and ready to go; have been for years. We rotate the food supplies so they won't spoil. We're a big family, so we're going to need every bit of what four wagons can carry to get us 1300 miles."

Case felt a little taken aback. He had no trouble understanding the desire to go to Salt Lake. But he was a lone man with nothing. It had been easy to head west; he had nothing to leave behind and nothing to lose. But these people had a beautiful home and every luxury they could ever want or need. Were they truly planning to leave it all behind? Of course they were. That was evident. But he had to ask, "Why haven't you left before now?"

Ben stopped what he was doing to stand beside Case and stare at the stationary wagons. "They wanted to join the Saints long before I came along. But every time they prayed about it, they always got the answer to stay here. Until this last spring, we were the only Mormons in the area. It's been hard. But now we know we were meant to be here to help others going west from here. We'll be going next spring unless the Lord lets us know there's a reason for us to stay longer."

Case could think of at least a dozen questions he wanted to ask, but the most prominent was, "And when was that, exactly . . . when you came along?" He hurried to clarify, "You don't have to answer that if it's too nosy. My mother always said my curiosity made her crazy."

"Doesn't bother me," Ben said. "I was ten when James Barrington helped bury both my parents in the same grave; that was nine years ago last winter. Then he brought me home with him and gave me a life better than I'd ever imagined possible. And he gave me his name."

Case felt stunned. Again he had to choose words from a barrage of different thoughts. "And that's what you meant last night at the dinner table . . . about being taken in by such good people."

"That's what I meant," Ben said and went back to moving bales of hay from one place to another.

Case resumed helping him and asked, "How did your parents die . . . if you don't mind my asking?"

"Exposure . . . at Winter Quarters." He said it as if that should explain everything, but Case had no idea what he was talking about. Ben kept working and added, "I believe they lost as many as a thousand during that time."

Case's stomach tightened. What was he saying? "Forgive me," he said, "but . . . I don't understand. They?"

Ben stopped and looked at him, puzzled. "You don't know, do you?"

"Know what?"

Ben chuckled, but it was more in disbelief than any hint of mockery. "Sit down," Ben said. "We're way ahead of schedule." Case sat on a bale of hay, and Ben sat to face him, pulling off his gloves. "I guess you haven't had enough time among the Mormons to hear the stories."

"Apparently not," Case said, clearly apprehensive about what he might hear, but still more confused than anything. Too impatient to wait for a lengthy explanation, he asked, "What do you mean by exposure, Ben? Forgive my ignorance, but . . . exposure to what?"

"The cold. Most of the deaths could be traced back to that, one way or another. Winter Quarters was a temporary community where Brother Brigham gathered the Saints to prepare to go west. By the time everyone had evacuated Nauvoo, it was too late in the year to set out. Our journey from Nauvoo was long and cold, and my parents never recovered."

"Nauvoo?" Case asked.

"That's the city we built out of the swamp after we'd been driven from Missouri. We built a temple there, but we had to leave it behind—again."

As Ben's meaning began to sink in, Case felt literally ill. He listened in horrified awe to a brief version of the story of the great Mormon exodus, being forced and driven from one place to another, with lives being lost all along the way. Case had only known the Saints were gathering in the west because their numbers were becoming so great that they needed a place with a lot of space to grow and be together. While that was true, it was now evident they had been forced to go far into the frontier to be free of the unspeakable persecution that had followed them. Case learned that Ben had also lost each of his four siblings at different stages of the horror. And he recited the stories with no trace of bitterness or anger. Case stopped trying to hold back his tears and just let them flow. And Ben just kept talking. He concluded his tale by saying, "Father tells me that my survival—and my losses—are like some kind of symbol of the faith of our people." He chuckled. "I don't know about that, but . . . I do know that our blessings in the next life will be in proportion to what we have suffered for our faith."

"Then you will surely be greatly blessed."

"I've already been greatly blessed," Ben said. "I've often wondered why I would be left behind. And I've wondered why I was privileged enough to be rescued, while so many others continued to suffer. I've never known cold or hunger since I was brought here. For that alone I am deeply grateful." He looked directly at Case. "So, what's your story?"

Case chuckled tensely and wiped away his tears. "My story is nothing."

"I wouldn't say that," Ben said. "I know that look in your eyes. You don't sit at the supper table and look as if you've gone to heaven if you haven't been through hell."

"Hell is relative, I suppose."

"I suppose. For me, it seemed worse after it was over than it was when we were in the middle of it. God gave us strength and buffered our pain. But it wasn't that way for you, was it?"

Case chuckled again, amazed at this boy's insight and wisdom. He could only say, "I had no inkling of God at all until a month ago. I'm still feeling like I've barely come to life, and I often have no idea what to do . . . or how to behave . . . when I've spent my entire life being somebody completely different."

"Well," Ben smiled, "this is a great place to learn such things." He stood up and briefly put a hand on Case's shoulder. "He'll show up any minute. I think we should look busy."

"Right," Case said, and they went back to work, saying nothing for several minutes. Case was grateful for the silence, which allowed his thoughts to catch up just a little bit with everything he'd just learned.

As Ben had predicted, James appeared in the barn. He took a look around and said, "I might as well go back to bed."

"You might as well," Ben said.

Breakfast in the Barrington home helped Case begin to accept that being here was not a dream. He just quietly took it all in, while his mind mulled over the things Ben had told him that had happened to people who shared his newfound faith. He couldn't believe it! He wondered for a moment if he had the faith to remain true in the face of such horrors, then he recalled the deep conviction that had brought him this far and the mighty change of heart that had occurred within himself. And he knew beyond any doubt that he would do anything—*anything*—that God required of him, if only to know that he could hold that kind of peace and joy in his heart for eternity.

After breakfast, Case returned to the barn to finish the task he'd started. He'd not been there long when James came in and said, "I'd like you to drive Eleanore in to town." Case still hadn't gotten used to hearing this man, who had such an air of refinement, be so casual with given names with someone who was little more than a stranger.

"I need some things picked up that are too heavy for her to handle, but she needs to take care of a couple of errands herself. And I promised the boys I'd take them fishing this morning. Harness the wagon." He motioned toward a buckboard that was parked next to the buggy and separate from the wagons waiting to travel to Zion. "She'll be ready soon." On his way out of the barn, he stopped and took hold of Case's arm, looking him closely in the eye. "Take good care of her."

"I will," Case said.

Alone in the barn, he did as he'd been told, wondering over this display of trust from James Barrington. He knew well enough that the man didn't take the care of his wife and children lightly. He also knew that Eleanore Barrington was likely only a few years older than himself, and she looked young for her age. Would people see their being together for what it was—or read something into it that might create a challenge? He reminded himself that he was a hired hand, and he should simply do what he was told and stop trying to analyze it.

Case barely had the wagon harnessed when Eleanore Barrington appeared, looking lovely as usual.

"Good morning," she said brightly, and he helped her onto the seat.

"Good morning," he replied and sat beside her, taking the reins in hand.

They were barely past the house when she stated each stop they needed to make in town, and how to go about it in order to accomplish their errands quickly. Then she asked him about himself, but he didn't have much to tell her that he cared to talk about. He used the opportunity of some quiet between them to say, "Might I ask you a question?"

"Of course. Anything."

"Anything?"

"Well," she laughed softly, "if I don't care to answer it, I'll certainly tell you."

"Right." He laughed as well. "I'm glad to know that, because . . . I guess you could say I'm curious by nature, and sometimes I'd do well to keep my questions to myself."

"No, it's fine. Ask away."

"Your husband's a good man; I like him."

"Yes, he is," she said. "And I like him too. But that's not a question."

"I just can't help wondering why he's so firm on using given names. You people hardly know me, but he insists I use given names. I've just never known anyone like that. Even with the members, it's *brother* this or *sister* that, but . . ."

"There is a logical explanation," she said. "And there's a personal one that deepens his conviction on the matter."

"Maybe we should stick to the logical one."

"Do you know one of the greatest concepts at the foundation of this country?" Case felt intrigued and just waited for her to answer her own question. "It's that all men are created equal. My husband is firm on that being *mankind* and therefore it includes women as well. One of his biggest reasons for coming to this country was to be free of social distinctions. He doesn't believe that money or education or any other form of status puts one man above another."

"But . . . I'm working for him . . . and much younger. It only seems right that I address him in a way that shows my respect."

"Yes, and your respect is something he will require. But as long as you give it, and never break trust with him, he will always give it in return. Still, he wants it clear that you are equals and there is no differentiation."

Case still had trouble with this. "But . . . he's so much more educated than I am. He's refined and . . ."

"You're missing the point, Case. Whatever opportunities he may have had in his upbringing that were different from yours do not make any difference in God's eyes. He was firm on this before he became a member of the Church. In addressing other members as *brother* or *sister,* he still prefers given names. You'll notice he shows respect to others where it's appropriate. But in reference to himself and his family, he's adamant about using given names."

"Well . . . all right." Case chuckled. "It's a great principle, but I'm still a little baffled as to why he's so firm on it." He noted her expression and asked, "Does that fall under the personal part?"

"Perhaps. But I don't mind telling you, and I'm certain he wouldn't mind your knowing. But he might not appreciate your bringing it up."

"Whatever you feel is best. I'm not going to pry, Sister Barrington, or—"

"Eleanore," she corrected.

"While we're in town I think I'll keep it formal, if that's all right with you."

"Whatever you feel is best," she repeated, and he smiled at her. "It's no great secret, Case—at least not at our house—that my husband is an English lord."

Case felt astonished—and confused. "What does that mean, exactly?"

"He is titled, although becoming an American makes that title irrelevant. But in England, it was highly significant. He's an aristocrat."

"Wow." He let that soak in. "Really?"

"Really. He owned an enormous estate and a manor house larger than any structure I have seen since I've come to America."

"And servants?"

"Many of them; too many for him to know all their names. He was treated like royalty in that house."

"Unbelievable," Case muttered, then chuckled. "And Iris remembers living this way?"

"She does," Eleanore said. "She had a nanny and a governess and maids right and left. And she had enough clothes and toys for ten little girls."

"But it was all left behind."

"Most of it. We wanted to be Americans."

There were dozens of other questions Case wanted to ask, but he held back, not wanting to be too nosy—especially in regard to Iris. They drove in silence for a few minutes while Case wondered why his mind would be drawn to Iris so frequently. She *was* beautiful. And, of course, what her father had said about her had certainly left him intrigued. But he was likely most curious over how a woman could be raised by James and Eleanore Barrington and have such a chip on her shoulder. He would have preferred to remain indifferent, but had to admit that he wasn't. Maybe he simply wanted to gain her respect, or perhaps her trust. Both had been given out freely from every other member of the household. But perhaps he'd *never* get either from Iris Barrington, and he'd be a fool to try—or to care.

The errands in town went smoothly, and on the way home Eleanore told him the story of her own conversion—and her husband's. Mingled into it was the story of their getting married and coming to America, and their reasons for staying in Iowa City so long when the rest of the Saints had been gathering elsewhere. Case was certainly grateful they had. He felt something almost magical being among this family, and he was glad to know that God would love him enough to give him such a great blessing.

Back at the house, Case helped Eleanore down from the buckboard, and he carried her purchases into the house for her. Then he returned to the barn to unload the feed and supplies from the wagon until Jamie ran out to tell him it was time for lunch. Entering the kitchen, it became immediately evident that this meal was more rushed and simple than breakfast or supper. Stella had a plate of sandwiches set out, and Case followed Frederick's example of taking one with him in a napkin once the blessing had been spoken. He went back to the barn and managed to keep himself busy there for a couple of hours, then he started pulling weeds around the perimeter of the house while the children worked with their father in the garden. He got one side of the house done, then chopped wood until it was time to get cleaned up for supper. James announced in the midst of the conversation that the following day, everyone who wasn't needed to cook or watch the children would be painting the outside of the barn. He'd had the paint for weeks and was determined to get it done. The plan was to start on the west side in the morning and see how fast they could go.

The following morning, once the usual chores and breakfast were finished, Case found everyone near the barn except for Stella and Eleanore and the two youngest children. James gave instructions, told Frederick he was in charge, then walked away.

"Where are you going?" Iris demanded, with a hint of humor in her voice.

"I'm sitting this one out, precious," he said with no apology. Case realized then that James commonly called his oldest daughter that. "I've got other things that need to be done." He motioned comically toward the small army gathered with paintbrushes. "I'm certain you can manage. Frederick will make sure it gets done right; he always does."

"That's my job," Frederick said as if it were some royal duty.

Case noticed a confused glance pass between Iris and Ben, and he wondered if James bowing out of such an activity was so rare as to arouse attention from his children.

Once the painting got underway, Case ended up working near Iris, without even trying. He liked seeing her dressed in clothes that were probably her worst, with her hair completely covered by a scarf. "What?" he asked, pointing at her head with a paintbrush. "You don't want to become a redhead?" She gave him a patronizing chuckle and said nothing. She just moved to a different place to work that put some distance between them.

The painting project moved along rather quickly, in spite of the ongoing need to keep Jamie and Isaac from playing in the paint. Case and Ben did most of the work that required a ladder, and Frederick declared that it would need some touching up once it dried and they could see what they'd missed.

After lunch, Frederick asked Iris to work on smoothing over some places where the boys had been painting—which put her right next to Case. Hating silence, Case cleared his throat and asked, "So, where are you from?" He already knew the answer well enough from his conversations with her parents. But he wanted to hear what she'd say.

Iris's expression implied the question was inane. "Iowa, Mr. Harrison. This is my home." He couldn't helping noting her formal use of his name, especially when everyone else had made so much effort *not* to be formal. And every other Mormon he'd met—beyond the Barringtons—had called him *Brother* Harrison. But apparently that would still be too informal for Iris.

Case tipped his head and just smiled at her. "Clearly you did not learn to speak in Iowa, Miss Barrington. Your accent is . . . so . . . *cute.*"

She visibly bristled over that last word, which made him chuckle. But she only said, "We came from England when I was five. I barely remember it." A moment later she added, "And what about you, Mr. Harrison? Did you get that subtle southern drawl in Texas, or did you pick it up on your adventures elsewhere?"

Case felt stunned. The question itself was perfectly fine, but she'd spoken it with such an acrid voice that it reeked of insult. He knew he should ignore her attitude, but before he had a chance to admonish himself to do so, he said, "Oh, you *are* precious, aren't you, Miss Barrington."

"What's *that* supposed to mean?" she asked and stopped painting. She sounded insulted, and he felt pleased with himself. He figured one good turn deserved another.

"I simply said that you're precious, Miss Barrington."

"It wasn't *what* you said," she snapped, "it was the *way* you said it."

Case feigned an enlightened expression and said, "That's exactly what I was thinking about what *you* said, Miss Barrington. Have a *nice* day."

"What's *that* supposed to mean?" she repeated, anger making her eyes sparkle in the sunlight.

"Exactly what I said, Miss Barrington." He smiled. "You should learn to take people—and the things they say—without false assumptions."

Iris made an infuriated noise that made Case chuckle as she tossed down her paintbrush and hurried away at the very moment James appeared to check on the progress. Case pretended to be fully absorbed in his painting while he strained to overhear.

"Is something wrong?" James asked his daughter.

"No, of course not," she said with false poise. "Walk with me. I need a break."

Case glanced their way to see them walking, hand in hand, toward the woods. He heard them both laugh comfortably, and he wondered why it bothered him that Iris couldn't be that cordial with him. He told himself, not for the first time, that she was better left alone, and he'd do well to keep from engaging in *any* conversation with her. But that night he lay in his bed, staring toward the sky outside his window, unable to think of anything but Iris. It was too hot to sleep, and he felt certain that his preoccupation with her was more from boredom than anything else. At the very most, he simply considered it a challenge to win her approval, even if he couldn't figure why he cared. As he always did during moments of doubt or confusion, he took his mind back to the greatest moments of his life. His conversion to the gospel, and subsequent baptism, had made a useless life worth living. *Everything* had changed. The mighty change of heart that had occurred in him was, in his own opinion, every bit as profound as it had been for Alma the Younger in the Book of Mormon. Case had not seen angels or been struck down, but the change that had taken place within had been startlingly quick and complete. Not only had his heart changed, but his thoughts, his feelings, his attitudes, his purpose for living had all changed as well. At the time of his conversion, marriage had been the furthest thing from his mind. He'd never pondered it for even a moment prior to that time, so there was no logical reason that it would suddenly come up. But when he'd been confirmed a member of the Church, he'd been told in the blessing that his Heavenly Father had set aside and preserved a woman of exceptional caliber to be his wife for time and all eternity. He'd been told that he would be led to this woman, and he would know by the power of the Holy Ghost when he found the right woman as clearly as he had known the Church was true. Knowing in his heart that the promise of this blessing was true and real, Case felt no interest in a woman like Iris Barrington beyond a casual interaction. He considered it a personal challenge to win her approval, even though he had absolutely no idea why she was so disapproving. Beyond that, he had no use for her. Case distracted himself from thoughts of Iris by indulging in a recent fantasy of arriving in the Salt Lake Valley and finding there the woman of his dreams. The two goals meshed easily together, and he figured that by the time he was able to travel to Zion, he would feel a lot more prepared to consider marriage. He was still trying to become accustomed to the new him.

The heat became so annoying that Case pulled the feather mattress off his bed and dragged it out to the little balcony outside his room. It was barely big enough to accommodate the mattress, but being outside was far more pleasant. He got comfortable, enjoying the breeze that was more accessible now. But his mind still remained with Iris.

* * * * *

Iris let out an exasperated sigh and kicked the sheet off, but its absence did nothing to ease the sticky heat of August. She finally got out of bed and pulled on a lightweight cotton robe before she headed down the stairs and outside in bare feet. It was a common habit to roam the yard on hot nights when she couldn't sleep. She loved the sensation of walking in the cool grass near the house where the yard was neatly groomed. She wouldn't dare venture too far from the house in bare feet, but this part of the yard was perfect. She walked around the house more than once, careful to be as silent as possible, knowing that every window in the house was open, and she didn't want to disturb anyone else who was struggling to sleep in the heat.

Iris finally ended up on the side porch, cooler now and more relaxed, but not ready to go back into the house, knowing it was far more pleasant out here. Her reprieve was interrupted when she saw movement and turned to see Casey Harrison ambling toward her. She resisted the urge to snap at him and tell him to leave her in peace. As he stepped onto the porch, she noticed that his feet were also bare, and his shirt was only partially buttoned.

"Am I disturbing you?" he asked, and she could almost believe he'd be pleased to know that he was.

"Not at all," she lied.

"Mind if I sit down?" he asked, and she wished he wasn't so perfectly polite.

"Why would I mind?" she countered, which prevented her from having to lie again.

She wished that he might take the hint from the subtle bite in her tone, but he sat down and stretched out his legs, crossing them at the ankles. She pulled her robe more tightly around her, grateful that it was too dark to see anything but shadows of each other.

"Well," he drawled, "since it's apparently too hot to sleep, and we're both apparently prone to wandering around in the dark, I saw you sitting here and thought we might as well keep each other company in our misery." Iris said nothing, and he added, "Why is it that I get the feeling you don't like me, Miss Barrington?"

Iris was so astonished by the question that she had to repeat it twice in her head to be certain she'd heard him right. Not wanting to sound like a fool, she struggled for a suitable answer. "It's not a question of liking you, Mr. Harrison. But unlike my parents and my brothers, I'm not inclined to get attached to someone who will soon be moving on. Many have come and gone before you, and we're both well aware that your being here is temporary."

"Isn't your being here temporary as well?" he asked. Before she could answer, he added, "I mean . . . we're all headed to the same place eventually, right?"

"That's not the point, Mr. Harrison. If you—"

"And I'm sure you're aware that no companies will be leaving until spring. Surely you could endure me being around that long."

"I can certainly endure it," she said, trying not to sound as curt as she felt. "But don't expect me to get all affable."

He chuckled. "I have no idea what that word even means, Miss Barrington. I'm just a simple country boy."

"It doesn't matter," she said, knowing she sounded exasperated, but apparently that was cause for humor, because he chuckled again. She hurried to add, "If you're going to sit here, find something else to talk about."

"I can do that," he said. "Is it all right if I ask you a question?" Again he didn't wait for her to answer. "I admit to being ridiculously curious. It used to infuriate my mother."

"Truly?" Iris said with more than mild sarcasm, and again he laughed. She wanted to accuse him of mocking her, but she kept quiet.

"Forgive my ignorance, Miss Barrington," he went on, "and you don't have to tell me if you don't want to, but I couldn't help noticing that while you share a certain resemblance to your father, your coloring has nothing in common with either of your parents. And your mother is . . . what? About ten years older than you?"

"Twelve!" she snapped.

"Oh, twelve," he drawled as if that made a tremendous difference.

"You *are* ignorant, Mr. Harrison. And you're also prone to meddling."

"No, I'm curious; I already told you that . . . especially about people I like."

"If you're trying to say that you like me, then you are—"

"I didn't say I like *you,"* he said firmly. "But I like your family. I can't help being curious about how your parents came together. But she's not your real mother, is she?"

"She most certainly *is* my real mother!" Iris insisted with a vehemence that was made facetious only because she knew how the term was used in the family, but Casey Harrison didn't. She couldn't deny that she enjoyed telling the story, and she felt more relaxed as she added, "But she is not my *blood* mother."

"So, tell me about your blood mother," Case urged, secretly thrilled by the present opportunity. He'd realized in the last few minutes that he truly enjoyed teasing her enough to get a rise out of her, but he also liked the softness in her voice that he'd never heard before, and he hoped she would remain open with him for more than a moment.

"I remember very little of her." Iris's voice became distant. "She *is* where I get my coloring; she was blonde—and very beautiful, but—"

"Like you," he interrupted.

She glared at him but otherwise ignored the comment. "But she was a horrible person. I only remember her being impatient and unkind."

"Truly?" he asked, mimicking her sarcastic tone from when she'd said it a minute earlier.

Iris wondered if he meant to imply that she had inherited being impatient and unkind, along with her appearance. But again she ignored him and went on. "I always felt like she wanted nothing to do with us."

"Us?" Case asked. "Who besides you?" He knew the other children in the household all clearly belonged to Eleanore Barrington, except for Benjamin, who had been adopted. He'd never heard about anyone else.

The stark change in her countenance let him know he'd asked a forbidden question, and he feared she wouldn't answer it. But she stated in an even voice, "David . . . my older brother; he died when I was ten."

Case took in the information along with a new level of understanding. He stated rather than asked, "You were close." The ache her brother's absence had left in her heart radiated from her, even though he could barely see her through the darkness.

"Yes, very." She cleared her throat, and her aura became less tormented, as if she'd consciously closed something off inside herself. "As I was saying, my mother was a horrible person. She died in premature labor when I was nearly four. Like I said, I barely remember her, but what I remember was not positive. I remember feeling guilty because I was glad she'd died, but I pretended to love and miss her because I knew that's what was expected."

Case considered the depth of her insight and experienced an increased level of respect for her. He also considered her sudden openness and felt some hope that she wasn't nearly as crusty as she wanted him to believe. "And your *real* mother?" he asked. "How did she make her way into the family?"

"When my mother died she became our governess. I remember wishing she could be my mother because she was so kind, and we had such fun together. And then one day my father announced that we were moving to America, and not many days later he told us he was marrying the governess, and she would be our new mother. It was David who said over and over that he wished she *was* our real mother. He wished that some kind of magic might happen to make her our real mother. One day, after we were settled here, our father told us that something magic *had* happened. He said that the love she gave us made her more of a mother to us than our blood mother had ever been. And that's when it was officially decided that she was our *real* mother."

She was silent a long moment while Case took all of that in. He'd known from his conversation with Eleanore that James Barrington had been a wealthy and prestigious man, but he found it difficult to believe that Eleanore had once worked for him. He said with all honesty, "That's a beautiful story."

"Yes, it is," she said.

While Case was trying to think of some other matter of curiosity to satisfy in order to keep the conversation moving, she stood abruptly and walked away. "Good night, Mr. Harrison. Now that you've had a bedtime story, perhaps you can get some sleep."

"Perhaps," he said and watched her walk briskly away. He sensed that she was possibly embarrassed that she'd been so open. But he considered it progress. However this turned out, he figured there was a reasonable chance that he could have James Barrington kissing his feet, all in good time.

Chapter Three

THE MESSAGE

Case returned to his room and finally managed to get some sleep. At breakfast, Iris blatantly ignored him while she was perfectly polite to everyone else. Even then, she said very little and seemed much less happy and relaxed than the other members of the household. He couldn't help being intrigued about the reasons for her behavior, but once again settled himself with the idea that it was best left alone.

It wasn't difficult to keep his attention away from Iris when there were so many other facets of this family that left him utterly in awe. Throughout his childhood, he'd always believed there were families that lived much better than the one he'd been born into—mostly because his mother taught him that. Her strength and wisdom were the only things that had saved him long enough to discover the gospel. To this day, he couldn't imagine how she'd ended up with someone like his father. He'd been the meanest, most horrible man in the world; of that Case was certain. He'd wager that his father could surely put Iris's blood mother to shame—or perhaps it gave him and Iris something in common. He'd love to hear how James Barrington had initially been married to a woman like that. And now he was patriarch of a home with no yelling or screaming, no drinking and cursing, and certainly no beatings. Case had believed for years that his older brother had overcome their upbringing beautifully. He'd worked his way through college, married a good woman, and kept a good job. He didn't drink, and he didn't beat his wife or his kids. Yet for all of his brother's success, Case had still seen his overt lack of kindness toward his wife and children. There had been a great deal of arguing and contention in the home, and they all seemed relatively unhappy. But here in Iowa, Case had found something so close to heaven that it almost seemed unbelievable. Being in the Barrington household had shown Case that there was an entirely different level of happiness possible, even in this relatively miserable world. It took days for him to fully accept that people could genuinely be this happy. And as the reality settled in, he began to wish that he could be part of such a family forever.

Once the barn was painted, James found a number of other projects that needed to be done. He said more than a few times that he wanted the home and property to be in excellent condition, since it would be sold the following year. He also said that they would be going to Zion whether it was sold or not.

Case thoroughly enjoyed working with both Benjamin and Frederick. They were kind and friendly and enjoyed chatting while they worked. It was easy to guess that Frederick and his wife Lizzie had come from England with James and Eleanore, but Case liked hearing the story. He doubly enjoyed hearing it from Frederick, and then from Lizzie separately. Like James and Eleanore, these two had a beautiful story. And they were happy. Lizzie often helped her husband with his chores, or at least kept him company while he worked, and he would often do the same for her just so they could spend more time together during the days. Their daughter, Mary Jane, mixed well with the Barrington children and often helped to look after little Mariah, a job that she apparently enjoyed and was very good at. Mary Jane was a delightful young lady and very bright.

Case quickly became comfortable with the routine of the household and what James Barrington expected of him. Beyond a few usual tasks that he completed each day, often working with Ben or Frederick, he would frequently to do a number of odd jobs for James that required lifting something heavy or exerting strenuous effort. And Case was glad to do it. The only good thing his father had ever given him was an appreciation for the fulfillment of a hard day's work. Case and his brothers had been forced to work to keep food on the table, since the old man was usually drunk. But work was something he felt capable of. And considering how well James and his family had treated Case, he'd do just about anything for this man. Along with providing a roof over his head and three good meals a day, James insisted on paying him a weekly wage that Case felt guilty for accepting. They argued about it only once, until James insisted firmly that he would take it or work elsewhere. James told Case he might need that money someday, and maybe he was right. Case was so used to being dirt poor and barely surviving from day to day that it was an entirely new concept to actually put money away for the future. He did use some of it, however, to get himself some better clothes and a few other odds and ends that he needed. He was pleased, for the first time in his life, to own clothes that he could attend church in and not feel out of place. Of course, he'd never attended church until he'd joined this one, but it was still nice to feel dressed up on the Sabbath.

A couple of times a week, James asked Case to take the buckboard into town and pick up feed and supplies. On one of the first days of autumn that showed a hint of relief from summer's heat, Jamie asked if he could come along. Jamie and his brothers, Isaac and Joseph, had taken to following Case around when their own chores were done, mostly because they liked to provoke Case into tickling them, or getting into a wrestling match where all three boys would attack him at once. He'd pretend to be overwhelmed and terrified and then always turn on them and send them running and giggling. James told his son that it was up to Case if he took Jamie to town, then he said to Case, "But if you take one, they'll all want to go, and they're a handful."

"Oh, I think we can handle it," Case said. The boys cheered as they climbed onto the wagon, although Case had to help Joseph up since he was the littlest.

They had a glorious time in town, and Case bought them each some candy at the general store. On the way home, the boys sang silly songs and told ridiculous jokes that Case pretended were funny. From that point on, Case could hardly go anywhere without them, but he enjoyed their company. Occasionally he told himself that he shouldn't get too attached to the boys, or to any other member of the family. He wanted to believe that they would all end up in the Salt Lake Valley together and that they would all be friends for the rest of their lives. That's the way he wanted it, but he knew well enough that life didn't always give you what you wanted, and maybe that's how it would be. Iris had said that his involvement with this family was only temporary, but even if that were inevitable, he made up his mind to enjoy it fully while it lasted. And having the boys tag around with him became one of his greatest pleasures. They spent hours each day with school lessons taught by their mother, and they were each assigned chores suitable for their age. Beyond that, they were expected to spend some time in the garden each day helping their father pull weeds, and it wasn't uncommon for James to take them fishing in the nearby river or for a walk in the woods after their work was done. The remaining hours of the day when they might linger near Case were never too overwhelming, but James and Eleanore both told him numerous times that it wasn't necessary for him to always be looking after the boys. He assured them he didn't mind, and he wasn't afraid to tell them if they became too annoying. This comment provoked laughter from everyone but Iris—which was typical. And Case just habitually ignored the subtle pall that seemed to define her presence. Instead he focused on her three little brothers; in fact, he grew so attached to them that he wondered what he'd ever done without them.

Like the boys, every member of the household had his or her expected duties, and everyone worked hard. Stella was either in the kitchen in the house or out in the summer kitchen nearly every waking moment, putting on three lovely meals a day. The women could all be found working with her at any given time, and they also kept busy with other tasks around the house as well. The home and yard were kept perfectly tidy with the joint efforts of the entire family, and Case felt certain they could manage fine without him. But if James couldn't come up with a project for him to do, he found one himself, determined to earn his keep and more. One way that he felt especially useful was in accompanying James to Coralville, the Mormon settlement on the outskirts of Iowa City. James went nearly every day, taking different family members with him, but often asking Case to come along. They would occasionally pick up supplies in town and take them quietly to one family or another, and they never left without putting in some labor on someone's behalf, according to their needs. James told Case of their years of frustration in wanting to join with the Saints in other places, and how the Lord had repeatedly made it clear that they needed to stay in Iowa City. It had only been earlier this year that two gentlemen had come from Salt Lake, asking James and his family to help the Saints who were gathering here in their preparations to go west. As James candidly and humbly spoke of what had taken place in the past several months, Case was freshly amazed by this man. He was kind and generous and full of faith, and yet he was somehow unaware that he possessed these attributes. His humility was especially touching. Given the opportunity to follow James Barrington around while he quietly and discreetly used his time and resources to aid the struggling Saints, Case learned more about the power of serving others than he ever could have learned from a book. He admired this man more than words could say, especially when compared to the miscreant who had raised Case.

Each day except for the Sabbath was filled with hard work; however, it didn't take long to see that around here, play was as important as any labor. There was always time for reading, or picnics, or playing in the river, so long as everyone did what was expected of them. Case had grown up knowing how to work hard, but playing and relaxing had been regarded as akin to grievous crime by his father, and Case often found it difficult to stop working and join in with other activities going on, even when he was begged to do so by every member of the family—except Iris, of course. She would probably prefer that he work himself to death and never show his face for any family activity. He occasionally wondered about her attitudes, but the only answers he came up with left him feeling assured that leaving it alone was best. He had no desire to cross her, so he just ignored her.

The highlight of each day for Case, beyond the meals he shared with the family, was the way they gathered in the parlor each evening to read from the scriptures and pray. Each time it happened, he wanted to hold the feeling deep inside himself and keep it forever sacred. He wanted to create a home someday where these kinds of activities took place and where such a sweet spirit resided.

In keeping with his curious nature, Case found himself discreetly observing the relationship between James and Eleanore Barrington, including the way they interacted with their children. Again, he couldn't help but compare what he saw to the home he'd grown up in, and it was difficult for him to believe that people could be so kind and loving toward each other. He felt utterly humbled and thoroughly awed by these people, and yet he felt wholly unworthy to even be in their home. But he had to consider that it was a gift from God, and he could only offer thanks and do his best to accept such a gift graciously. He didn't know how long he might get to stay, but he looked at each day as a blessing, and each time he saw James Barrington kiss his wife's hand, or look into her eyes with overt adoration, he counted it as one more drop in the bucket of joy that counteracted the ugliness he'd seen between his own parents. He wanted to be like this man, to someday love a wife that way, to be that kind of father. Beyond basic reading and writing, Case knew he was an uneducated man, but more than any kind of schooling in worldly matters, he desired to be educated on how to make a good life. So he took it in, one minute, one hour, at a time, while the people around him were oblivious to his purposeful observations.

By the first of October, Case had been working for the Barringtons for two months, and he couldn't possibly comprehend life before then. His conversion and baptism were pure memories that remained close to his heart. His immediate journey to Iowa City to join the Saints was somewhat of a blur of passing scenery while his mind and his spirit had attempted to comprehend how dramatically he had changed. And life prior to those changes had also become a hazy blur, most of it ugly and unpleasant and best not thought about too much. He prayed every day that he might be able to remain close to this family, but knew in his heart that such a miracle might not be part of God's plan for him. However, there were many months left until spring, and only then would he know what course to take from there. He'd quickly grown to care for every member of the household, and they in turn had been generously kind and gracious toward him—except for Iris. But after knowing her for two months, Case felt disarmed to realize that all of his efforts at ignoring her and disregarding her attitude toward him hadn't helped the matter at all. He was still prone to thinking about her far too much, and there was no logical reason for this. She *was* crusty, and she certainly didn't like him; she'd made that unmistakably clear. But even if she did, he was little more than a vagabond, and she was elegant and refined. All humor aside in recalling James's challenge regarding his daughter, Case knew he could never be the kind of man worthy of a woman like Iris Barrington—even if she *was* crusty. His minimal attempts to make conversation with her always ended in disaster. If others were around, she would be barely polite, and if no one else could hear, she could be downright rude. He knew there had to be more to her disdain than simply her desire to remain aloof from someone whose presence was only *temporary*. But he had no desire to even ask.

A week into October, Case walked into the barn in the middle of the afternoon to find James kneeling on the ground, struggling to breathe, both hands pressed to his chest.

"What's wrong?" Case demanded, kneeling beside him.

A glance showed that James was embarrassed, annoyed, and afraid all at once. Through his wheezing he managed to say, "I'll be all right in a minute."

Case felt assured by his confidence, but not willing to leave him alone, even though he had no idea what to do if he were *not* all right. Gradually the wheezing merged into normal breathing, and James sat hard on the ground, exhausted. Case sensed that James might prefer to be left alone and pretend the episode hadn't occurred. But Case cared for this man far too much to ignore something that was obviously a huge concern.

"You want to tell me what just happened?" he asked, sitting beside him.

"Not really," James said, "but if I don't you'd probably go blabbing to my wife and get me in trouble."

"Are you saying she doesn't know about this?"

"Oh, she knows," James said. "At least she knows I have difficulty breathing if I overexert myself. But since I've promised her I wouldn't overexert myself, she wouldn't be very happy to know that I had. I didn't intend to. I try to be careful. But sometimes I just . . . forget."

"If Eleanore knows, then you've surely seen a doctor."

"Two of them. It's a condition called asthma, and there's nothing that can be done."

"Are you saying it's fatal?" Case asked, pleased that his voice didn't betray how sick he felt at the thought of losing this man he'd grown to care for and respect so quickly and so deeply.

"Eventually, yes," James said tonelessly. "As one doctor put it, not being able to breathe is certainly fatal. But it only happens when I get overexerted, so I just need to . . ."

"Not get overexerted, obviously."

"I'll be more careful," James said. "And Case," James put a hand on his arm and looked at him firmly, "I don't want my children to know. Not one of them; not even a hint. Do you understand?"

"I understand that you're asking me to keep this in confidence, and I hope you know that I will. I would never betray your trust in any matter."

"I know that. I just wanted to make it completely clear . . . I don't want them to know."

"May I ask why? I mean . . . if this is serious, shouldn't they have some awareness of the problem? If it could be fatal, shouldn't they have the opportunity to be prepared for the possibility of . . ." He couldn't finish that thought.

"Perhaps eventually," James said. "For now, I don't want them to know. They'll just worry. And I don't want anyone fretting or fussing over me."

"Does anyone know besides your wife?"

"Frederick. He keeps me in line when he's around."

"Now I can keep you in line when he's not," Case said, trying to lighten the mood.

James smiled. "Yes, I suppose you can. Just don't let it go to your head, boy."

"Don't you worry, old man," he said with overt facetiousness, "I know my place around here. Even though I know your secrets, I'm still willing to kiss your feet."

"I thought it was the other way around," James said.

"What?"

"That I am supposed to kiss *your* feet." Case felt completely confused until James added, "Are we talking about Iris?" Only then did his mind go back to their first conversation.

He hurried to say, "No, no. No, no, *no!*" He laughed. "I'm afraid you'll have to find some other poor soul to feed to the vultures. She's too much woman for me."

"Oh, I wouldn't say that," James said almost under his breath as he came to his feet. Case jumped up and took his arm, trying to help him. James shrugged him off and added, "I can stand up just fine, boy. Don't start coddling me, or I'll give you a bloody nose."

"You wouldn't."

"No, but I don't want you to forget that I'm capable. You may call me 'old man,' but don't start treating me like one."

"Fair enough," Case said.

Lying awake in his bed that night, Case considered what he'd learned about James Barrington today. He was grateful for the comfortable camaraderie that had developed between them that had made it possible to frankly discuss James's health issues. Case prayed that the symptoms wouldn't get out of hand, and that this great man could live for many years to come. He thought of how it would break his heart to lose James now, and he couldn't imagine how it would affect all of these other people who had been a part of his daily life for years. Case wondered if his greatest purpose for being here was to help keep James healthy by doing work he could no longer do. Whether that was the case or not, he intended to keep himself between James and overexertion every minute of the day, if possible.

Over the next several days, Case realized that James had already been doing just that for weeks now. He could see now that there had been purpose in the way James had avoided being involved with certain projects, and how he'd asked Case to do tasks that he normally would have done. That was why he'd been sending Case into town to pick up feed and supplies, because they were heavy and required some serious lifting. And Frederick was clearly busy doing *other* things that James was trying to discreetly avoid. It was evident that his family was accustomed to seeing him work hard, and he was diplomatically trying to avoid having them notice a problem, using the need to keep a new employee busy as an excuse. Case suspected that James had similar motives in encouraging him to play with the boys. It was evident they were accustomed to wrestling, tickling, and playing heartily with their father. But James had gracefully eased Case into that position, and instead would sit and watch them play, always with a smile on his face, as if he could enjoy it every bit as much from a distance. Of course, Ben and Frederick played with the boys, too. But Case had apparently come along just at the right time to be some kind of temporary replacement—at least until James felt it was right to let his children know there was a problem. Case didn't necessarily agree with James keeping his illness a secret, but he respected his desire to do so and simply did his best to keep doing what he'd been doing in order to keep James Barrington healthy and strong.

With autumn well underway, other tasks and even some of the children's lessons were put on hold to focus fully on the harvesting and preserving of all the family had worked together to grow throughout the summer. Case enjoyed being put to work in the garden, as well as in the kitchen. Eleanore made it clear, with good humor, that any man worth his weight would not be above bottling fruits and vegetables. He wholeheartedly agreed, even though it was evident that Iris did not. She put a great deal of effort into finding things to do in order to avoid being where Case was. But sometimes Eleanore asked her specifically to do a task that made it impossible to avoid him. Case thoroughly enjoyed forcing her through meaningless conversation while they worked side by side when other people were around, which prevented her from telling him to shut up and mind his own business. Seeing the way she behaved so differently toward him, as opposed to anyone else, Case made up his mind that she was simply a shrew—and a very good actress—and that her parents were somewhat blind to her true character.

Iris was grateful to finally be done cutting up the carrots as her mother had asked her to do so she could go back out to the garden and pull more of them out of the ground. This allowed her to get away from Case's continual barrage of questions and his nearly constant smile. What could he possibly be smiling about all the time? She couldn't begin to imagine.

During the time that Case had been working—and living—among her family, Iris had struggled daily to remain indifferent to his presence. But she simply couldn't. She felt uneasy around him, and knew that was surely an indication that she shouldn't trust him. Consequently, she didn't like him. She refused to put any effort into analyzing the reasons any further than that. She only knew that she preferred to avoid him, but even when he was nowhere in sight, she would often find herself thinking about him and about all the things she didn't like about his being here. The very fact that she wasted so much thought on him made her even more angry.

Iris eased into the garden, appreciating the autumn breeze that helped counteract the high sun in a cloudless sky. She bent over to start pulling more carrots from the ground, and a moment later she heard Case say, "You look like a flower, Miss Barrington, out here in the middle of the garden all by yourself."

Iris heard the subtlest hint of sarcasm in his attempt to be polite and complimentary. But that was the tone he *always* used with her, whether anyone was around or not. And since no one was around, she told him exactly what she thought. "You're not only impertinent, Mr. Harrison; you're also delusional."

"You're using big words again, Miss Barrington," he said and started uprooting carrots at the other end of the row. "How many times do I have to remind you that I'm just a simple farm boy?"

"But you *can* read," she said. "That's something, I guess. Perhaps you should start reading books with bigger words."

"You mean words like *Zarahemla,* and *Liahona?* I know what those words mean."

"How clever of you," she said, her sarcasm deepening.

"You know," he said, "even if you *didn't* look like your blood mother, I'd know you must have somebody else's blood in you; you sure didn't get that sassy impudence from your father, *or* Eleanore."

Case heard an astonished gasp but didn't bother looking at her, even when she said, "You are the most arrogant . . ."

"What?" he asked, turning then. He straightened his back and put his hands on his hips, staring at her hard. "I'm an arrogant what?"

Iris made a huffy noise and glanced at the ground. "Being a Christian woman, I can't say it."

Case actually laughed. "A *Christian* woman? Is that what you said? My dear Miss Barrington, I can assure you that Jesus would never speak to any human being the way you do. And that makes *you* a hypocrite." He forced a smile and left the garden. "Have a nice day, and keep your opinions to yourself so I can too."

Iris felt so infuriated she wanted to scream at him, but his accusations of hypocrisy kept her silent. Instead she put more energy into pulling carrots out of the ground while she thought about pulling hard on Casey Harrison's thick, wavy hair.

That evening at supper, Iris couldn't even look at Case without recalling the aggravation he incited in her. She was relieved to have the meal over, and she zealously set to work scrubbing all of the pots and pans that were dirty, if only to avoid being anywhere near Case.

Then he showed up next to her with a clean dishtowel, offering to dry what she was washing.

"I can manage, thank you," she said tersely.

"I'm certain you can," he said and proceeded to dry a pan. "In fact, I think you're very good at proving how well you can manage just about anything. But I'm not here to help you. I'm here to help Stella."

"And you're both very good at it," Stella said from behind, and Iris felt embarrassed to realize they'd been overheard.

"It was an excellent supper, Stella," Case said. "Thank you."

"You always say that," she said with a girlish giggle.

"It's always true," Case said, and Iris resisted rolling her eyes. She wondered if she was the only one around here who could see through his flattery and smooth words. Stella stopped talking, and Iris was relieved when Case did too. While others moved in and out of the kitchen, working to clear the table and clean up the meal, Case put his attention to teasing and flattering everyone else, which kept Iris from having to converse with him. And then it was just the two of them with Stella again. Not for the first time, Case started asking her questions about her homeland of Ireland, which was fine with Iris, if only because it kept him from asking her anything at all. After the pans were all washed and dried, Stella kept talking, using animated gestures, telling some funny stories from her childhood. Case leaned against the counter, listening with a silly smile on his face. But then, he usually had a silly smile on his face. Iris sat down to listen, realizing she'd never heard Stella go into so much detail about her life in Ireland. She'd only heard bits and pieces before, and she had to concede that Case was gifted at getting people to talk.

Later that evening, when everyone was gathered in the parlor, reading from the Book of Mormon, Iris found some pleasure in seeing Case put on the spot in the same way he was so good at doing to others. Frederick asked Case what his favorite story was in the Book of Mormon, and he looked utterly flustered for a few seconds before he answered in a voice that was more soft and timid than Iris had ever heard him use. "It would be Alma the Younger," he said, looking mostly at the floor.

"Why is that?" Lizzie asked, and Iris sensed Case's nerves heightening.

Iris felt certain that Case didn't know nearly as much about the book as he might have let on all these weeks while he'd sat through these reading sessions, saying very little. But she felt grateful no one could read her thoughts, and more than a little guilty over her attitude when Case uttered with a crack in his voice, "Because I know that the mighty change of heart he talks about is real. I know what it's like to lead a deplorable life one day, and the next thing you know, you're a completely changed man."

Iris felt increasingly uncomfortable with the ensuing silence, especially in light of her own mixed thoughts and feelings. Without bothering to premeditate her words, she asked Case, "What sort of deplorable life?"

She saw mild alarm in Case's eyes the same moment her father said, "I don't think that's necessary for any of us to know, or even appropriate to ask."

"I don't mind her asking," Case said to Iris's father while he stared at her. "But let's just say it was too deplorable to talk about in mixed company—or at all."

"There, it's in the past," Eleanore said and smiled at Case. "How wonderful for you to have experienced such a miracle in your life."

"Yes," Case said. "Yes, it is."

The discussion went on while Iris's thoughts wandered between her dislike of Casey Harrison and her wondering about his deplorable past. Was she the only one who felt any concern at all that he might return to such a past, whatever it may have entailed? She was startled by her father requesting that she offer the prayer tonight, and she hurried to utter one silently first, asking that her negative thoughts might not inhibit her being able to pray appropriately on behalf of her family. When everyone moved from their seats to kneel in a circle in the usual manner, she was startled to find herself right next to Case. It had never happened before. He looked at her with a trace of humor in his eyes as he took hold of her hand, and she fought to focus only on the prayer and nothing else.

Case was completely unprepared for the way he reacted when Iris's hand slipped into his. It was the first time he'd ever touched her, but he never would have expected such simple physical contact to affect him so deeply. It was as if their touching ignited some deep, obscure memory that he couldn't quite recall with his mind but which he felt in his heart. The words of her prayer became distant and almost hazy while he attempted to figure what such a sensation might mean. And yet he felt the spirit of the prayer surround him, as if the very act of her praying showed him the glory and potential of Iris's spirit. All of his weeks of attempting to be indifferent to her, of teasing her for the sake of getting her riled, of wondering how a Barrington woman could be so crusty, all fled out of him, and in their stead, a rush of pure energy and information flowed in to fill the void. He was startled by a constriction in his chest and a quiver in his stomach, the combination of which was something he'd never experienced before. In the time it took his heart to beat only once, he was able to comprehend a message of eternal consequence. *She was the one!* His being here now was not happenstance, and the crustiness that was so aggravating was the very thing that had preserved her for him and him alone. He didn't know how he knew it, but he knew it. He knew it as surely as he knew the gospel was true and that God was real and living. All at once he felt enormous peace to think that he *would* be given the magnificent blessing of being a part of this family eternally, and he was also overcome with deep wonderment on how it might come to pass when the obstacles presently felt so immense. But a heartbeat later he knew that it didn't matter *how;* he only needed to trust in God to show him the way, one step at a time, and to remember, no matter how difficult the journey might become, that the message had been given to him as clearly as it had to Moses or the brother of Jared.

Suddenly the amen was spoken, and Case was made aware of time again, as if he'd been momentarily transported to another dimension. He couldn't recall anything that had been said in Iris's prayer, but he firmly echoed her amen and resisted letting go of her hand long enough to turn and look at her, attempting to comprehend what he'd just learned. She turned to silently question his holding onto her hand. He immediately let go, but it was enough to be able to see her eyes. And he couldn't help smiling. *She was the one.*

"Is something wrong?" James asked, and Case realized he was being addressed. He then became conscious of his own labored breathing. When he didn't answer, James said, "Case, are you all right?"

"I'm fine," he said. "I just . . . had a little trouble . . . catching my breath."

James's eyes narrowed, and he almost scowled, as if to question if this was some attempt at humor on Case's part in relation to James's own breathing difficulties.

Case just discreetly returned his gaze and added, "I'm fine now. Thank you." He then turned to Iris and said, "That was a beautiful prayer. Thank you."

Iris only hurried from the room, and Case resisted the urge to run after her and declare his intentions here and now. He reminded himself of the need for patience and went to bed. But hours later he was still wide awake, gazing into the darkness, attempting to accept what he'd just learned about Iris Barrington. He couldn't believe it! And if the experience he'd been given had not been so undeniably real, he would feel prone to dismiss it in light of the cold, hard facts. Iris hated him. And if he were totally honest with himself, he couldn't deny that he wasn't terribly fond of her. He'd felt intrigued with her right from the start, and she was certainly beautiful. But he'd never once felt attracted to her in the slightest. He certainly couldn't say that he loved her. Did God expect him to marry a woman he didn't love? Would he ever be able to break past Iris's churlish behavior, or was that simply something he'd have to live with? He was willing to do whatever God asked of him, but he wasn't terribly keen on spending the rest of his life with a woman who didn't like him and wasn't afraid to say so. Of course, something had to change. She certainly wouldn't agree to marry him under such circumstances. *He was little more than a vagabond, and she was elegant and refined.* Where would he possibly begin to try to win the heart of such a woman? When another hour of thought produced no answers, he prayed for the purpose of putting the matter in God's hands, and finally fell asleep.

Chapter Four
FALLING

Case lost count of the days that he spent attempting to see Iris through new eyes. He found great comfort in the spiritual glimpse he'd been given of her glory and potential; otherwise he'd be certain he'd lost his mind. No matter how hard he tried, he couldn't quite mesh this woman with that one. The Iris who blatantly ignored him in spite of many attempts on his part to be kind was not a woman he wanted to be with forever. He continued to pray day and night for guidance and hope. He felt hope only in knowing the witness he'd been given. But he felt no guidance whatsoever. He finally felt compelled to ask for some advice from someone he respected who had a great deal of life's experience behind him. Case just wasn't sure how to discuss such a matter with the father of the woman who was the source of the problem. He would do it very carefully, he concluded, determined to keep the conversation vague.

With the desire to speak to James alone, he felt sure his prayers were being heard when James asked Case to ride into town with him; everyone else was too occupied elsewhere to come along. James had something personal that he needed to take care of at the bank, but he also needed to pick up some supplies that would be too heavy for him to lift.

They were only a couple of minutes from the house, seated side by side on the buckboard, when Case said, "Can I ask you something?"

"Of course," James said easily.

"If you pray for guidance concerning a specific matter, and you're not getting any answers, what do you do?"

James turned to look at him and asked, "Are *you* the one praying for guidance, or are we speaking hypothetically?"

Case chuckled. "I have no idea what that means."

"Are you speaking in a general sense, simply for the sake of understanding the principle, or is this personal?"

Case had no trouble admitting, "It's personal." But he had to add, "I don't feel prone to discussing the issue. I just need to understand why I'm not getting any answers. Am I doing something wrong?"

"If you're doing your best to live the gospel, and you're praying with sincerity, you're not doing anything wrong. You're entitled to the guidance of the Spirit."

"Then why am I not getting any guidance; any answers?"

"It's been my experience that there are generally three possible answers to a prayer, Case. Yes, no, or not yet. If you're not getting the answers, then it's not yet time for those answers to come. I'm not certain what exactly you're talking about, but I would guess you just need to be patient and allow things to work out in God's way, and in God's time."

Case was almost startled by how easily James had answered the question, and by how clearly it made sense. He chuckled, feeling some relief, and said, "Thanks. I think that's exactly what I needed to hear."

James chuckled as well. "Glad I could help."

The remainder of their time together was filled with *hypothetical* discussion on gospel principles and their application to life in a way that Case was only beginning to understand. He felt added gratitude for having such a man as a friend, and for all he was learning through their association. Watching James walk into the bank while he waited outside, Case was struck with a quickened heart at the thought of having this man become his father-in-law. The very idea seemed incomprehensible and at the same time utterly wonderful.

On the way home, after all of their errands were completed, a thought occurred to Case, and he asked, "So . . . do you think . . . hypothetically speaking . . ." He chuckled at hearing such a word come out of his own mouth; just associating with James Barrington made him feel smarter. "Do you think," he repeated, "that if we know something is right, or . . . meant to happen . . . that it will . . . as long as we have faith?"

"Since we're just speaking hypothetically," James chuckled as if he sensed that it was more personal than that for Case, "then I would have to say that we are certainly blessed for being faithful, and that by trusting in God, our lives will turn out the way they should. However, we are only in control of our own actions, and we cannot control the free agency of another human being. Even God can't do that."

Case felt startled by that concept, and it took him a few minutes to let it settle in. He finally asked, "So . . . are you saying that . . . even if something is . . . well . . . meant to be . . . that a person can . . . make the wrong choice?" As he said it, he could only think that this meant Iris could very well choose to never have anything to do with him. And if that happened, what would the result be for him? He knew that God wanted him to marry this woman. Would he end up alone if Iris chose a different path?

"Yes," James said, "but God still knows the outcome. He knows everything from beginning to end." Case felt confused but couldn't put together a specific question. He was relieved when James added, "Our free will is a very important part of our life's experience, Case, but God still knows us well enough to know the choices we will make, and what the outcome will be. And He provides for us, even when things don't work out the way we believe they're supposed to."

Case picked up on something in James's voice and pointed out, "I thought this was hypothetical." He enjoyed using the word. "This sounds pretty personal to me, like you know from experience." James looked at him as if he'd been caught off guard and Case added, "Of course, you don't have to tell me, but . . ." He knew he didn't have to remind James of his own curious nature, but he needed to remind himself to be polite and not too forward.

James was silent for more than a minute, and Case felt certain he would let the subject drop. Then he said with a somber voice, "It's no great secret in this family that I was married before; that my first wife died, and that she was a difficult woman. When I married Iris's mother, I truly believed she was the right one. I believed that together we could make a good marriage and raise a beautiful family and be happy. And I believe we could have—if she had upheld her part of the bargain. But she chose not to, and I had no control over that. I wondered a thousand times if I'd made a mistake, but in my heart I know I did the best that I could, and somehow it needed to be that way. God knew what the outcome would be, even if I didn't. I believe we can only trust in Him and do the best we can, given our circumstances, whatever they may be."

Case allowed that to settle in, while James gave him the silence he needed to do so. They were nearly home before James said, "Are you all right?"

"I'm fine, why?" Case asked.

"You seem terribly . . . distracted."

"Just trying to figure it all out," Case admitted. "This kind of stuff is all new to me; not just the gospel, which is of course, but . . . well . . . the life I grew up with wasn't real conducive to teaching a man the right way to live, and to treat people, and to . . . allow them to make their own choices."

"If it will make you feel better, the life I grew up with wasn't either." Case was stunned and turned to make certain he wasn't joking. James went on to say, "You look surprised."

"I am."

"Do you think because I was raised with plenty of money and lots of education that my life was therefore right and good?" Case didn't reply because he knew the answer was obvious, and he felt a little foolish to realize that maybe he *had* thought that. James added, "My parents were cruel to each other and to me. It wasn't easy learning how to *not* be like them." A few seconds later James chuckled and said, "Now you *really* look surprised."

Case chuckled. "I just didn't think you and I could have that much in common."

"Oh, my boy," James laughed deeply, "we have *very* much in common."

"Do we?" Case asked, disappointed to realize they were home.

"Just give it time," James said and got down from the wagon. Case thought about that while he unharnessed the horses and unloaded the wagon. That was the answer to *all* of his questions and concerns. He just needed time.

* * * * *

November brought winter with it, and no change in Iris's behavior—or the way Case felt about her. He kept praying for answers and guidance, and kept telling himself to be patient. While he could readily admit that Iris was an attractive woman, he didn't feel at all attracted to her. Intrigued, yes. Fascinated, certainly. But attracted? No. Deciding it would be best to feel attracted to a woman he intended to marry, he prayed that if this was indeed the right course, that his feelings for Iris might give him some indication that this was the goal he should pursue. Only a few days later, he went to the office to speak to James, and instead found Iris there, sprawled on the couch, reading. Her stockinged feet were dangling over the arm of the couch, and he took a moment to just look at her while she was unaware of his presence. The sound of his approach had been lost in the boys' running up the nearby stairs. And while he watched her, it happened. His chest constricted, and his stomach quivered—not unlike the moment when he'd known that Iris was the woman God had chosen for him. But now he could only think of how beautiful she was, and for the first time ever, he felt a desire to touch her face and hair, to hold her in his arms. He didn't need to analyze his feelings to realize that this was certainly attraction, and to know that this was an undeniable answer to his prayers. Then Iris peered over the top of her book, as if she'd sensed that someone was there. She gasped, then glared at him and sat up abruptly.

"What *are* you doing?"

"I was just . . . looking for your father," he said quickly, hearing a subtle tremor in his own voice. "Obviously he's not here."

"Obviously," she said, and he hurried away.

Once out the back door, Case had to lean against the side of the house for a couple of minutes and catch his breath. The intrigue he'd felt with her right from the start had blossomed suddenly and brilliantly into feelings he had no idea what to do with. Realizing that her feelings for him were clearly still the same, he actually had tears burn his eyes, then he muttered into the winter breeze, "Be careful what you pray for, Case."

* * * * *

Iris found it difficult to concentrate on the book she was reading for several minutes after Case left the house. Seeing him there had startled her, but she had also seen something different in his eyes that left her disconcerted. She convinced herself that it was only her imagination, but that evening at supper, he behaved completely differently toward her. There was an absence of his usual teasing, and he made no effort to infuriate her, even when she goaded him in a way that had become typical between them. For days this new behavior continued, and she felt angry over the amount of mental effort she was putting into trying to figure out the reasons. She was sorely tempted to just ask him, but had no desire to open any such conversation with him. She could admit, however, that she'd come to rely on their senseless bantering. And now he hardly spoke to her at all, as if he were almost afraid of her. She wondered if she'd done something to *really* offend him and whether he was somehow angry with her. But she didn't sense anger. She was most disappointed to realize that since he'd actually done what she'd wanted him to do all along—just leave her alone—she didn't necessarily like it.

* * * * *

Case began to wish he'd never asked to feel this way about Iris. He could barely eat and hardly sleep. He felt completely obsessed with her, and kept wondering what it would be like to hold her, kiss her, share his deepest feelings with her. He imagined them married, having children, sharing life in every respect. Then he'd see her in the yard or across the table and be convinced that he was out of his mind. He prayed every day and tried to let go of the matter and put it in God's hands, but his heart was involved now, and he felt more impatient than ever. He wondered if she would ever feel for him the way he did for her, and he had trouble believing that might be possible. He wondered if she would ever consider marrying him simply for the sake of practicality. He knew that many marriages took place for that reason, but he couldn't imagine Iris settling for that either. Any way he looked at it, he couldn't begin to fathom how all of this might turn out.

A couple of weeks after Case's feelings for Iris had come to life, he noticed that Eleanore didn't look well as she sat down at the breakfast table. He sensed concern in James's eyes, which remained more focused on his wife than usual. Then Eleanore left the table abruptly with her hand over her mouth. The chattering in the room completely stopped as concerned glances were exchanged in every direction. It was Jamie who said, "Is Mom pregnant again?"

All eyes turned to James while the silence ensued. He cleared his throat and said, "Yes, she is."

"Oh, that's wonderful news!" Stella said, and the others agreed, but some at the table appeared less enthusiastic than others—most specifically James.

A few hours later, Case found the opportunity to be alone with James in the barn, and he simply had to say, "Forgive me if I'm being too nosy, and just tell me to mind my business, but . . . I sense you're not entirely happy about your wife's pregnancy."

James gave him a sharp glance, and Case felt sure he *would* tell him to mind his business. But his eyes softened, and he looked away. "The prospect of having another child brings me great joy, but I always worry for Eleanore's health. She's had some problems along the way, more with some pregnancies than others." He sighed loudly. "And we were planning to head west with the next company going out. But I won't have her making the journey while she's pregnant, or giving birth somewhere on the plains. So, we'll have to wait. It will set us back. The baby isn't due until July, and that's far too late to leave, in my opinion. Which means we'll be waiting another year." Case thought that was the end of the explanation, but James sighed and added, "Or . . . she may lose the baby, as she has several times, and when the time comes to leave she won't be pregnant at all."

"Several?" Case echoed, sounding more incredulous than he'd intended.

"That's right," James said and left the barn. Case continued with his tasks while his mind worked through this new revelation. He had looked at this family and wrongly assumed that their lives were good and always had been. Of course, he'd known about David's death and that prior to James and Eleanore coming together there had been challenges in James's life. But the thought of them having lost several babies gave Case a certain heartache on their behalf. He prayed that this pregnancy would go well, and felt sure that it would all fit in with James Barrington's desire to take his family to Zion.

With Eleanore's pregnancy, Case saw a shift take place in the household. She rarely made it to breakfast, did very little around the house, and she didn't look at all well. He could understand James's hesitance in taking her across the plains in such a condition, and he prayed that it would all work out well.

Case also prayed—almost continually—for guidance regarding Iris. He was surprised when, after weeks of no information in that regard, an idea came firmly to his mind. Apparently the time was right for him to cross a bridge. He needed to attempt to close this gap between them and let her know something of his feelings. The problem was that he didn't know exactly how to go about it. He didn't know what to say or how to say it. Apparently that part was up to him. He just kept praying that the Spirit would guide him to do the right thing at the right time.

On a sunny day when Eleanore was feeling unusually well, Case chopped wood while he watched everyone gather into the buggy and the buckboard to go on an impulsive trip to town for some shopping and lunch. Eight different people asked him to come along, but he declined, insisting he didn't feel up to it, telling them he had other things that needed to be done. It was difficult to explain that he just felt like he should stay.

"There's no work that can't wait," James insisted while Eleanore stood beside him, silently echoing a firm desire for him to come with them.

"It's not that," Case said. "Thank you . . . truly. I just . . . have some things I need to take care of." They both looked doubtful and questioning, staring at him with an intensity that forced him to finally admit, "I just . . . feel like I shouldn't go."

There was a moment of silence before James said, "That's an answer I can accept." Eleanore smiled at him, and they both turned to leave. James hesitated and turned back long enough to say, "As long as you're here, you can look out for Iris."

"She's not going?" he asked, wishing he hadn't sounded so alarmed. He wasn't sure he wanted to be here alone with her. That fact alone made him question his reasons for staying, but he had to conclude that the feelings were still the same. He needed to stay. And maybe that was the reason—a thought that actually terrified him. Was this the answer to his prayers?

"No," Eleanore said. "Her reasons sounded a great deal like yours." She tossed him a subtly conspiratorial smirk before she headed toward the buggy at her husband's side. For the first time it occurred to him that others might have sensed his feelings for Iris. At the very least, Eleanore had. He couldn't figure out any other reason for such a look. And knowing that she knew made him all the more nervous.

Case stood and watched them ride away, then the silence of their absence felt almost eery. He looked toward the house and wondered what Iris might be doing—or thinking. Was there some deep significance in their both being here, with no one else around? He'd been feeling for days that he needed to talk to her. But he didn't want to, and he certainly didn't feel ready. Was this opportunity meant to give him the shove that he needed?

For more than two hours, Case kept busy while his mind stewed over the situation. He told himself over and over that Iris didn't want to hear what he had to say, and attempting to say it would only create more challenges between them. He convinced himself the time wasn't right, and he kept himself occupied with a variety of tasks. Then the thought came to him strongly that he needed to talk to her, and it needed to be now. He felt hesitant to even go into the house with no one there but her, certain she would accuse him of some ludicrous violation of her privacy. But the thought came again, and he couldn't ignore it. He didn't know what he was doing, or what the outcome would be. But if Nephi could act not knowing the outcome, surely he could too.

Case went quietly through the back door and took off his coat and gloves. He also removed his boots, since they were a little muddy. He hoped she would be on the main floor in one of the rooms that he'd commonly visited. He couldn't fathom hollering her name up the stairs, hoping she might hear him. He heard a little noise from the front of the house and concluded that she was either in the parlor or the library. He walked slowly and noiselessly up the hall, trying to figure what he might say to her, how he might begin. His mind felt completely empty, and he prayed that the words would come as he needed them.

Case peeked into the parlor and saw that no one was there. He peered around the corner of the open door of the library to see Iris on a ladder that was leaned against the high book shelves. She was apparently dusting. He'd barely caught a glimpse of her when she reached too far and the ladder tipped. His desire to speak to her became immediately irrelevant as he rushed to stop her from falling. But it was too late for that, and he could only do his best to break her fall. She screamed, then noticed him there just before he grabbed her and hit the floor with her landing mostly on him. In a fragment of a second, Case saw the ladder coming down after her and abruptly rolled over to put his body between her and the inevitable blow. She screamed again as the ladder collided with his upper arm and a portion of his back. Case groaned from the impact and struggled to get hold of the breath that had been knocked out of his lungs. He glanced at the ladder laying against him, and the placement of Iris's head buried beneath his shoulder. It was readily evident that if he'd not been there, it would have fallen on her face. He tried to push the ladder off with his left arm, since his right was beneath Iris. He felt some relief that the arm couldn't be broken since he was able to move it, but the pain was a good indication that he was badly bruised. He awkwardly kicked the ladder off, then he had to take a moment to breathe deeply and assess the level of pain. He became less mindful of his pain as he became aware of Iris's sharp whimpering. He moved onto his side and saw both fear and relief in her eyes.

"I could have been killed," she said breathlessly.

"Maybe not killed," he said, "but not necessarily in good condition."

"What are you doing in here?" she asked, incredulous but not angry.

"Apparently God has some reason to spare you." She looked confused, and he added, "I felt like I needed to come and talk to you." Iris let out a sigh that turned into a sob. Like some kind of delayed reaction, she started to cry.

"Hey," he said, "it's all right. You're all right."

"I know," she said and cried harder.

Case felt no desire to move, motivated as much by being close to her as he was by the throbbing in his back and shoulder that encouraged him to remain still. He prayed he wouldn't regret it when he wiped Iris's tears that were running over her temples and into her hair. When she didn't protest, he gingerly touched her hair, hardly daring to believe he'd been given such a privilege.

"Hey, it's all right," he said once again, more softly. Her crying quieted, and he expected her to tell him to leave now that the crisis was over. Her eyes showed a sudden awareness of his fingers in her hair, and he waited for something angry or accusatory to fly out of her mouth. But her eyes connected with his in a way that had never happened before—in a way he'd never imagined possible. She said nothing, but she didn't need to. No matter how cantankerous she'd been with him—or would yet be—he knew in that moment there was something more, something different, hidden beneath the surface. She *did* feel something for him; he could see it, and he knew it. He knew it the same way he'd known from that life-altering moment that this was the woman God had preserved for him. The pain seemed to rush out of him, and he could only feel his heart overflowing with love for this woman—almost against his will. His emotions prompted him to a boldness that he never would have exhibited according to any rational judgment. He touched her face, and she took in a ragged breath. But still, she didn't object. And she showed no sign of anger.

Iris took in the fact that Casey Harrison was touching her—and she was allowing it—and she wondered if the fall had addled her brain. Then it occurred to her that she was not only unopposed to his being so near, she was actually enjoying it. The thought was shocking. How could it be true? She was *attracted* to this man? It seemed impossible, especially when she'd put so much effort into not liking him. Had she felt this way all along, or was it something that had just surfaced since she'd nearly died a few minutes ago? While she was struggling to understand what she was feeling and why, she realized by the subtle change in his expression what he was going to do next. One moment she was ready to slap his face and tell him that his intent to kiss her was appalling, and the next she wanted him to kiss her so badly that she could hardly breathe. She saw him close his eyes, but couldn't bring herself to do the same, fearing she might become lost in something out of her control and never find herself again. The moment his lips touched hers, her breathlessness amplified. She'd not been kissed in years, and that had been by a man who had broken her heart. Why was she doing this? What was she thinking? He kissed her meekly and opened his eyes for just a second before he closed them and kissed her again. Her stomach quivered, and she became conscious of her heart beating in a way that made her wonder if it might not have done so for a very long time. "Iris," he murmured close to her lips, and then into her ear, "Oh, Iris." The shiver that skittered down her back startled her to the realization that she was behaving like some kind of madwoman.

"Don't," she said and eased away to put distance between them. But then he was looking into her eyes, asking her silent questions that she couldn't answer. Suddenly afraid and not willing to analyze it, she pushed him away abruptly, and he groaned as she jumped to her feet.

"Hey, careful, lady," he snarled, mostly teasing. "That shoulder just saved your face."

"I'm sorry," she said and hurried from the room, crying before she made it to the top of the stairs.

Iris rushed into her bedroom and closed the door, as if doing so could put a barrier between herself and what had just happened. She kept seeing herself coming down from that ladder and having it hit her, as if she were being shown how it might have occurred if Case hadn't been there to save her. She wondered if her reaction was rooted in panic and shock, but her deepest instincts led her to believe she truly could have been killed, or at the very least permanently injured. Such an experience would be difficult to take in and of itself, but it had quickly become complicated by the way Case had touched her face and looked into her eyes. And he had *kissed* her! And she had *let* him! She couldn't believe it. Had they both gone mad? Short of insanity, what could it possibly mean? Was he some kind of rogue or scoundrel, accustomed to taking advantage of such an opportunity to tease a woman or test her response? Or was there some kind of feeling behind what he'd done? The memory of his eyes left her completely unable to credit his actions to anything unsuitable or improper. So, what did *that* mean? Did he care for her? Was he attracted to *her?* "Oh, help," she muttered aloud. She'd only realized minutes ago that she felt attracted to him. How could she possibly come to terms with evidence that he felt the same way? And perhaps more frightening, was it possible that he loved her? How could he? She'd given him no reason to. She certainly hoped he *didn't* love her, or even that he might believe that he did. She had no desire to contend with such issues with this man, knowing she would only break his heart and leave him hating her, as she'd somehow managed with many who had come before Casey Harrison.

"Oh, help," she muttered again and dropped to her knees beside the bed, praying for understanding and guidance. She prayed and pondered her feelings for several minutes before she found peace with the realization that she didn't have to figure it all out right now. In fact, all that mattered for the moment was the fact that she'd left the poor man lying on the floor in pain, and he could surely use some help. She felt more foolish for having left him there than she did for letting him kiss her, which motivated her to hurry back to the library. She couldn't deny a desire to be in the same room with him, and she rationalized that she simply wanted to get to know him better. Surely it was a good thing to learn more about a man who had saved her life, in spite of her skepticism over certain aspects of his character. Going down the stairs, Iris was displeased to realize the family had returned in the last few minutes, and her opportunity to be alone with Case would be impossible. But perhaps that was best, considering her present state of confusion.

* * * * *

Case watched Iris leave the room and resisted the urge to curse, knowing it was unseemly for a Latter-day Saint. He attempted to stand up, and it took more effort to resist the urge to spout off an inappropriate word—the kind that had flowed so freely in the home he'd grown up in. He groaned instead and had to sit on the floor for a minute to get his equilibrium. Unfortunately, it was more from the pain than from the realization that he'd actually kissed Iris Barrington. He focused on the kissing in an effort to divert his mind from the pain, and it worked. Butterflies swarmed in his stomach, and a little chuckle escaped his lips. He touched them briefly, thinking of how they'd made contact with hers. He closed his eyes and thought of touching her face and hair, and the sensation inside him heightened. The moment hadn't ended well, but in his opinion it was a glorious step in the right direction. For the first time since he'd been told in no uncertain terms that this was the woman God intended for him to marry, Case actually felt some real and tangible hope that it could be possible for her to accept that idea. They had a long way to go, but at least now she had some indication of his feelings for her. And he absolutely knew that she felt something more for him than the disdain she carried so proudly. He'd seen it in her eyes and felt it in the subtle response of her kiss. Thoughts of it made him chuckle again. Then he heard evidence that the family had returned and quickly struggled to stand, not wanting to be found on the floor of the library in this condition. He got to his feet, steadied his equilibrium, and moved toward the couch, quickly assessing that nothing was broken. He'd had broken bones before and knew the difference. Everything was movable, and there was no sharp or intense pain anywhere. What he felt was more a throbbing ache, which he knew well enough would get worse before it got better. He was badly bruised. But he'd survived the equivalent before, more times than he could count. At least this time his bruises had served some purpose in sparing Iris. He would gladly endure the pain, knowing that it was him feeling it, and not her. Once on the couch, Case had to contend with that unsteady feeling again, and he put his head down in an effort to alleviate it. He heard the children scattering through the house, filling the previous silence with shouting and laughter, and he knew the adults would be close behind. Not wanting to be found here like this, Case stood up carefully, but immediately sat back down. Thoughts of bringing attention to his injuries and having these people fuss over him brought on a sudden queasiness. But with his head between his knees, he didn't realize it was too late until he heard Eleanore say, "Are you all right?"

Case lifted his head slowly, not wanting to make the matter worse. He saw Eleanore's concern, which turned to alarm when she noticed the fallen ladder. "What on earth happened?" she demanded, far more distressed than angry.

"I . . . uh . . ." Case struggled for the right words, not wanting to say anything that might make Iris look bad in regard to the incident. He pressed his hands over his face, as if to help him think more clearly. "Well . . . I came in, and . . ."

"It was my fault," he heard Iris say, and he turned to see her standing beside her mother. "We need to send for the doctor."

"No, we do not!" he insisted, startled by how brash he sounded. It only took a second for him to know that his response had more to do with memories than with the present circumstances. In a dramatically softer voice he added, "I appreciate your concern, but I can assure you that nothing is broken. Just give me a few minutes, and I'll be—"

"A few minutes?" Iris countered, and he looked at her again. She was back to her cantankerous self. "You'll be lucky if you can get out of bed in a few days. Stop being so proud and just—"

"Will someone tell me what happened?" Eleanore asked.

Case and Iris exchanged a glance, as if to gauge which one of them might speak first. He saw something conspiratorial in her eyes, perhaps bordering on amusement, and he wondered if she had found something pleasant in the episode. He hoped so, because he certainly had. He was determined to let her explain. He'd already tried without much success. Before she could speak, James appeared beside his wife and asked, "What's wrong?" He looked at the ladder, then at Case sitting on the couch, looking a little pale, and added, "What happened?"

"That's what I'm trying to figure out," Eleanore said and turned to glare at Iris with a silent demand that she offer an explanation.

"It was my fault," she repeated. "Case appeared by some miraculous means, at exactly the right moment, to keep me from having a terrible fall. I was on the ladder and . . . reached too far . . . and it fell."

"Good heavens," Eleanore muttered.

James added, "Are you all right?"

"I'm fine," she said, then turned to look at Case. "But I know *he's* not. He couldn't possibly be. So tell him to stop being proud and stubborn and send for the doctor."

"I'm *fine,"* Case insisted. "I'm a little bruised, that's all. I've done all kinds of work with bruises before; I can do it again." He wanted to stand up and prove that he was stable, but he felt his pulse throbbing in the muscles of his shoulder and knew if he attempted to stand he would only end up looking like a fool.

Almost like a child tattling, Iris added, "After he broke my fall, the ladder landed on him. He *can't* be fine."

"I'm sending Ben for the doctor," James said and left the room before Case could protest again.

Chapter Five
RISK

"You should lie down," Eleanore said, moving toward Case.

"I just need a minute to get my bearings," he said.

"So lie down and get your bearings," she insisted. "I'll get you a pillow and some—"

"There's no need for that," he argued. "I'll just go to my room and get some rest, and I'll be fine tomorrow."

"If you're bruised, you'll be worse tomorrow," Eleanore said. He knew she was right, but he hated the thought of these people fussing over him, especially when he was supposed to be working. "You need to stay in the house where we can look after you. This couch isn't pretty, but I'm told it's fairly tolerable to sleep on. I'll get you some pillows, and we'll get you comfortable. You're staying here until the doctor says it's all right for you to be walking around and going up those stairs."

Eleanore left the room, but Iris remained where she was. After a moment of silence, Case looked up to find her staring at him, biting her bottom lip. Their eyes connected, and he would have given a month's wages to know what she was thinking. His heart quickened at the memory of their kiss, and at the same moment, she looked away as a subtle blush covered her face. Were their thoughts the same?

"Forgive me," she said, and he wondered if she was talking about the fall or the kiss. Wanting no regret over the kiss, he was relieved when she added, "I was being foolish, and the results could have been disastrous if you hadn't come along when you did. I know you're in pain, and I know it's my fault. And I'm sorry."

"There's no need to apologize, Iris. It was an accident. I'm glad I was here when you needed me. I can assure you I've been bruised before, but never for such a grand purpose. I'll be fine."

He'd said it to give her some assurance that he felt confident it wasn't the big ordeal she was making it out to be, and to share with her his confidence that he knew he would recover. But he saw something inquisitive come into her eyes, and the very idea of offering any further explanation put his stomach in knots. He looked away and felt those knots begin to tighten when she said, "That's the second time you've said something about such things happening before." He squeezed his eyes shut against the memories and cringed when she added, "But you don't want to talk about it."

"That's right; I don't."

"Do you believe I'll think less of you?"

"Absolutely. Anyone would."

Iris sat down across the room. "So this is part of your deplorable past?"

He opened his eyes to look at her. "Yes, but it's exactly that—in the past. The moment I was baptized, all of that was washed away. It's no longer relevant."

"Except that it's a part of who you are," she said, and Case felt himself shudder. That very idea was the most deplorable of all. "And clearly from that look on your face, it's not nearly so much in the past as you would like it to be."

Case looked away, not wanting his thoughts read so easily. He hated the course this conversation was taking, but didn't know how to get out of it. They'd kissed, and he'd taken the pain of her fall, but that didn't mean he could trust her with his deepest, darkest secrets. He reminded himself that he had nothing to hide, and he'd long ago taken the attitude that he'd rather have people know the truth and be repulsed than to live in fear of people inadvertently finding out the truth. If Iris couldn't accept him in spite of his deplorable past, he could never risk sharing his past life with her. Still, the very thought of saying it made him a little queasy. Imagining Iris's likely repulsion enhanced the feeling.

When she said nothing more and the tension became unbearable, he attempted to be glib. "If you're waiting for me to spill my past at your feet, you might be waiting a long time. What reason do I have to trust you with such things, Iris?" Then he became more serious. "How do I know you won't one day turn and use such information to incriminate me?"

He saw guilt and regret pass through her eyes and found some comfort in that. She looked down and wrung her hands together slightly. "You're right. I've given you no reason to trust me." She looked back up with a challenging expression in her eyes. "I just wonder if you're willing to take the risk."

Case took her words deeply to heart. He was willing to risk anything—everything—to have her in his life. Would it take spilling his heart and opening himself completely to bridge this chasm between them? He knew that such risk would likely end up coming back to bite him in one way or another. His childhood had taught him that. But Iris was not his father, and he was not the man he used to be. If she needed some evidence of his trusting her—even when she hadn't earned it—he was more than willing to comply, in spite of the knots in his stomach. While he was wondering exactly what to say, she muttered almost lightly, "So . . . is your experience with such things a result of barroom brawls? Fighting in the streets, perhaps? Or maybe it was fighting for sport?"

Case swallowed carefully, but had to admit to the truth of his thoughts. "If you weren't so beautiful, your judgmental attitude would be entirely appalling." He could guess by her expression that she was delightfully startled by the compliment and confused over her own judgmental attitude. He felt surprised to realize that he was now able to read her so easily when he'd spent months trying to understand her with no success. He knew a tremendous shift was taking place between them; he only wished it didn't require his sharing what he knew Iris was waiting to hear. At least her judgmental attitude gave him some incentive in wanting to straighten her out.

"If only," he hurried to begin before he lost his nerve. "I could brag about fighting for sport and barroom brawls. I spent a lot of time in bars, Iris, but it wasn't to fight. It was to forget." In the midst of such a confession, he wondered if she'd noticed that he'd started using her given name. He liked saying it and was glad to be done with formality, whether she was or not.

Trying to focus on the topic again, he forced himself to move on, if only to get it over with. He took a deep breath and just said it. "My father drank a lot; all the time. And he was mean when he was drunk. He'd take it out on whoever happened to be close by when the mood would strike him." He paused and tried to ignore the horrified expression on Iris's face. Such a thing had clearly never occurred to her, and he felt some regret over exposing her to the reality that such evils of life existed. But now that he'd started, he had to finish. "My brothers and I were good at running and hiding, but sometimes he'd catch one of us off guard." She gasped, and he could feel it sinking into her. She put a hand over her mouth, and he asked gently, "Do you want me to stop?" She shook her head, and he reiterated, "You don't have to hear this, Iris. It's in the past and—"

"Just tell me," she said, and he saw her visibly struggling for composure. If nothing else, her emotional reaction was somewhat comforting.

Again Case took a deep breath and forced the words out of his mouth. "He'd keep kicking and punching until he passed out, but no matter how battered we were, he expected us to be up at dawn, out in the fields doing the work he couldn't do because he was too drunk or hung over to stand up straight." He cleared his throat tensely. "That's it, really. That's explanation enough. Now I can be grateful for what I learned and put it in the past."

"What you *learned?"* she asked, sounding barely calm.

"I learned how to work hard. I learned that all pain goes away eventually if you let it. And I learned that a human being is capable of surviving anything short of death. I'm still alive, which proves it."

Case saw her scrutinizing him as if they'd just met all over again. He wondered if her new opinion of him would be better or worse than the old one. She finally said, "Forgive me . . . for my judgmental attitude."

"Forgive *me."*

"For what?" she asked, surprised.

"For exposing you to such things. A lady so fine as you should not have to even know of the ugliness of life."

She glanced away. "Why are you being so kind to me? I can't think of any reason why you should be. If I—"

"Sorry it took me so long," Eleanore said, coming into the room with two pillows and some bedding.

Distracted from a conversation that had been way too deep, Case became more aware of the pain, especially in his shoulder and upper back on the left side, where the ladder had fallen. Eleanore put the pillows at one end of the couch and said, "Now lie down and rest until the doctor comes."

"I'm fine," he said gently. "You're very kind, but—"

"Stop being so stubborn and lie down," she said with a motherly smile, taking hold of his shoulders gently to urge him to do so.

Case was startled by the pain provoked by her touch and responded with a sharp moan before he could even think to exert more discipline.

"Good heavens," Eleanore said and abruptly pulled her hands away.

Iris saw the evidence of Case's pain in his face, in spite of his efforts to mask it, and the gist of their conversation fully sank into her. It suddenly took all her willpower not to burst into audible sobbing. She'd experienced a huge gamut of emotions since she'd fallen from that ladder, and she was finding it difficult to even remain standing as her tumbling thoughts and roiling emotions swirled inside her. She was relieved when her mother said, "Iris, get me some salve, some towels from the kitchen, and a big bowl of snow."

Iris hurried from the room but had to take a minute to lean her back against the wall and catch her breath. Out of Case's sight, she was able to let her guard down enough to allow it all to penetrate her reeling brain—and her heart. Everything he'd said about his past increased her new understanding of that look in his eyes. His taking the pain of her fall merged with the way he'd touched her face—and kissed her. All of it together left her knowing only one thing for certain. She would never be the same. She didn't know what it all meant—or at least what it meant to her—but she knew that Casey Harrison had opened her eyes to things she'd never considered before. A harsh sob rushed up from her chest, and she had to put a hand over her mouth to stifle its sound, knowing she was still too close to the open library door. She heard her mother telling Case to take off his shirt so she could see the damage, and Case protesting in return. Iris forced her emotions to a place where she could examine them later and hurried farther down the hall, knowing her mother would surely win the argument.

Iris was glad for an excuse to go outside and get some snow. The cold air made it easier to calm the rumbling inside of her. She scooped handfuls of snow into a bowl, knowing from past experience with the many minor injuries of three little brothers that cold helped counter the swelling associated with bruises and muscle aches. She quickly got the salve and some towels and succinctly answered Stella and Lizzie's inquiries over Case's injuries before she returned to the library. Approaching the door, she could hear her father saying, "That's a pretty heavy ladder. We can be grateful it wasn't worse."

Iris hesitated at the door as her mother said, "And it's a long way that Iris could have fallen. That top book shelf is quite high. She could have been seriously hurt . . . or worse."

Iris took a step to enter the room, then hesitated again as Case spoke. "I'm glad Iris is all right. I'm glad I was there. But I'm certain it's not as bad as it looks. I'll be fine, and you're making way too much fuss over this."

"Oh, admit it," Eleanore said more lightly. "It's good to have someone taking care of you. Everybody needs that in their life."

"I can't deny that," Case said, "but that doesn't mean you have to make such a fuss."

At a pause in the conversation, Iris entered the room, unable to see Case at all, since he was on the other side of her parents, who were hovering over him. When they heard her and turned, Case came into view, shirtless, with a glowing purple bruise over his left shoulder and upper back. She gasped, and he looked at her for only a moment before he turned away, embarrassed.

"Oh, good," Eleanore said and took the salve from Iris. "Let's get some of this on it first. This is obviously the worst of the problem."

"It looks horrible," Iris said, setting down the towels and the bowl of snow. "I *feel* horrible. It's my fault."

"We've already had this conversation," Case said and winced only slightly when Eleanore began carefully rubbing the ointment over the bruised area. James stood the ladder up and muttered something about being grateful it hadn't been worse.

Hearing the cry of a child from somewhere in the house, Eleanore put the jar of salve in Iris's hand and said, "Here, you can do this. Then get some cold on it. I've got to get Mariah down for a nap."

Iris wanted to shout that she would be more than happy to watch her sister, as opposed to doing this task, but she said nothing. She was just getting up the nerve to actually take over her mother's task when her father left the room, saying he'd come back to check on Case after the doctor had seen him. It became more difficult for Iris to resist the urge to shout. She wanted to say that she couldn't be left alone with this man, especially under such circumstances, and in charge of a task that required touching him. She forced any thoughts of kissing or attraction or deeply emotional conversations out of her head and dug a fair amount of salve out of the jar with her fingers. Trying to concentrate only on the assignment, she gently rubbed the ointment over the bruised area. Concentrating became more difficult when she allowed her eyes to wander over his neck, his hair, the side of his face that was visible from where she stood. He seemed deep in thought, and she wondered where his mind was. She considered what he'd shared with her about his past and felt a little queasy. She could imagine him feeling the same, having such memories dredged up by the present experience. That alone increased her regret.

"Forgive me," she finally said.

"We've already *had* this conversation, too. There's nothing to apologize for."

"I realize the injury was an accident, and I've already apologized for my judgmental attitude. But . . . I need to apologize for being so . . . insensitive . . . about your past."

He turned his head to look up at her, as if to assess if she were being sincere. He looked straight ahead again. "As I saw it, you were not at all insensitive over what I told you."

"But before you told me, I was."

"That was being judgmental." He sounded subtly facetious. "And you already apologized for that."

"Well, I'm certain I've been insensitive somewhere along the way. And I'm sorry."

Again he looked at her, but only for a moment. "Apology accepted. Now, I think there's probably plenty of that stuff on there."

"Oh, of course," she said and set the salve aside, wiping her fingers on one of the towels she'd brought before she wrapped it around a handful of snow and pressed it gently to the bruised shoulder.

Case winced more from the cold than any pain. But at least it gave him something to distract him from her nearness, her attention, her changed attitude. His heart quickened, knowing this was not just his imagination. To relieve the silence, he said, "And the cold is supposed to do . . . what?"

"It helps keep the swelling down, which is supposed to make it less painful."

"That would have been nice to know when I was a kid," he said.

Iris tried to come up with a comment regarding what he'd confessed about his childhood, but what could she possibly say in regard to something so horrible? Instead she asked, "How are you feeling? Does it hurt much?"

"Other than that shoulder, it's not too bad," Case said. "And that only hurts when I move it or touch it."

"Oh, only then?" she asked lightly. He chuckled, but it sounded tense. They both remained silent while she adjusted the cold towel to a different place on his bruised skin. She felt some relief when she heard sounds indicating that Ben had returned with the doctor. She left the room as the doctor came in, closing the door behind her.

Iris was sitting in the kitchen with her parents when the doctor came to give his report. Nothing appeared to be broken, and there was no sign of any serious injury or anything to be concerned about. He advised them to keep doing what they were doing for the bruises, and to put Case's left arm in a sling until the pain of the contusions eased up. The sling would take the weight off the shoulder and keep Case from using it until it healed. The doctor suggested having him take it easy for a few days, and felt certain that doing so wouldn't be difficult. "I suspect," he said, "that when he wakes up tomorrow he's going to hurt a lot worse than he does now."

Iris suppressed her feelings of guilt over that very thing and watched her father settle generously with the doctor before he walked him outside. Her mother stood up and said, "I'll help Case get what he needs. Would you mind watching out for the children until supper?"

"Not at all," Iris said, a little disappointed not to be assigned to see what Case needed. But on the other hand, she wasn't certain she could endure much more strained silence, considering all that had happened between them this afternoon.

* * * * *

Case was finally left alone in the library with strict orders to stay down and rest. He had been tucked beneath a blanket on the couch, with a clean sheet beneath him and soft pillows under his head. His arm was in a neatly made fabric splint tied behind his neck, and there were cold towels laid over his shoulder and upper back. His efforts to assure Eleanore that he could rest in his own room and that he didn't need all this attention were thwarted rather forcefully. He had to remind himself to be gracious, but it felt strange to be so coddled. Never in his entire life had any injury or illness been treated with so much concern or interest. And never in his life had he been seen by a doctor for anything. His father had forbade a doctor to enter his home, even for serious injuries. But those injuries were usually a result of his violent behavior, and he hadn't wanted to draw any attention to it.

Now that he was alone, Case's mind began to absorb the fact that today's incident had triggered something inside of him that he didn't want to acknowledge. He knew now that the reason he'd felt so lightheaded and unsteady was more related to his emotions and memories than to the physical pain. And having to verbalize the source of that to Iris hadn't helped any. Or maybe it had. Maybe it had been good for him to say it out loud. Still, he didn't want to think about that time in his life. It was behind him, and that's where it needed to stay.

Case certainly felt stiff and sore from his body hitting the floor to break Iris's fall, and his shoulder wasn't at all happy with the battle it had waged with the ladder. Still, Case felt certain he could get up and do *something,* and he felt both restless and guilty. He'd wager that James spent more on the doctor's visit than Case made in a week. He felt guilty for that, too. But both he and Eleanore had insisted that they considered it a privilege to care for him, and they were grateful for his sparing Iris from any injury.

As his thoughts turned to Iris, Case let out a weighted sight that merged into a delighted chuckle. When he'd felt compelled to talk to her, he never would have predicted such an outcome. But it had turned out fairly well, in his opinion. He'd take the injuries all over again just to be able to kiss her the way he had. And her change in attitude—her kindness and apologies—seemed nothing less than miraculous. He prayed and thanked God for such miracles, and asked that he might be able to get back to work very quickly. Sitting around like this for very long could incite him to madness.

When he heard evidence down the hall that supper was being put on, he got carefully to his feet and removed the sling enough to gingerly get his arms into his shirt. He put the sling back on, amazed at how much it hurt to move that shoulder even a little. The sling did alleviate some of the pressure, and he was grateful for the doctor's suggestion in that regard. Walking into the dining room, Case was assaulted with a gentle scolding from Eleanore, with Stella insisting that she was going to bring his supper to him in the library.

"It's far too boring in there," Case said. "And I'm capable of getting up and coming to the table."

"Fine, then," Eleanore said, "but you be careful."

"I promise," he said to her, and she smiled. But she looked tired, and he knew the pregnancy was affecting her more than she likely let on most of the time.

The children were characteristically noisy and full of the usual antics when they came into the room. It was evident that James had explained to the boys what had happened to Case, but they were still full of questions and wanted to see the big bruise they'd heard about.

"Later," Eleanore said. "It's time to eat."

After everyone was seated and the blessing on the food had been spoken, Lizzie took it upon herself to dish up Case's plate and cut his food into bite-sized pieces, since he could only use one hand. He warded off any embarrassment and simply thanked her. Throughout the meal, Case enjoyed the usual chatter and bantering that went on at the supper table. Iris was typically quiet, but in the middle of a bite of mashed potatoes, he looked up to see her watching him. Instead of the glare he'd become accustomed to, she smiled slightly, then looked away, but not before he caught a distinct sparkle in her eyes. It *was* a miracle. He thought of how it had felt to kiss her, and his heart did an unexpected flutter.

When supper was over, James walked Case back to the library, resisting all argument that Case could go to his own room and sleep. "We're just going to keep you close for a couple of days," James said firmly. "Is there anything you need from your room? Anything we can get for you at all?"

"No. No, thank you," Case said. "I'm fine."

Alone again, Case decided to find a book worth reading in order to kill some time. He looked at the clock and wondered how long until the family gathered to read from the scriptures and pray. At least he'd be close by for that. He was glad to find a novel that quickly interested him, and was surprised at the passing of time when Jamie came to tell him to come across the hall for the usual evening ritual. Nothing was out of the ordinary except for the way Iris kept glancing discreetly at him, and he did the same in return. If only he had any idea what she might be thinking!

After prayer, Iris went to put the little ones to bed, knowing her mother was especially tired. Case thanked everyone for their help and was touched by Ben's firm offer to do all of Case's chores for the next few days, or until he could manage.

"I'm certain I can do *something,"* Case said.

"Not for a while, you can't," James said, and Case was tired of arguing with him.

When no one else was close enough to hear, Case whispered to James, "Now, don't you go doing anything stupid while I'm laid up. You be careful and take care of yourself."

James looked at him hard and said, "I will if you will."

Case sighed. "Fine. I will if you will."

He settled back onto his makeshift bed in the library. There was a single lamp burning nearby, and he read some more from the novel he'd started earlier. Hearing a light knock on the door, he felt sure Eleanore had come to check on him, but it was Iris who peered inside once he'd declared that he was decent.

"Sorry to bother you," she said.

"You're not bothering me." He set the book aside.

She closed the door and leaned against it. "So . . . how are you feeling?"

"I'm fine," he insisted with comical exaggeration, which made her chuckle. More seriously he added, "As long as I don't move it or touch it, I'm fine."

"Then you mustn't move it or touch it."

"Impossible to avoid to some degree, I'm afraid. But it will heal soon enough. How are *you?*"

"Me? Oh, I'm fine. I just . . . need to say something."

By her hesitancy, Case wondered if this would have anything to do with what had occurred between them earlier. He wondered if she would tell him that it had been a mistake, that she wanted nothing to do with him in that regard.

"Have a seat," he said and motioned to a chair across the room. But she sat at the other end of the couch where he was sitting, on top of the bedding Eleanore had carefully tucked around the cushions.

Iris fought to subdue her nervousness and reminded herself of the motivation that had driven her to come here and open this conversation. The day had been far too eventful and filled with way too much to digest. But there was one point in particular that was bothering her. "What did you want to talk to me about?" she asked straightaway.

"Excuse me? *You* came in here to talk to *me.*"

"I came to ask what you wanted to talk to me about . . . earlier . . . when you came to the library. After you saved me, you said you needed to talk to me. But then . . . I was crying, and then . . . we were kissing, and . . . then I left and . . ." She hesitated when she saw him smile. "Is something funny?"

"No. I'm just glad to hear you admit that we were kissing. I was afraid you'd prefer to pretend it hadn't happened."

"Maybe I would."

"Maybe I won't let you."

She felt herself growing warm and knew she had to stick to the point. "What did you come to talk to me about?"

Case sighed and wished he could find the courage to say what he'd been hoping to say when he sought her out earlier. But it was easier to say, "Maybe I didn't really need to talk to you; maybe I was prompted to find you in order to save you."

Iris looked down, feeling guilty all over again for the pain she'd caused him. Without looking up, she said, "But . . . there must have been something you wanted to say."

"Yes. Yes, there was. But now I'm thinking it's likely better left unsaid . . . at least for now."

Her eyes became inquisitive, perhaps frustrated, then she chuckled. "I think your curious nature has rubbed off on me."

"What you mean to say is that you're dying to know what I was going to talk to you about."

"Yes, I suppose I am."

Case weighed his instincts carefully. Just because they'd shared a tender moment and a couple of kisses didn't necessarily mean she was ready to hear how he really felt about her, or the full measure of his intentions. He didn't want to scare her off after they'd finally made such progress in a matter of hours. But oh, how he wanted to kiss her again! Then it occurred to him that something in her eyes was encouraging him to believe that was what she wanted, too. He hoped he was reading her right when he held out his right hand and said, "Come here."

Iris looked at his hand, then his face, while an uncontrolled swarm of butterflies took flight in her stomach and fluttered through her every nerve. She fought the urge to cry and wondered over such a reaction. Was it residue from her own brush with serious injury earlier today? Had his saving her given them some kind of connection that hadn't been there before? Was it some combination of guilt and gratitude because he *had* saved her? Or was there something more? He'd kissed her, and she'd allowed it. And most startling, she'd enjoyed it. The moment kept coming to her mind, even more than the moment of falling off of the ladder and seeing it come down after her. But she felt so out of sorts with herself that she didn't know if she was overreacting to her fear of what could have happened to her if he'd not shown up. And perhaps this sudden sense of dependence on him was part of that overreaction. Or maybe she was trying to analyze the whole thing far too much. Maybe there was nothing deeply significant about this sudden attraction she felt. And maybe there was. As she reached out and put her hand into his, she honestly didn't care. She was only grateful to be in this moment and to feel what she was feeling. She saw him smile at the same moment he squeezed her hand, tugging on her arm to urge her closer. With the way the arm in the sling was resting on the arm of the couch, she felt certain that moving it would cause him pain, so she eased next to him, and he let go of her hand to put his right arm around her shoulders.

"Do you need me this close to talk to me?" she asked, hearing a dreaminess in her own voice.

"No." He smiled again. "No, I don't."

This time Iris closed her eyes as he bent to kiss her, fully allowing herself to become lost in the sensation. She put a hand to his face, loving the feel of his stubbled skin beneath her fingers. This kiss was lengthier than the earlier ones, but still meek and unassuming. He drew back, and she opened her eyes to see him watching her, silently questioning her, but she couldn't figure out what the question was exactly. For more than a minute they just gazed at each other, as if doing so might allow their minds to catch up to this moment and accept it, or perhaps understand it. Iris came to no conclusion beyond surprise at her own feelings—and behavior—and a startling awareness of how utterly handsome this man was.

When the silence between them became heavy, Iris finally said, "So, what did you want to talk to me about?"

Case chuckled. "You can't stand it, can you. I realize now what you're doing. You're only letting me kiss you so you can lure information out of me."

"No," she said with a seriousness that she hoped would let him know she meant it, "that's not why I let you kiss me."

"Why, then?" he asked with the same seriousness.

"I have no idea," she said and urged her lips to his, as if that might help answer the question.

Case smiled as their lips parted. "But you know it wasn't to lure information out of me?"

"That's right."

With their faces only an inch apart, he said, "Maybe it's better if I just keep my thoughts to myself."

"You don't *want* to tell me."

"I do," he insisted. "But . . . saying it involves some . . . risk."

"You think I'll be angry?"

"Maybe. Or maybe there's more risk for you in *hearing* what I have to say than there is for me to say it."

Iris thought about that and said, "So the level of risk depends on . . . what?"

Case shrugged without moving his left shoulder. "I don't know. Perhaps . . . how much a person is willing to open his heart. That takes risk, doesn't it?"

Iris felt a physical response that made the answer to the question obvious. "Yes, it does."

"Truthfully," he went on, "I've never opened my heart to a woman before, so I'm certainly not an expert."

"Oh, *I'm* an expert," she said with a facetious edge that kept the admittance from getting too close to that bitter, frightened part of herself she didn't care to look at right now.

"And you're really willing to risk hearing what I have to say?" he asked.

Iris was surprised at how long she had to think about that. But her concerns were overruled by her curiosity. "I really am."

"What if you don't *like* what I have to say?"

She had to think about that even longer, but decided to take it on as it came. "Then I may never speak to you again," she said with a sober face, then she laughed.

"I don't think that's funny." Case attempted to sound severe while his heart pounded as he considered the context of the conversation. "I'm certain you are completely capable of never speaking to me again." He kissed her brow. "But I think I prefer it this way."

"I think I do, too," she said and settled her head on his shoulder. "I'm willing to take the risk, Case. Just say what you need to say."

Case closed his eyes and attempted to accept this as reality. Iris Barrington was snuggled close to him with her head on his shoulder, willing to hear what he had to say. He quickly gauged his instincts, wondering if it was truly the right time to say what he *really* wanted to say. If she reacted badly, things between them could be worse than ever. But it felt right, so he made up his mind to just say it and get it over with, and he'd deal with the repercussions as they happened.

Chapter Six

PRACTICALITY AND CONVENIENCE

Iris waited with a quickened heart for Case to speak. She wondered what could be so serious, then it occurred to her that perhaps he was just teasing. "I was going to ask you to marry me," he said, and she laughed until the obvious became evident.

She lifted her head to look at him. "You're not laughing."

"No. No, I'm not."

Iris's heart began to pound. "You're serious." She made a noise of disbelief and put some distance between them, as if that might help her see him—or his intentions—more clearly. "Until today, I didn't even *like* you."

"I know."

"But you were going to ask me to *marry* you?"

"Yes. Yes, I was."

"Why?"

Case searched for the right words. "Because I've believed for some time now that it's the right thing to do."

Iris tried to accept him having such feelings for *some time* now, but she couldn't even comprehend it. "I . . . I don't understand." She felt flustered and overwrought. "What . . . what exactly are you saying, Case?"

"I'm saying that I believe it's right for us to be married."

"Just like that?"

"I suppose that depends on you. I'm willing to take that risk. Are you?"

Iris stood up, and Case prayed silently that this conversation would end well. He fought away his panic and focused on trusting in the Lord, and remembering what he knew to be true in his heart. He also reminded himself that he could not control Iris's free agency. He could only hope and pray that, with time, she would come to know what he knew.

Case watched her pace the room a couple of times before she said, "That's not *risk,* Case, that's insanity. We can't just up and get married as a matter of convenience or practicality."

"Sure we can . . . if we both know it's right."

She stopped pacing and looked at him as if he'd completely lost his mind. "These things go in order," she said. "My parents taught me very clearly the difference between infatuation and love. This . . . attraction we feel for each other doesn't necessarily mean anything at all."

"But love can grow with time, Iris, as long as it's given the right ingredients. Lots of people get married out of practicality."

"Is that how it was with your parents?" she asked, and Case bristled far more than he could ever let on. She didn't know the half of it, and he had to remind himself of that. In truth, he hoped she never did.

He could only say, "That's not fair."

"It's probably not," she said, "but it makes a fair point."

"Yes, it makes a fair point, but not the one you're trying to defend. My mother married my father because she fell in love and was blinded to every evidence of his true character. She would have done well to be a little more practical. What we have that they didn't have is the knowledge that God will guide us to what's right through the Holy Ghost. And when you know something's right, you do it—even if it isn't easy."

"So, you're saying you believe it's right for us to get married."

"Yes. Yes, I am."

"And you're saying you're willing to marry me, even though it might not be easy."

"Well, this conversation is a good indication of that."

Iris willed herself not to get defensive and make a fool of herself. "You're trying to aggravate me; you're testing me."

Case chuckled. "No, I am not. I'm simply stating what I see to be true. Is it some great secret that you and I aggravate each other without even trying? I'm not naive enough to think that would instantly go away because I put a ring on your finger. But I believe we can make a good marriage and raise a good family, because down deep we both want the same things."

"What's that?" she asked as if she felt certain he had no idea what she wanted.

Case answered firmly. "We both want to live the gospel and to be gathered with the Saints. We want the blessings of eternity more than the comforts of this life. We don't want to be alone in this world or the next one."

Iris sat down. He *did* know what she wanted. But she still had an arguable point. "I will marry for love, Case, *and* practicality. We *do* want the same things, but I don't believe that's enough. My parents married for love, and I will do the same."

"And was that your blood mother or your real mother who married for love?"

He saw anger in her eyes. "That's not fair."

"No. No, it's not." He found great pleasure in repeating what she'd said a minute earlier. "But it makes a fair point. Your father loved the woman who gave birth to you, but obviously that didn't work out the way he'd expected. Maybe marrying for love isn't all it's reputed to be."

"Obviously, that depends on the person. You've seen the example in this house of people who love each other. How could I settle for anything less than that?"

"I wouldn't want you to. But we both have to be practical enough to fall in love with someone who shares our most basic values and has the character to be everything we need to raise a good family."

Iris thought about that. "I can agree with that."

"You don't think you could ever come to love me?" he asked, certain she would break his heart then and there.

"I don't know," Iris admitted, then her stomach quivered as she considered the depth of feeling beneath his question. "Are you saying that you love *me?"*

Case looked away abruptly, hoping to hide any truth she might see in his eyes. He wasn't ready to expose that part of himself; not yet, not under the circumstances. He hurried to say, "I'm not saying any such thing. I'm saying that I believe it's right for us to be together."

Iris didn't want to, but felt she had to ask, "Is this really about me and you, or is it about me being the most practical way for you to become a part of this family?"

Case turned back to face her, astonished and trying not to feel hurt. He swallowed carefully and gave her a straight and honest answer. "I love being a part of this family, Iris, but I would never manipulate you into marrying me for any such purpose. If you haven't noticed, I can be a part of this family with or without you. One thing has nothing to do with the other."

Iris looked down. "You're right, of course. I'm sorry. It's just that . . . well . . . we don't even know each other; not really."

"Then we should get to know each other. And when you think this . . . attraction we feel . . . has turned into something more . . . you let me know."

She looked at him. "I think I can live with that."

"Fair enough."

"But . . . what if it doesn't? What if it never turns into something more . . . for one or the other of us . . . or both of us?"

Case shrugged, his confidence aided by the spiritual manifestation he'd had, and the evidence of miracles in that regard that had already occurred. "I guess that's a risk we'll both have to take."

Hearing him put it that way, Iris wondered if she was really willing to take such a risk, to open her heart to this man when her instinct was to not trust him. But she *wanted* to get to know him, and in the deepest part of herself, she wanted to trust him. She just didn't know if she could. However, there could be nothing wrong in giving the matter time to learn whether or not that might be possible.

With the air between them cleared, Iris took advantage of the moment and just sat beside him again, slipping her hand into his. "Thank you," she said, "for saving me today."

"A pleasure," he said and lifted her hand to his lips.

She wanted to sit and talk with him, but her mind was busy trying to catch up with all that had been said between them already. She finally broke the silence to tell him good night, once she'd made certain he had everything he needed. But as tired as she was, it felt like hours before she was finally able to sleep. Casey Harrison had asked her to marry him. It was as wonderful as it was terrifying. She hoped and prayed that with time, the wonderful would overpower her fear, and not the other way around. She asked herself if she *could* love him, or if she already did. She honestly couldn't say one way or another, but perhaps that was best for now. For now, she would simply enjoy getting to know him and savor the way she felt in his presence, or even just thinking about him. Finally she slept, with a smile on her face.

* * * * *

The following morning, Case woke up feeling far more stiff and sore than he'd expected. All pride aside, he couldn't deny being grateful to know he'd been given orders to take it easy. The very thought of attempting to do any of his expected chores made him a little queasy when it hurt just to move. He could hear noises in the house to indicate everyone was awake and bustling around, but he couldn't talk himself into the effort of getting up and making himself a part of it. In order to distract himself from his inability to move, he guided his mind to the memories of his precious time with Iris the previous day. As long as he remained still, nothing hurt. He felt himself smile, then he chuckled with no one there to hear it. He offered his usual morning prayer right where he was, certain God would understand his reasons for not being on his knees. And he expressed deep gratitude for the progress he'd made with Iris that had obviously been guided by God's hand. He finished his prayer, then just lay there, his eyes closed, pondering his feelings for Iris and wondering what the future might bring. At the moment, it felt as if everything would just neatly fall into place from here. Surely, with time, he could prove to her that he was everything he claimed to be, and that she could trust him enough to pledge her life to him. And with any luck, she would learn to love him, and their marriage could be more than a matter of practicality for her.

Hearing a knock at the door, he called, "Come in," but he resisted moving more than to turn his head to see who was there. His heart quickened to see Iris with a smile on her face.

"Good morning," she said and set a breakfast tray on the table in front of the couch.

"Good morning," he said, staying where he was if only to avoid drawing attention to how much it hurt to move. "You don't have to wait on me, you know."

"I know, but Mother insisted you would likely be better sticking close to bed today, and I volunteered."

"How thoughtful of you." He took her hand and she sat on the edge of the couch beside him. He kissed her hand, then touched her face. "You're beautiful when you smile, Iris. You should smile more."

"Yes, I'm certain I should."

"I mean . . . you're beautiful even when you *don't* smile, but . . . when you smile . . ." He wanted to sit up and kiss her, but he felt frozen with sore muscles. He was deeply relieved when she bent over to kiss him.

"Enjoy your breakfast," she said. "I'll check back to see if you need anything."

"Thank you," he said as she moved toward the door. "For the kiss, especially."

"My pleasure," she said and left, leaving him to wonder if this was a dream. The pain he felt in just sitting up in order to eat let him know that it wasn't. But even that made him chuckle.

A while after he'd finished eating, Iris came back to get the dishes and asked, "How are you feeling today?"

"Since I'm committed to honesty, I have to say that I'm pretty sore . . . but it will pass."

She sighed. "I'm sorry for—"

"You need to stop repeating yourself, Iris. You just keep bringing me food, and I'll sit here and let it pass. Next week at this time, neither one of us will hardly remember this happened."

"Oh, I don't know about that," she said and tossed him a saucy look on her way to the door. "Is there anything else you need?"

"No. No, thank you. But thanks for asking."

Ben came in to see how he was doing, and they talked over a game of checkers. A while later the boys came in, asking all kinds of questions and looking pleasantly horrified to see the bruise that they begged him to show them. After twenty minutes, their father came in to tell them they'd bothered Case enough and he needed to rest.

"They're fine," Case insisted, enjoying the entertainment of their antics.

"You can come back later," James said to his sons. "You all have chores and schoolwork to do."

The three of them didn't complain, because they knew their father wouldn't tolerate it, but they sulked away as if they were being sent to prison, which made Case chuckle.

"Sorry," James said.

"They're fine, really."

"How are you? And don't lie to me."

"I don't lie," Case insisted and gave him the same answer he'd given Iris. "As long as I don't move, I'm fine. So . . . I'm just going to stay here and avoid moving as much as possible. And tomorrow I think I'll need to start moving just to get rid of the stiffness."

"Maybe the day *after* tomorrow," James said. "We'll see."

"So, you're my warden now?"

"Something like that," James chuckled. "Do you need anything?"

"No. No, thank you. Iris already asked."

James lifted an eyebrow and smiled, but he made no comment before he left the room.

A short while later, Frederick and Lizzie came to check on him and stayed to visit a short while. Stella brought his lunch and came for the tray, also staying to chat for a few minutes. And Case had to keep insisting that he truly didn't need anything more than the abundance of care and company that he was already receiving.

That afternoon, Mary Jane came to visit him for a while, and he enjoyed talking with her as he never had before. Soon after she left, the boys came again with the purpose of entertaining him by acting out stories from the Book of Mormon. Their favorite was the story of Ammon cutting off the arms of the men who tried to steal the sheep. Case thoroughly enjoyed the entertainment, but it made him laugh far too much—and it hurt to laugh. Iris came and shooed the boys away, telling Case that they were more easily taken in small doses.

"So, if you sent my court jesters away, will you entertain me instead?"

"Certainly," she said, and they played three games of checkers before she asked, "Do you know how to play chess?"

"If I don't, will you teach me?"

"Certainly," she said again, and they worked at it until she left to help put supper on. When she brought his meal to him, she brought enough for herself, and they ate together while sounds of the family talking and laughing in the distance added to the pleasant atmosphere. She asked him questions about himself and his life, some of which he answered eagerly; others he gracefully skirted around or gave answers that were true but not too deep. He asked her questions as well, and he sensed that she was answering in the same way he was. But still, it was progress in getting to know each other better, and he was enjoying every minute of it.

Iris left to help clean up the kitchen, and Eleanore came in, looking tired and pale, which reminded him of her ongoing struggle with her pregnancy. She suggested that the family read scriptures and pray in the library so he wouldn't have to move so far, but Case insisted that he needed to move around a little and was settled in the parlor before the others arrived. Iris sat beside him, as opposed to making an effort to sit as far away as possible. He felt tempted to hold her hand, but wasn't certain if she wanted him to do so in the presence of others, so he didn't.

Case managed to get to his knees for prayer without drawing too much attention to himself, but getting back to the couch after family prayer took great effort, and he felt conspicuous. He decided to just stay there until everyone else left, then make the trip across the hall to the library without anyone watching. Lizzie offered to put the children to bed since Eleanore was tired, and she specifically assigned Iris to see that Case had what he needed before she went to bed. Case found himself sitting there with Iris beside him, and James and Eleanore sitting close together on the opposite couch. For the sake of making conversation—and to satisfy his curiosity—Case asked questions about their life in England, and they were soon talking freely of the situation there. Case marveled at descriptions of the manor house they'd lived in, and found it difficult to believe that Eleanore had once worked for James Barrington in a household with many other servants. When he commented on that, Eleanore said, "Oh, I worked there for years before he even knew I existed."

"How *did* he come to know of your existence?" Case asked.

"I know this part," Iris said to her father. "You interviewed all of the women in the household to find a governess after my mother died, and she's the one you knew was right for the position."

"Yes, that's true," James said, "but that's not the first time she'd come to my attention."

"He found me in the library one night," Eleanore said. "I was there to read from the Bible, but I wasn't supposed to be. I was afraid he'd have me expelled from the household—but obviously he didn't."

"So, how exactly did you fall in love?" Iris asked, tossing a brief, conspiring glance toward Case. Clearly she meant to prove a point in light of their recent conversation. But he was surprised when she added, "I don't think you've ever actually told me."

"I don't know that there's much to tell," Eleanore said. "I just . . . realized that I loved him, and—"

"So, that's it? You were taking care of his children, which meant you saw each other a lot. And you just . . . realized you loved him?"

Case saw James and Eleanore exchange a look that indicated some confusion, which prompted the same expression on Iris's face.

"I thought you knew," James said.

"Knew what?" Iris asked, sounding mildly panicked.

"You were so young when we got married, but . . . I suppose I just assumed . . . that you knew."

"Knew *what?*" Iris repeated, as if she were terrified to hear some devastating news.

It was Eleanore who answered the question, but she did it with a smile, as if she found great pleasure in telling Iris what she wanted to know. "I didn't fall in love with your father while I was the governess, Iris; it was long after that. In fact, I remember clearly the moment it came to me. I had suspected before then, and I'd struggled with understanding my feelings. But the moment I knew was a moment I'll never forget." Her eyes became nostalgic, and she took hold of her husband's hand while they exchanged a warm smile. "It happened in the barn. Something changed, and I just knew that I loved him with all my soul."

"Wait a minute," Iris said, her confusion deepening. "You mean . . . here? This barn?"

"That's right," Eleanore said.

Iris stated the obvious. "But . . . you'd been married for months before we arrived here, and—"

"That's right," James said. "And that's what I thought you knew. When we got married, I don't think either of us ever expected to actually love each other." Iris gasped and glanced at Case, as if to gauge his reaction. He only smiled and lifted his brows quickly, which provoked a subtle scowl from Iris. She turned back to her parents as James continued. "I asked her to marry me because I knew she had the qualities I wanted in a wife, and I'd seen how well she cared for my children. We wanted the same things. I believed we could make each other happy."

"But you didn't love her," Iris stated, incredulous.

"Truthfully, Iris, I believe I did, but I couldn't see it and I wasn't ready to admit it. I viewed the situation from a purely practical perspective."

"And you?" Iris asked her mother, as if she were on trial.

Eleanore shrugged. "I would have been a fool to turn down such a proposal. A wealthy, handsome man was offering to take care of me for the rest of my life and take me to America, where I had longed to go. But I wasn't willing to accept his offer until I knew, beyond any doubt, that it was the path God wanted me to take. That's what made it possible to marry a man I felt nothing for beyond respect."

"Nothing?" Iris asked. "Not even . . . attracted to him?"

"Not even a little bit."

"Oh, now that's just being cruel," James said lightly, and Eleanore chuckled before she gave her husband a quick kiss.

"That problem didn't last long," she said.

"Why is this so . . . unsettling for you?" James asked his daughter.

"I just . . . always assumed that you'd fallen in love before you were married, and that's why you got married. It's just . . . strange to realize it wasn't the way I'd thought it was."

"We both knew it was right," Eleanore said, as if she sensed that Iris's understanding of that point was important. "But at the time, yes, it was a matter of practicality and convenience. I wanted to go to America. He needed a mother for his children." She looked again at James. "And now that I've spent more than half of my life with him, I feel terrified to even wonder what my life might have been like if I had turned down his proposal. He's the greatest thing that ever happened to me."

James smiled at his wife. "It's the other way around."

An almost reverent silence settled over the room while the love James and Eleanore felt for each other almost seemed to make them glow.

"You look tired," James said and came to his feet. "I think it's time I put my wife to bed."

"I think you're right," Eleanore said and stood also. They embraced briefly before they left the room holding hands, saying good night to Case and Iris.

As soon as they were alone, Iris said, "Don't you dare say you told me so."

"I would never say that, but . . ."

"You told me so?"

"I wasn't going to say that."

"What *were* you going to say?"

"I was going to say that you have to admit it's excellent evidence that a marriage can succeed based on practicality and convenience, as long as two people go into it for the right reasons."

"Yes, I have to concede that. But I can also choose to love the man I marry *before* I marry him."

"Fair enough," he said.

She stood and held out a hand for him. "Come along. I won't be able to sleep until I know that you're comfortable and you have what you need."

"Is this guilt over my ailments, or concern for my welfare?" he asked, coming carefully to his feet.

"Probably both," she said. "But don't get too supercilious over that."

"You're using big words again, Iris."

"It means you'd do well to stay humble."

"Of course," Case said and pretended to have more difficulty walking than he really did, only so Iris would help him. He liked having her arms around his waist, and he enjoyed the opportunity to lean on her just enough to take in how it felt to have her so close to his side. Once she had him settled in the library, she gave him a quick kiss on the cheek and told him she'd see him tomorrow. Case couldn't wait.

The next day went much the same as the day before. Case could feel a little bit of improvement, but still preferred not to move too far.

In the middle of the afternoon, Case was immersed in the novel he was reading when he heard a knock at the door.

"Come in," he called, and James entered the room.

"How are you feeling?"

"A little stiff and sore, I'll admit, but it's not too bad. It's certainly not bad enough for me to be sitting around doing nothing."

James sat down. "Just give it another day or two, and then I'll feel better about putting you back to work."

Case made a scoffing noise. "You're just doing this to torture me, aren't you? You know sitting around like this is making me crazy."

James chuckled. "Sometimes we just have to let others take care of us, for a change."

"And you're an expert on that?"

"I'm learning to be," James said with some chagrin, and Case knew what he meant.

"How are you doing with that?"

"I'm fine," James said. "I've been very careful and haven't had any episodes for weeks. Frederick is keeping close track of me."

"That's good, then."

A moment of awkward silence preceded James saying, "I've noticed a rather significant change in Iris the last couple of days; all of us have noticed, actually. You wouldn't know anything about that, would you?"

"What kind of change?" Case asked, pretending innocence but dying to know what others might have observed.

"Well, she's cheerful, which is generally rare. And . . . I guess that covers it, really. She's more cheerful than I've seen her since . . ."

"Since what?"

James looked at him with narrowed eyes. "Since her heart was broken one time too many."

Case looked away, wondering if that was a threat not to break his daughter's heart, or some expression of hope that Case might be able to mend it. Case said nonchalantly, "Have you asked Iris about this miraculous change?"

"I have."

"And what does she say?"

"She said that perhaps her nearly dying has given her a new appreciation of life."

Case chuckled. "You don't really believe she would have died falling off that ladder, do you?"

James answered more seriously than Case had suspected. "Depending on how she'd landed, I think it's possible. What if she'd hit her head or her neck on something on the way down?"

Case hadn't thought of that. He could only say, "I'm glad I was here, but I was here because I felt prompted to be here. It was God who saved her."

"I agree with that. But you can take credit for listening to the Spirit and following it. And your humility over the matter is touching."

Case couldn't comment; he felt mostly embarrassed over the ongoing attention to the matter. He was glad when James changed the subject.

"I suspect there's more to Iris's change of attitude than her brush with death."

"Do you?" Case asked, not certain he was ready for James to know about his evolving relationship with Iris—or his intentions. Or perhaps he was more concerned about Iris not wanting her parents to know at this point.

James gave him that authoritative look he was so good at. "I can tell something's changed between you and Iris since you saved her from that fall. I don't need to know what, exactly; that's between the two of you. I just need to clarify something."

"Say anything you need to," Case said.

"On the day you first came here," James began, "when I said what I did about . . ."

"Kissing my feet?" Case guessed when he hesitated.

"Yes, that." He sounded relieved to get to the point without any further explanation. "I don't want you to think that I would lightly marry my daughter off to just anyone. If you'll recall, I said if she'd have you I'd kiss your feet."

"Yes, I recall that part too—very well."

"I knew then and I know now that she wouldn't have a man unless he measured up to a very high standard. Sometimes I've wondered if it's a little *too* high. Whether or not that's true, you need to know that I would gladly accept and respect her choice because I know she won't choose lightly."

"Considering the kind of woman she is beneath all that crustiness, any man would have to work pretty hard to even aspire to being worthy of her."

"May I ask if you're aspiring to that?"

"You may certainly ask, and the answer is yes. Yes, I am."

James smiled, but there was concern in his eyes. "You have a way of saying all the right things, Case, but you've given me no reason to believe you aren't genuine in what you say."

"I'm not certain Iris thinks so. I don't know if it's possible to convince her that I don't say something unless I mean it."

"She's smart, and she has good instincts, but fear and hurt can get in the way of those instincts. I know from experience. I pray every day that she can get beyond the past hurts and learn how to trust again. One day I hope she will come to realize that the good Lord knows your heart, and if you're the right one for her, that she'll trust in Him enough to hear what He has to tell her."

"I pray for the same," Case admitted.

James looked him in the eye. "You're a good man, Case."

"I try to be, but . . ."

"We're all trying. Just . . . keep at it, and . . . remember, for all her snap and fire, she's fine and precious. Be good to her."

"On the chance that she'll have me, I'll certainly do my best."

"Do you love her?" James asked.

Case hesitated, wanting to be honest with this man who had become as much a friend as an employer and a father figure. But he wasn't ready to cross certain boundaries just yet. He cleared his throat, then chuckled tensely. "Do I have to admit that to her father before I have a chance to admit it to her?"

James chuckled. "No, I guess that wouldn't be quite right, would it?"

"She's softened toward me a great deal," Case said, "and I'm thankful for that. But I believe she needs time . . . and I'm willing to give it to her. For now, I'm just going to be her friend and do my best to let her learn to trust me. I don't know what's happened in the past to make her so afraid to trust; it really doesn't matter. I just intend to prove that she *can* trust me, and whether or not we end up together, I'm hoping you'll always let me be a part of your family. It's the greatest blessing I've ever known in my life. I've wanted to say that to you for a long time now. I'm glad to finally have the chance."

James smiled, and tenderness showed in his eyes. "It's a privilege to have you as part of our family, Case, and you will always be welcome with us, wherever we may be."

Case suddenly felt too choked up to speak, mostly because it was evident that James really meant it. He wasn't just saying something kind for the sake of kindness. He really meant it. And Case could only hope to live his life in a way that exemplified so fine a man. Case had lived most of his life with no one to look up to, no man he could call a hero in his life. He'd had no example of how to live that hadn't felt repulsive to him. The gospel had changed him, but taking hold of it had left him reeling, not quite knowing how to apply it in life when the life he'd been accustomed to had no place for the gospel in it. But God had led him to James Barrington, who had given him a place in his home and his family. His gratitude was beyond description, and as emotional as he felt, he could only nod and say, "Thank you." His voice cracked as he added, "That means a great deal to me." He had no desire to let this conversation become mushy, but he felt strongly compelled to add, "I hope it's not inappropriate to say that . . . you're everything I wished my own father would have been . . . except that when I was a kid, I had no idea that a man could be any other way."

James smiled. "No, I don't think that's inappropriate at all. And it's nice to hear, actually. As I've mentioned before, my own parents had some challenges. I put a lot of conscious effort into becoming something different than their example taught me to be. I've worked hard to be a good husband and father. Eleanore tells me I'm happy because I deserve to be, because I've made the right choices. I don't know about that. But I do believe that we can change; we don't have to be the result of bad breeding, if that makes any sense."

"It makes a lot of sense to me."

When nothing more was said, James asked, "Do you need anything?"

"No. No, I'm great. But thank you . . . for everything."

"You're welcome." James stood. "You take good care of my daughter, now."

"I'll do my best . . . provided she'll let me."

James chuckled and left the room.

Chapter Seven
PERFECT WINTER

Case was grateful to start feeling back to normal and able to return to his room and take care of himself. He eased into the work routine slowly and got pretty good at doing some tasks with one hand, but when the other was finally usable, he was grateful to be able to work with two. At first he had to go easy and could tell when he'd overdone it, but every day he felt a little better.

The best aspect of his life, however, was the way that Iris had become a pleasant part of it, as opposed to their just getting on each other's nerves. She started going into town with him when he'd go on errands, and the boys usually went with them. The change in her behavior quickly became evident to everyone in the household, and they all commented individually on how nice it was to see her happy again, and voiced their suspicions that it had something to do with him. Case took no credit; he just enjoyed every minute he could spend with Iris between their each having work to accomplish. At first she seemed to prefer that her family not know that their relationship had romantic implications; then one evening she took his hand when she sat beside him for scripture study in the parlor, and from that day on, they held hands whenever they were together, no matter where they were or who was around. They occasionally went riding together or for a walk in the woods, in spite of the cold temperatures. And they shared long talks, usually late at night by the fire in the library, discussing their childhood memories, their hopes for the future, and sharing deep discussions of gospel principles. The more time that

Case spent with her, the more he wanted to be with her forever. And he sensed that she felt the same way, but something held him back from taking the step of making it official between them. Instead, he just enjoyed every day and the time they spent together, certain that the Lord would let him know when to take the next step. Occasionally, he would give in to the temptation to kiss her, but not nearly as often as he would have liked, and he was careful to keep his passion bridled, not wanting to offend this amazing woman, or make her feel uncomfortable with him in any way. But he couldn't help wondering what it might be like to be married to such a woman, and to share his life with her in every respect. It was a day he longed for, and he prayed continually that it would all come together in the way he envisioned it in his mind.

While cold weather kept them indoors more, Case enjoyed playing with the boys in a different way than the roughness they indulged in outside. They played games and read together, and Case did more reading on his own than he'd ever done. He considered the Barrington library priceless, and he felt privileged to be able to use it, and to be given the time to do so when there truly was nothing else that needed to be done. During working hours, he kept to the usual tasks and also shoveled snow and chopped a lot of wood. And he did everything he could think of to earn his keep and keep James healthy. The holidays came and went, weaving a magical thread into Case's life as he spent the Christmas season with a family that seemed too good to be true, immersed itself in celebrations of Christ's birth and life in ways that he'd never imagined. Christmas had never even been a part of his childhood; it had been the same as any other day. Being a part of the preparations and gaiety of the event caused Case to feel like he was living in some kind of dream that he never would have had enough imagination to comprehend.

In the middle of February, the thought occurred to Case that this had been the most perfect winter of his life. In spite of the harsh Iowa cold that he was sorely unaccustomed to, he'd never felt happier. And he told Iris so late one evening while they sat close together on the couch in the library, with the fire casting strange shadows around the room. They talked of marriage in hypothetical ways, never particularly applying it to themselves, but still in a way that gave him hope of moving in the right direction. She spoke of her father's two marriages, making comparisons of the betrayal and horrible behavior of her blood mother, as opposed to Eleanore's integrity and kindness. Case spoke of his own parents and how miserable and afraid his mother had been, and how it had impacted him and his brothers.

"You've never told me about your brothers," she said. "You told me you have two brothers, but I've never heard anything about them."

"One is married and lives back east. He's a lawyer."

"Oh, you *did* mention him. You were staying with him when you met the missionaries."

"That's right."

"So, he's doing well?"

"Well enough. He's certainly come a long way from what we were raised with, but I still don't agree with the way he lives his life."

"What do you mean?"

"Let's just say he's not very kind to his family, and I don't think he's very happy. I didn't realize it was possible for a family to be happy until I came here."

"I'm glad you came here," she said and snuggled closer to him.

"So am I," he said and pressed a kiss into her hair.

"And your other brother?"

Case sighed and pushed away related memories that he didn't want to think about. "He's dead."

"May I ask how?"

"I'd rather not talk about that," Case said with a firmness that Iris understood. There were things she would also prefer to avoid talking about.

She simply said, "I'm sorry."

"For what?"

"That your family life was so . . . hard."

"It's in the past. It doesn't matter any more." He added lightly, "Your father said he would adopt me, so it's all good."

Iris tightened her arm around him and said, "Maybe he won't have to."

Case took in her words and her nearness and wanted to propose here and now, but he knew the time wasn't right. He just held onto the hope of the implication and enjoyed the moment. He shifted so that he could see her face, then pressed his fingers over her soft skin, and into her hair.

"Oh, Iris," he murmured and kissed her, inhaling her sweet aroma, "I've never felt this way before. Never has any woman stirred me the way you do."

She smiled and said, "If you keep saying things like that, you may just get to keep me, after all."

"I'm counting on it," he said, and kissed her again.

* * * * *

As signs of spring appeared, Case began to feel restless about his future. His plan had been to go west with the first company heading out. But now he had no intention of going anywhere without Iris, which hopefully meant that he would be staying with the Barringtons indefinitely. His relationship with Iris felt solid and secure, but nothing specific about marriage had come up in months. Case had come to feel completely comfortable among the family and in their home. He'd gained a personal relationship with each member of the household and felt personally invested in their lives, as they were in his. He'd even come to love little Mariah, and had personally helped care for her as well as her brothers. The children were all wonderful and close to his heart. Eleanore began to look pregnant, but as her size increased, her illness eased, and she started to look better, which she told him was typical. She also told him that every passing month that she remained pregnant increased the chances of her giving birth to a healthy baby. He prayed that was the case. Seeing James and Eleanore together, and hearing them talk about the forthcoming arrival of another child left Case wanting to move forward with his own life. He wanted to share that kind of relationship with Iris. He wanted to have children of his own, and to know the full joy of living that could only be found through such a relationship.

Following much deep thought and many prayers, Case felt confident about taking the next step with Iris. She'd wanted time for them to get to know each other better. They'd done that. He hoped that he had proven in the eight months he'd been here that he was a man who lived by the principles he believed in, and that he could work hard enough to care for her no matter what life might bring.

One evening after the rest of the family had dispersed following prayer, Case urged Iris out to the side porch with him. Even though it was chilly, it was a beautiful night, and they sat close together, holding hands, with a lamp burning nearby that he'd brought out with them. He uttered a silent prayer, then pressed into the topic he needed to open up. "We've had a perfect winter, Iris; at least it has been for me."

"Me too," she said with a smile.

"Let's make it a perfect spring; let it be perfect for the rest of our lives."

"Now, we both know *that's* not possible."

"Of course, struggles and challenges will come up . . . but we can face them together, Iris." He kissed her hand and lowered his voice. "Marry me; marry me soon."

Iris was so startled that it took her a moment to just close her astonished mouth and look away. She chuckled tensely. "I . . . hadn't expected this. I . . . I . . . I'm not sure I'm ready for this."

"Why? How ready do you need to be?"

She looked at him again. "More ready than this."

"Talk to me, Iris. Tell me what's holding you back."

"I . . . don't know. I'm just not ready. And you're just going to have to accept that."

She stood and walked into the house, and Case hung his head, letting out a weighted sigh. He prayed that she would soon come around, but something deep in his gut led him to believe that it was going to get worse before it got better. He could only pray that, in the end, she would come to her senses and they could share a good life together.

Another month passed while Case waited and watched Iris for clues. She seemed a little more cautious, perhaps, since their discussion of marriage had come up. But beyond that, everything seemed right between them; at least it did to him. He hoped he wasn't making false assumptions or setting himself up for some kind of imminent disaster. His deepest instincts told him something wasn't right between them, but he had no idea how to find out what the problem was. He asked Iris several times if something was wrong, or if there was something she needed to talk to him about. She always insisted there was nothing, that everything was fine. But he didn't feel prone to believe her. He began lying awake at night, recalling her distrusting and judgmental attitude with him prior to the magical moment when everything had changed. After playing it over and over in his mind, he realized that he had no idea what had changed, and he could only come to the conclusion that *nothing* had changed. He pondered over whatever it was that was at the source of her ill feelings that still existed inside of her somewhere, and the more he pondered, the more it became clear to him that eventually he would have to face Iris's ugliest self. But perhaps there were ugly things inside of him that also had yet to be faced. And maybe that was what frightened him most of all. In spite of the fear, however, he could feel the Spirit guiding and preparing him for what seemed inevitable. They could never be fully happy together until they could be happy with who they were as individuals, and come to terms with where they had been.

On one of the first truly warm days of spring, early in April, Case asked Iris to take a walk with him, praying that the results of this conversation could bring them closer together and not drive them further apart. Once they were seated close together on the ground in a pleasant sunny spot near the river, Case took her hand and said, "Talk to me, Iris. Tell me what makes you so hesitant to marry me. Is there something about me you don't like or—"

"No, it's not that."

"Then what?" he asked, but she didn't answer. "Is it still about trust? Is there a reason you feel you can't trust me?"

"Maybe it's men in general."

"I'm not 'men in general,' Iris. You know me better than that. What will it take to prove myself to you?"

She sighed and looked away. "Maybe it's more about me than you."

"Whatever it is, let's talk about it. Get it out in the open. There's no need for secrets between us. There shouldn't be anything that we can't talk about if we can accept and respect each other." He sensed her softening and added, "Tell me."

"I don't know." She shrugged. "I just . . . I admit that I have trouble trusting any man after what happened, but . . ."

"You've never told me what happened. You don't have to if you don't want to, but . . . maybe you'd feel better."

She shrugged again. "It's not complicated, really. I grew to love someone, and I thought he was the right one for me. We courted a long time, and I thought I really knew him. He was showing an interest in the Church, and he gave me every reason to believe he would be baptized and we would be married. But it kept getting put off. Then my parents saw him with another woman. Turns out there had been many women. Some months later I heard that some woman was pregnant with his baby, but he abandoned her; left town. Thankfully that wasn't me." She blew out a ragged breath. "After that, it seemed every man I made any effort to get to know quickly illustrated by his behavior that he was dishonest, or shallow, or held such archaic views on a woman's place that I couldn't tolerate him. I guess that's why I'm surly. I just . . . don't want to be hurt again."

"Do you believe I'll hurt you?" Case asked.

"I don't know," she said, looking into his eyes. "There are times when I think that if I lost you it would kill me, and maybe that's why it feels safer to never really have you in my life."

"But I already am. You've already opened your heart to me, Iris, far more than you realize. You must believe me when I tell you that I would never betray you, never lie to you; that I would devote my life to living the gospel and making you happy."

Iris sensed his sincerity and wanted to believe him, but fear and insecurity seemed to overpower her other emotions. While she couldn't fully admit that she could believe what he was saying, she also couldn't deny how drawn she was to him. "Maybe it's more than that."

"What? Tell me."

Iris wondered whether or not she *should* tell him. But perhaps this was a good test of the trust between them. If she could trust him enough to share this burden, and if he could keep her confidence and accept her anyway, then perhaps they could move forward.

"When I was sixteen, I went through a . . . rebellious stage, I guess you could say. I became involved with a young man. I was foolish and headstrong. He took advantage of me. What happened between us was . . . well, it . . . never went all the way . . . but it went way too far, and . . . I thought I'd come to terms with it, but . . . maybe I haven't. I still feel guilty when I think about it. I did all the things I know we're supposed to do to repent of sin. I had no religious leader to confess to, because we were the only Mormons here, but I told my parents everything. I believed at the time that God had forgiven me, but it still haunts me, and . . . maybe I just . . . don't feel worthy to . . ."

"To what?" he asked, but she couldn't answer. "It's in the past, Iris. It doesn't matter to you and me. In the grand scheme of eternal life, it's nothing. It was taken care of according to God's requirements. You just need to let go and forgive yourself."

Iris took in his words and wanted to believe them, but she was distracted by something in his attitude. "You sound as if you're speaking from experience."

"Yes, I suppose I am."

He looked away, but not before she saw shame in his eyes. Iris felt a little startled at the implication. "You're talking about a woman. There's a woman in your past." Guilt rose quickly into his eyes before he stood and took a few steps, turning his back to her. She didn't like the jealousy she felt at the thought of him being with someone else in the way that he was implying, but now that the door had been opened, she needed to know all of the truth. She stood beside him and said, "You never told me about your past loves."

"According to this conversation, I would say we're even on that score."

A thought occurred to her that she found disturbing. "You *did* tell me that you'd never felt for any woman the way you feel for me."

"And that is true."

"But—"

"You're telling me about *your* past loves. For me, love never had anything to do with it."

Iris took a sharp breath. "What are you saying?"

Case struggled with his fear, his regret, the guilt he knew he shouldn't be feeling in light of the changes in his life. But she had a right to know, and in his heart he'd known this conversation was inevitable. She'd once told him that his past was a part of who he was, and he knew that was true, even if he'd become a different man. He said a quick prayer and drew a deep breath, figuring he'd do well to just get it over with. "I told you my past was deplorable, Iris."

"But . . . I thought you meant . . . what your father did to you; the poverty, and his drinking, and the way he treated you."

"Well, that's all certainly deplorable, but . . . once I left home, I just started drinking, trying to forget. But when a man is drunk, he does all kinds of regrettable things."

Case saw her move a step away from him, as if he were suddenly repulsive. He looked into her eyes, attempting to take in her overt disgust, and he wondered if he had just lost her. Was this that point at which free agency might change the outcome? Would she choose a different life because she couldn't live with his past? He didn't know the answer. He only knew that if she couldn't accept him in spite of his past, he could never live with it. He drew courage and resigned himself to getting this over with, praying this didn't mean resigning himself to live without her. He reminded himself that God had known about his past when he'd let Case know that Iris was the right woman for him, but he also had to concede that Iris had her free agency, and he couldn't begin to understand what God might expect both of them to learn through this experience.

"What do you need to know, Iris?" he asked.

Iris considered the question deeply. What *did* she need to know? Was it need, or was some other emotion driving her desire to hear a truth that shouldn't matter? She felt sick to her stomach and utterly betrayed as her instincts told her the truth even before she clarified, "There was more than one woman?"

Case looked at the ground, unable to face her as he answered, "Yes."

Iris didn't want to say it, but she had to be unmistakably clear. "And you're talking about being completely intimate with these women?"

Case sighed loudly but kept his eyes down. "Yes."

Iris's heart thudded, and the sickness in her stomach heightened. But she had to ask, "How *many* woman, Case?"

He looked at her then, his eyes pleading. "Oh, Iris, it was before I was baptized, before I found the gospel. I felt no value as a human being, had no understanding of the sacredness of such things. I didn't know any better."

"Your brother was raised the same way you were. Did he—"

"Don't you dare try to compare him to me. He lived his own version of a sordid life before he got married, and I have no reason to believe he's faithful to his wife. He's *nothing* like me. He never has been. Just stick to me and you, Iris."

"Fine. How many women, Case?" she repeated.

Again he dropped his head and blew out a breath so painful that he had to put a hand over his chest. *Just say it,* he told himself three times before he could get the words to his tongue. "More than I could count," he said and heard her gasp. He hurried to finish. "Mostly because I was too drunk to remember most of them." He could hear her struggling to breathe and attempted to soothe the horror by pointing out, "It's in the past. It shouldn't matter."

"Maybe it shouldn't," she cried, showing more evidence of anger than hurt. "But it does. It matters to me."

"Why? So you can condemn me for my bad choices? So you can have a reason to not trust me, a reason to justify the fear you've been holding onto all along?"

"That's not fair!"

"Fair? The gospel is about redemption and forgiveness. But you're putting me on trial here for something that took place in another realm for me. I was a different man."

"Still the same man who is asking me to share your bed and have your children."

"Only under the right circumstances. Don't go twisting this to suit your anger or—"

"Don't *you* go twisting it to use against me. I believe in redemption and forgiveness, Casey, but that doesn't mean I can live with giving myself to a man who has been in more women's beds than he can count or remember. How do I know you won't revert to that again one day?"

Case felt so hurt and utterly devastated he could hardly breathe. "How could you even ask me that? How could you *think* that I . . . that I . . . would *ever* go back to that kind of life? If you can believe such a thing is possible, then you don't know me at all." He heard his voice crack at the end, and felt hot tears in his eyes.

"That is evident," she snarled. "I don't know you at all."

Suddenly lightheaded and nauseous, Case watched her walk away. What had he done? The regret over his former life now felt equivalent to his regret over having to tell Iris about it. He was grateful to be in the woods and completely alone when he dropped to his knees and pressed his head almost to the ground, groaning from the physical pain consuming him. "Dear God, help me!" he muttered. "What have I done? Oh, what have I done?"

Case wrapped his arms around his middle and rocked back and forth while the passing of time drowned in his tears. He marveled that the pain could be so physical, and he prayed for relief from such suffering as his perfect winter came crashing down around him as surely as the snow had melted with the spring sun. His tears finally dried up, and he sat on the ground in a state of shock that he'd only felt once before. He frantically pushed those memories away, not willing to associate that moment with this one. When he began to feel cold, he realized he'd been out here a long time. Not wanting James or anyone else to worry or think he'd abandoned his work, he collected his thoughts, gathered his composure, and headed back to the house.

Coming out of the woods, Case concentrated his efforts on appearing as if nothing were wrong or out of the ordinary, while inside he felt as if he might crumble if someone looked at him sideways. Then he looked up and saw James on the back porch, his arms folded, looking straight at him. He'd been waiting for Case to come back.

"Is something wrong?" Case asked.

"That's what I was going to ask you," James said, halting Case's intent to apologize for slacking on his work when he should have been back a long time ago. "Where have you been? I've been worried. You look terrible."

Case turned his back to James to hide the new onslaught of tears. James stood just behind him and asked with compassion, "Is that the answer to my question? That you can't even answer the question without falling apart?"

"I'm not . . . falling apart," he barely managed to say without crying audibly.

"And I thought you'd never lied to me."

"I haven't," Case said and coughed to avoid sobbing. "I already . . . fell apart." He sobbed against all his efforts. "The pieces of me are scattered somewhere in the woods . . . where she told me that she . . . that she . . ."

James took hold of his arm and guided him back toward the woods. Case managed to add, "I don't think we'll be able to find the pieces."

"We can't," James said, "but the Savior can."

The very idea provoked another sob from Case's throat. As soon as they were in the trees, out of sight from the house, Case abandoned his battle for composure and dropped to his knees again, crying like a baby. He couldn't recall crying this much when his parents had died. But then, he'd been relieved on his mother's behalf, and grateful for his father's absence. He could find no positive point in his present pain. He was barely aware of James kneeling beside him and putting a hand on his shoulder. When Case finally managed to stop sobbing, James asked, "What happened?"

"Where's Iris?" he countered, wondering if she'd said anything. He knew it was inevitable for James and Eleanore to know the heart of the problem. He just preferred to have it come from him, as opposed to them hearing it through the perspective of Iris's anger.

"She's locked herself in her room; won't come out, won't talk." Case was surprised when he added, "Has she done what I feared she would do?"

"What's that?" Case asked, looking at him.

"Has she found some reason not to trust you?"

Case squeezed his eyes shut and groaned. "Yeah, I'd say she's found a reason; a really big, ugly reason."

"Do you want to talk about it?"

"I'd rather have you hear it from me than from her. At least if I tell you, it's between friends and won't be considered as gossip."

"Tell me whatever you feel you need to."

Case looked at him. "Then find a new job? Somewhere else to live?"

"You should know me better than that. There's nothing you can tell me that will make me feel any differently about you, Case. The reasons that would compel me to kick someone out of my home are things that I don't believe you're capable of. If I'd had concerns about such things, I wouldn't have kept you around this long. Just talk to me."

Case sat on the ground and pressed his hands through his hair. James sat beside him. Case felt surprisingly calm—most likely in shock—as he spoke. "I asked her why she was so hesitant to marry me."

"You asked her to marry you, then?"

"Yes, a month ago. She told me she needed time. She admitted to struggling with trust. I asked her today about the reasons. She told me about some things from the past; things you apparently know about. She said that you did."

"Yes."

"I've wondered all along if it was right to tell her about my past. I didn't want to burden her with it, but on the other hand, maybe it's something a wife should know. I guess I said enough to make her suspect. She asked, so I told her. I never imagined she would react that way. I've put it behind me, and God has too. I just believed she would see it the same way."

"I can only assume you're talking about women," James said, and Case nodded.

Case repeated what he'd told Iris, and how he felt about it, not wanting any room for misunderstanding between him and James when this inevitably erupted even further. Case had expected James to be kind following his confession; he'd declared that nothing would make him treat Case any differently. But he was completely unprepared for the way this man put his arms around him with a fatherly embrace and let him cry like the child he'd never been allowed to be with his own father.

Once he'd had another good, long cry, James spoke to Case about the power of redemption through the Savior, and that he needed to remember that his sins truly were behind him. He said that he could understand why learning something like this could be difficult for Iris, but that it wasn't her place to hold it against him or say the things she'd said. They both agreed that there was more to what was troubling Iris than either of them understood, but that only made the problem worse. And neither of them knew what to do about it. Case believed, in his deepest self, that this was the end for them. She would choose not to marry a man like him, and he would move on. He only hoped that he could learn from this experience whatever God wanted him to learn.

When there seemed nothing more to say, James insisted that Case come back to the house and get something to eat, and he felt certain Ben and Frederick would cover his chores. But Case protested, not wanting to go in the house or see Iris tonight, and he felt certain some work would help clear his head. It was the only way he knew how to keep putting one foot in front of the other.

* * * * *

Iris stood at her bedroom window and watched Case and her father talking just outside the barn. Her father gave him a firm embrace, then Case went into the barn, and she could hear the back door open and close below. She wasn't surprised to hear her father's footsteps on the stairs, nor his knock at her bedroom door, but she wondered if he would take Case's side in this argument. The very idea bristled her nerves and beckoned her defenses firmly into place.

"Come in," she called, remaining at the window, her back to him.

She heard the door open and close, then there was a long pause before he said, "Are you all right?"

His concerned words and compassionate tone softened her defensiveness a little. "Not really, but I'm not sure I want to talk about it."

"Well, then." He sat down. "Let's talk about something else."

Iris knew this tactic well. If they got talking and eased the tension, then he could bait her into the topic that needed to be addressed. But perhaps that was just as well. If he'd heard Case's side of the story, he certainly needed to hear hers. And since he was determined to talk, she decided to be the one to pick the topic. "How did you feel when you found out that my mother had been unfaithful?" she asked.

She turned to see that he looked taken aback and mildly upset by the question. But he answered straightly, "It was horrible; it was the worst thing that ever happened to me. There's no describing that kind of betrayal, and how deeply it hurt."

"Then you understand how I feel."

"About *what?*"

"About Case and the women without number that he's been involved with, most of whom he can't even remember."

"I can understand that this would be difficult for you, Iris, but your comparison is unfair. This is *nothing* like that. *Nothing!*"

"It is very much like *that,*" she retorted. "I feel betrayed and—"

Iris felt a little startled by the way her father stood and took a step toward her, his expression intense. "Now, you listen and listen well,

Iris. Your mother had exchanged vows with me. She had promised to honor me and our marriage, and to pledge herself to me and me alone. I was her *husband.* What happened in Case's life happened a long time ago, and—"

"Not *so* long ago."

"It happened before he was baptized, and it's in the past. For you to dredge it up and persecute him for it is completely out of line. You have a right to some difficult feelings over learning something like that about the man you love, but—"

"What makes you think I love him?"

"Now you're just making a fool of yourself. No one gets this angry over such a thing without loving someone. As I was saying, you have a right to some difficult feelings, and it's natural to need some time to come to terms with them, but you need to keep perspective. He had no commitment to you at the time, and he didn't know any better. You cannot possibly judge such choices, especially when you consider the way he was raised."

"Must that always be an excuse for his behavior?" Iris asked, not caring if her anger made her look like a fool. She refused to believe that it meant she loved Casey Harrison.

"It's not an excuse, Iris, it's a *reason.* And his behavior since he committed his life to living the gospel has never been anything less than it should be for a righteous man. Frankly, I find it difficult to believe that you would behave this way toward him."

"I could have guessed that you would side with him. He's been currying favor from you since the day he got here."

An anger flared in James Barrington's eyes that Iris had rarely seen. But his voice was steady and calm. "I do *not* take sides for the sake of it, and I never have. I side only with the truth, Iris, and you should know that. And *no one* has ever *curried favor* with me and gotten away with it. My relationship with him has *nothing to* do with you, and requires no judgment from you. I have no idea where such an attitude would come from in you. This is not how you were taught, Iris."

"Well, maybe I got it from my mother," she snarled and left the room, only able to feel frustration in not having gained any of the compassion or empathy she had hoped to get out of the conversation. She grabbed a shawl and went out the front door, needing some air but determined to avoid going anywhere near where Case might be. She didn't know if she could ever face him again.

Iris returned from a lengthy walk and went straight to her room, hoping her mother wouldn't be too unhappy with her for not offering her usual help with putting supper on. In truth, she didn't feel at all like eating and didn't want to go anywhere in the house where Case might be. She knew she couldn't avoid him forever, but she was determined to at least avoid him today. She hoped he might be humiliated enough to just leave here and look for work and lodging elsewhere. But then, he surely knew he would never have it so good anywhere else. James Barrington treated him practically like a son, a fact that now made Iris feel even more betrayed for reasons she had no desire to look at. She only knew she wanted him to leave and never come back.

Iris paced her room and stewed, knowing that supper was taking place downstairs and no one had bothered to come looking for her. She felt certain it would be good for her to get on her knees and pray, but she didn't feel like praying and therefore avoided doing so.

When her mother brought some supper to her room, Iris thanked her, then said, "I'm sorry I didn't help downstairs. I just . . . can't see him."

"That's going to be difficult to maintain when he lives and works here, Iris. You've got to face him sooner or later."

"I know. But . . . I can't tonight."

"That's fine. That's why I brought you some supper. But Case didn't show up to eat either."

Iris sighed and sat on the edge of the bed, and Eleanore sat beside her. "You know what happened," Iris said.

"Your father told me everything. Are you all right?"

"No," Iris said, and then she just cried with her mother's arms around her. And while she was crying, her father came in and sat on the other side of her, telling her everything would be all right. She could only be grateful to know that even when he didn't agree with her, he loved her no less.

Chapter Eight

THE FAVORED CHILD

Case was grateful for the supper that Frederick brought to his room. He didn't feel like eating, but he knew that he needed to, and he hoped it would ease the queasy feeling in his stomach. Frederick offered some compassion and asked if there was anything he could do. But it was evident he didn't know what the problem was. Still, his kindness was appreciated, and Case knew that if he *did* feel like talking, Frederick would be glad to listen, and he would likely be as accepting and kind as James had been. But Case just wanted to be alone and attempt to understand all of this. He prayed over his meal before he ate it, then he got on his knees and stayed there until he found himself drifting to sleep and crawled into his bed. There he cried again, wishing he didn't care so much what Iris believed of him, and wishing even more that he didn't love her. It would all be so much easier if he didn't love her.

* * * * *

Case saw Iris at the breakfast table and resented the way his stomach quivered and his heart quickened. He said good morning to her, but she blatantly ignored him, and for the first time in months, a cold aura once again hovered around her. This began an all-too-familiar pattern that Case loathed. He only attempted once to talk with her and was told in no uncertain terms that she had nothing to say to him. He prayed night and day to understand and find some hope, and tried very hard to resign himself to living without her, but he just couldn't find peace with letting go. And as long as Iris felt this way about him, he could never find peace with holding on. He felt stuck in the middle of an unsolvable problem, only able to keep putting one foot in front of the other with the hope that something would change, and soon, before he lost his mind.

On a pleasant day in the middle of April, Case and Frederick were on the roof of the house, doing the standard spring repairs following the snows of winter. They talked and laughed in a way that helped Case not think about Iris or feel sorry for his own broken heart. Frederick said he was going down the ladder for more shingles, and a minute later Case heard him fall and cry out in pain. He moved to the edge of the roof, consumed with panic, grateful to see Frederick moving and conscious. But he was also clearly in pain.

"What happened?" Case demanded, moving quickly down the ladder.

"I don't know," Frederick said and groaned. "I just . . . lost my footing. I think my leg is broken," he declared and groaned again.

"Just try to stay still," Case said, kneeling beside him. "We'll get the doctor. Are you hurt anywhere else?"

"I don't . . . think so," Frederick said, "but . . . oh! Blast! It hurts!"

"Yeah, I know what you mean. I'll be right back."

Case found Ben and told him to get the doctor and to hurry, then he found James and Eleanore and told them what had happened before he rushed back to find Frederick struggling to breathe evenly while pain consumed him. When James arrived with Eleanore close behind him, he asked what had happened, then he declared with some anger that he was going to ban ladders from his home.

"Oh, we'll just *fly* up to the roof when we need to fix it," Frederick muttered.

"Or we can just go to Zion and leave the ladders here," Eleanore said.

"Not for at least a year, we won't," James said firmly, glancing at his wife's rounded belly.

"And perhaps when we acquire a new ladder there, it won't be as dangerous as the ones we have here," Eleanore added facetiously.

"Perhaps," James said as if he truly believed it. Then Lizzie and Mary Jane came out of nowhere, both needing to be calmed down when they found Frederick injured and suffering.

It seemed forever before the doctor arrived, then he guided the men in helping Frederick to his bed in a way that would prevent pain and further injury. Once there, the leg was set and splinted, and Frederick was given something for the pain that would help him sleep. He was left in the care of his wife and daughter, and Case made a point of seeking out James for a private conversation. He found him at his desk in the library, and closed the door as he said, "Could we talk . . . alone?"

"Of course," James said. "How is Iris?"

"Ignoring me," Case reported.

"Don't give up on her just yet."

"I didn't come to talk about Iris," Case said, and James looked surprised.

"I came to make it clear that having Frederick unable to work is not an excuse for you to start doing any more around here than you already do. If I have to follow you around like a lost puppy to keep you from lifting more than a basket of eggs, I will."

James leaned back in his chair and chuckled. "It sounds a bit like you're giving me orders, boy."

"You bet I am, old man. At least when it comes to that."

"You never told Iris . . . about the problem."

"Of course not. Did you think I would? You asked me not to."

"No, I didn't think you would. And if she had known, I'm certain I would have heard about it. I wasn't asking, I was stating a fact. I wanted you to know that I'm grateful you didn't tell her. I know the two of you talked a great deal, and . . . it could have slipped out. But I'm grateful it didn't. I don't want her to worry."

Case looked down. "Like I said, I didn't come to talk about Iris."

James sighed loudly. "I get the impression you want to keep me alive."

"Yes. Yes, I do."

"That's somewhat comforting to hear from someone who will inherit a large sum of money when I die."

"What?" Case practically shrieked, as shocked as he was angry. In a more controlled—and quiet—voice, he said, "What on earth are you talking about?"

"I added you to my will," James said as if it were no different from saying that they were having stew for dinner.

"Why would you do such a thing?" Case demanded quietly. "It's ludicrous."

"I don't take well to having my judgment questioned, Casey."

"Forgive me. I'm not trying to be rude. I just . . . don't understand. Why would you do this?"

"A number of reasons, actually. Iris is the least of them, but one of these days she is going to get it in her head that you're just being nice to me because I'm a wealthy man, and she'll want to believe you're doing it so you can get a piece of the pie."

"How do you know she'll—"

"I know her. But now that this is done and final, you and I will both know that no matter what she might think or believe, you're only being nice to me because you want to be. The hard fact is that whether you're nice to me or not, you're still going to get an inheritance."

"Why would you do something like that?" he asked again. "I feel . . ."

"What?"

"Insulted . . . that you would think I'm here because I'm some kind of gold digger."

"If I thought that were even remotely possible, I can assure you I never would have included you in my will, Case. The truth of the matter is that I've grown to love you like a son, and I just feel like this is the right thing to do. I'm really hoping my will won't become necessary for a good, long time yet. But when it is, whatever happens, I want you to know that you're there because I care for you as one of my own, not unlike Ben, and I want to know that you will be provided for. That's all. There's no need to discuss it again, and I'm not going to remove your name, no matter how much you complain, or how badly you treat me."

"I could never treat you badly."

"I know that," James chuckled. "Now stop taking this conversation so seriously. I'm certain you have work to do, especially if you intend to follow me around like a lost puppy." Case got up to leave, not certain what to say, and thinking it might be best if he didn't say anything at all. As he opened the door, James added, "Oh, and . . . Frederick was going to take the boys fishing in morning while I take Eleanore into town. Would you mind doing that? I'm certain you can keep them from falling in the river."

"I'd be happy to; they're great kids."

"Yes, they are." He chuckled again. "And they wear me out. I'm getting too old to play with them the way boys should be played with. I think it's a great blessing they have you around. They could use a big brother." He sounded mildly sad, and Case felt the same way. It was evident James wanted to be able to do things with his sons the way any father would. But his health had to be preserved. Case could only be grateful that he was here to help buffer the problem. He felt suddenly emotional and hurried from the room, trying to comprehend the words James had used in the conversation. *Love you like a son. Care for you as one of my own. They could use a big brother.* His only thought about the money was how utterly unworthy he felt of such an offering, and how irrelevant it seemed in light of all else this man had given him. He prayed that James Barrington would live for a very long time.

* * * * *

Iris watched Case leave with her brothers to go fishing and felt irritated by the fact. When they came back hours later, all full of laughter and teasing, she felt downright angry. Over the next several days, her anger deepened as she observed Case's interaction with the rest of the family, feelings she'd struggled with the previous fall concerning his behavior with her father and brothers. She had forgotten all about such concerns during the months that she had actually liked him, but with the recent changes in their relationship, her eyes were opened again to behavior that could only have one possible motivation. She felt utterly disgusted at the effort Case put into seeking favor with her father, following him around like a child and stepping in to do every little thing for him, like some kind of servant attempting to gain favor with a king. And more and more he was playing with her brothers, or getting them to work beside him, the way her father used to do. Case's efforts to usurp their father's place in their lives infuriated her beyond all reason.

After days of making a mental list of all the reasons why Casey Harrison had ulterior motives, she found him in the kitchen with her mother, laughing together as if they were the best of friends, and the following morning he drove her into town, just the two of them. They returned full of smiles, and Iris bristled when she saw from her window the way he took Eleanore's hand to help her down from the buggy, and then kissed it.

"He's completely unbelievable," Iris muttered under her breath and hurried out to the barn where she knew he would be unharnessing the buggy. Once through the door and assured that no one else was there, she repeated her most prominent thought to him. "You are unbelievable!"

Case turned to look at her, then he comically looked around as if to imply that she couldn't possibly be speaking to him.

"Yes, I mean you!"

"You're actually speaking to me," he said with cool nonchalance as he continued with his chore.

"Someone's got to. You can't get away with it, you know."

"Get away with what?" Case asked without looking at her. He loved her so much that he hated her.

"The way you are trying to curry favor with my father. Do you think if you ingratiate yourself with him long enough that some of his money might end up in your pocket?"

Case was so stunned he could only turn and stare at her. He was amazed at how accurately James had predicted this moment, although he suspected Iris's father had likely had some clues. He wondered what Iris might have said to him. But in that moment he felt even more insulted and hurt than he had when she'd implied that he would revert to his old ways and one day cheat on his wife. He reminded himself to stay calm and not take the bait of getting into an argument with her. He only said, "If that's all you can see from what's going on around here, Iris, then you're even more judgmental than I ever imagined."

"Don't call me judgmental when your behavior around here is so visibly appalling."

"And how is that?" he asked, trying to sound bored, wishing she would just leave him in peace. He far preferred her ignoring him to this kind of drama.

"You've turned my brothers against me."

Case actually laughed at the ludicrousness of such an accusation. "I have *never* said a word to them about you; not a *word.*"

"They said they were mad at me because I didn't like you anymore. You must have told them *something.*"

"Your imagination is incredible, Iris. They asked why you and I weren't doing things together anymore; I told them I didn't know. Whatever they said beyond that came from their own appraisal of the situation." He added with deep sarcasm, "Imagine them assuming that you didn't like me anymore. I wonder where they would have *ever* gotten that idea."

As if she had no more defense on that topic, she moved on to the next one. "You were flirting with my mother!"

"I was *not!*" he snapped and realized he'd taken the bait. He couldn't believe she would even think such a thing, let alone say it.

"You *were!* And don't try to deny it. I saw the way you were teasing her, making her laugh."

Case let go of an astonished chuckle. He truly couldn't believe what he was hearing. "Is that against the law in this family?"

"You were *flirting* with her!"

"No, I was *not!* Whatever you may or may not have perceived, my intentions with her are not even the tiniest bit inappropriate. I respect her. Pardon the comparison, but she's like a mother to me."

"She's only a few years older than you."

"She's a happily married woman, and I am not the kind of man who would even *think* of flirting with a married woman—*especially* a woman who treats me like her own son."

"I saw the way you held her hand."

Case shook his head and resisted the urge to yell at her. "I was helping her step down from the buggy, Iris."

"And you *kissed* her hand."

"I would kiss my own mother's hand if she were alive. Do you make this up as you go along, or do you lie awake at night and let your imagination run wild with things to accuse me of?" He took a step forward, and she took a step back. "Your accusations reek of ridiculousness, Miss Barrington. If you're going to put me on trial, at least come up with a case that's got some substance behind it. Even *if* I were prone to flirt with a married woman . . . *if* I were a philandering cad who behaved inappropriately with other men's wives—which I am *not*—your mother is not the kind of woman to stand for such behavior. She is far too wise and discerning to not see past such intentions. And she is far too committed to her marriage, and deeply in love with her husband to ever give *any* man a second glance. Do you honestly believe that she would feel comfortable around me if she had the slightest inclination that I might be *flirting* with her? In spite of being near the same age, I still see her as a mother figure, and you are way out of line to even *think* that it would be anything else." He shook his head again, taking in the flash of anger in Iris's eyes and the stubborn set of her face as it became evident she had no retort. "You're going to have to do better than that if you really intend to condemn me and have me banished from your home."

Case told himself he should walk away before he said anything more, something he might regret. But he felt so furious—and hurt—over her accusations, that he couldn't even move. The very idea that she would even *think* he would behave in such a way left him feeling sickened and betrayed. He reminded himself that it was ludicrous to feel betrayed by someone who boldly claimed to have no respect for him anyway. But it still hurt.

Realizing he had work to do and she was where he needed to do it, he forced a steady voice to ask, "Is there something else, Miss Barrington, or might I return to my chores?"

"Yes, actually. One of these days my father is going to realize what you're trying to do, and he's going to be as disgusted as I am. You can't just move in here and start acting like his son, expecting to gain some favor with him. He's too wise to stand for it indefinitely. Your days here are numbered."

Case said nothing. No words could begin to express how he felt, and there was nothing he could say in his defense that would make any difference. He felt an added measure of disgust and disbelief when she added, "Your silence implies that you have no rebuttal."

"I have no rebuttal that would make any difference to whatever you have deluded yourself into believing. You have no idea what you're talking about."

"If you think that—"

"Is there a problem here?" James asked and startled them both.

Case said nothing, wondering how much he had overheard. Iris turned to her father and said, "If you can't see the problem here, then there really *is* a problem."

Case was surprised to hear James say in a calm voice, "Stop persecuting the poor boy and go help your mother."

Iris made a disgusted noise and left the barn. Once the door had closed behind her, Case said, "How long were you there?"

"Long enough to know that she *does* believe you're after my money, and she also thinks you're flirting with my wife."

"And what do *you* think?"

"I was wise enough to see through such behavior before she was even born. You already know what I think." He folded his arms and added, "I'm going to tell her the truth."

"About *what?"*

"The reason you do so much for me."

"No," Case countered. "Let her think what she wants. Better that she think ill of me than worry about you."

"Is it?"

"For now, yes."

"I'm not so sure," James said. "This kind of poor communication should be cleared up."

"This isn't about poor communication, James. This is about judgment and prejudice. And I don't want her to know; not yet. If she can't learn to see me for who I really am, then anything else is irrelevant. And even if she didn't believe all these horrible things about me, she would still be unwilling to let go of my past. I don't want her to know," he repeated.

"That's pride talking."

"Is it? Maybe it's protection." He sighed. "Maybe it's better this way. I love her, James. But I can't live with a woman who treats me like that."

"And you shouldn't. I love her, too, but I cannot make sense of why she would behave this way. We'll just keep praying for her. In the meantime, take good care of my wife and children. Whether I'm around or not, they need you. I need you. I'm grateful you're here."

James left the barn and closed the door. Case resisted the urge to curse, and he groaned instead. He'd never imagined that loving someone could be so hard. But he couldn't deny how abundantly blessed he was. James Barrington was a kind and generous man who had a great deal of compassion for Case's situation. He might never earn Iris's respect, but he'd earned that of James Barrington. How could he not be grateful for that?

For days, nothing changed in Iris's attitude toward Case. She was mildly irritable with everyone, but wouldn't even speak to—or look at—Case. He just tried to ignore the fact that she was ignoring him and keep track of James and the boys. Frederick was completely down in bed for a week, and then the pain let up enough that he was able to start moving around on crutches. After another week he started venturing from his own home into the big house during the days so that he could share meals, study, and prayer with the others, but he wasn't capable of doing much of anything beyond sitting at the kitchen table with his foot propped on a chair so that he could help Stella with some odd tasks here and there.

A week into May, Case finished the usual early-morning work in the barn without seeing any sign of Ben, which was unusual. He didn't mind doing the work; he just wondered if something was wrong. When he took buckets of fresh milk into the kitchen, he was surprised to find no one there, and no evidence of breakfast cooking, as it normally would have been. He left the milk there and moved quietly up the hall toward the sound of voices at the front of the house. Then he heard crying; more than one person crying. He stopped, heart pounding, wondering what had happened. He hesitated to intrude, but his concern and curiosity compelled him forward. He moved discreetly into the doorway of the parlor to see James with one arm around Eleanore, the other around Iris, and Ben sitting across the room. The men were gravely solemn, the women crying. He guessed that the children were still asleep, or at least still upstairs. And Frederick and his family probably hadn't come to the house yet today. But where was Stella? The pounding of his heart increased, and the words leapt out of his mouth. "What's happened?"

They all looked up to see him. Only Iris looked quickly away, burying her face against her father's shoulder. A long moment of silence compelled Case to add, "Forgive me for intruding. If it's none of my business, then—"

"You're not intruding," James said. "Of course you need to know." A tremor rose in his voice. Stella . . . died in her sleep." Case sucked in his breath and couldn't let it out. How could this be possible?

They'd just been talking and laughing in the kitchen last night while he'd washed a couple of pans. He hadn't known her nearly as long as everyone else here, but he'd grown to care for her, nevertheless. She was more a part of this family than he was, beyond any doubt. He just couldn't believe it.

James went on. "It was Iris who found her." Iris cried harder, and James tightened his arm around her. Case felt envious of James for being the man who could comfort her grief. "We . . . don't know what happened. Iris got up early to help in the kitchen. When Stella wasn't there, she went to check on her, and . . ." It took him a moment to gain his composure enough to finish. "It would seem she just . . . went to sleep . . . and never woke up."

While Case internalized his shock over Stella being gone, he tried to imagine how traumatic this must be, especially for Iris. He wanted to be able to talk to her and hold her hand. He wanted to be a strength to her in her time of need, whatever that need might be. Perhaps if he hadn't once been in that position, he might not feel so lost and helpless over not being there now. As it was, his grief over Iris's banishing attitude toward him felt as stark as his grief over Stella's death.

Case felt awkward and mildly out of place as the family coped with Stella's sudden demise. Perhaps it was simply because he'd come into the household after Stella had, or perhaps it was something more. As always, James and Eleanore insisted that he remain involved in every facet of what the family was doing. They had a way of keeping him in the circle of their household that often left him overcome with gratitude. But at the same time, Iris was intently proficient at making him feel unwelcome, as if he had no right to be grieving for Stella, or to be there at all. He felt more like an outsider while he observed the grieving of these people for someone they had cared for deeply.

The funeral was beautiful and touching, and there was no questioning the peace present as Stella was buried in the woods, near David's grave. But there was still sorrow over her passing and the separation between this life and the next one. He agreed wholly with James, who more than once expressed his gratitude for the understanding that the gospel had given them of eternal life and the Resurrection, but it was still difficult to be without loved ones. He spoke of David's death with the same mixture of sorrow and gratitude, and Case couldn't help thinking of his own loved ones that he'd lost. But he couldn't talk about that. He doubted that he would *ever* be able to talk about that.

Throughout the course of dealing with Stella's death, Case saw a different side of Iris. It was as if her grief was too consuming for her to put any effort into being obnoxious with him. She simply pretended he wasn't there. Following the burial, everyone worked hard to get life back to normal, while it was impossible to avoid noticing Stella's absence. Iris, Lizzie, and Eleanore began spending more time in the kitchen to take over Stella's duties, but everyone knew they were struggling to manage between the three of them what Stella had done so gracefully on her own. There was joking about the decrease of quality in the cooking, and while the food was perfectly fine and no one really cared about that, they all missed Stella's gift in putting on fine meals as much as they missed her sweetness and her tender nature.

The strain on the family began to show with Stella gone, Frederick laid up, and James trying to discreetly avoid doing anything that took any exertion. Eleanore was also restricted due to her pregnancy, and James didn't want her spending too much time on her feet or overdoing herself in any way. Case noted the way James solved two problems by insisting that he help more in the kitchen in order to keep her from doing so much there, which kept him from doing work outside that required more physical effort. His excuse of staying close to Eleanore in the kitchen made it easier for him to ask Ben and Case to do everything else without anyone getting suspicious.

The grief over Stella's death was still fresh when Case entered the barn to see James sitting on a bale of straw, his head in his hands, straining to breathe.

"What have you done to yourself?" Case insisted and startled him.

"It's not that," James said and lifted his head, discreetly wiping tears. "I'm fine . . . I'm breathing, at least."

"What is it, then?" Case asked. "Or is it—"

"It's all right for you to ask, Case." James cleared his throat and sat up straight. "Word from Salt Lake."

When he hesitated, Case asked, "Is it your friends there? Are they—"

"They're fine, as far as we know. But there were two companies; handcart companies . . . that left here late last July—right before you came here to work."

"I remember. I felt frustrated at the time, wishing I'd gotten into town a few days sooner so I could have gone with them." James's eyes widened. "Obviously I needed to be here."

"Obviously," James said and took a ragged breath, as if he were now more burdened than he'd been before. "They got into trouble. Winter came in too fast; there were other problems. I don't know the details. The prophet sent rescue parties after them, or they *all* would have died."

Case heard the deeper message. "How many *did* die?"

James sniffled and hung his head again. "I don't know exactly. A couple hundred, I think. Many more were permanently maimed from the frostbite. They were starving and . . ." He sniffled again. "I was worried when they left. But their faith was stronger than any logic regarding the journey, it seemed." He wiped his face with his shirt-sleeve. "I'm certain their sacrifices will be long remembered and revered, and I pray that no other companies run into such disaster." James stood as if to end the conversation. He put a hand on Case's shoulder and added, "And I'm grateful you didn't get to Iowa City a few days earlier."

Minutes after James left the barn, Case attempted to accept and understand such a horrible event, and how the people must have suffered. He considered his own position and wondered why he would have been spared. When the questions had no answers, he just got down on his knees and prayed that those who had survived would be comforted and blessed, and that their sacrifices *would* be remembered. He prayed that he would live his life in a way that honored such sacrifice. Then he got up and continued with his work.

On a cloudy afternoon a week after Stella had been buried, Ben went into Coralville to do something on his father's behalf, while Case stuck to the usual chores, attempting to avoid going anywhere near Iris. But he found it impossible to avoid thinking of her while he chopped wood with excessive vigor, wishing the physical labor would drive her out of his head. He'd prayed to be free of thoughts of her—and feelings. But if anything, they had only increased. Either God was trying to tell him he *should* be thinking about her this way, or he was losing his mind.

* * * * *

Iris discreetly watched Case chopping wood from an upstairs window while the children played noisily in the room. She wished she could feel as indifferent toward him as she pretended to be. Instead she felt confused and lost, drowning emotionally in waves of fear and anger that she couldn't make sense of. She missed the time they'd spent together and the comfortable relationship she'd developed with him. But that had been shattered, and she couldn't see any possible way of putting it back together.

Mary Jane came in and told Iris that her father wanted to talk with her.

"Thank you," Iris said, and this girl who was as good as her sister smiled and hurried away, likely to help her mother in the kitchen. "You watch out for the little ones," Iris said to Jamie on her way into the hall.

Jamie made a noise to indicate he'd heard her, and Iris went downstairs to find her father sitting behind his desk in the library, gazing at nothing. She wondered where his thoughts were while he looked so troubled.

"You wanted to talk to me?" she asked, and he turned.

"Yes. Come in." He stood and kissed her cheek, and they sat at opposite ends of the couch. "How are you?"

"Is that what you wanted to know? How I am?"

"That's one thing," James said without apology.

"I'm fine," she said.

"You're lying," her father countered.

"I'm *not* lying."

"Then you're using *fine* in a relative sense while you ignore everything about your life that makes you unhappy."

Iris looked away. She'd always known her father was perceptive and unafraid to say what he believed. But in her present state of mind, the truth pierced her more deeply than usual. Her mind went naturally to Case, and she resisted the temptation to tell her father exactly what she thought of him. She wanted to ask the wise and insightful James Barrington if he had any idea that he'd be more wise not to be so trusting of Casey Harrison. But she said nothing, not wanting to talk about it as much as she didn't want her father trying to convince her of the opposite. She felt certain he would see the truth eventually.

Much to her relief, the conversation began far from Case. Her father asked how she was dealing with Stella's death, and they spoke of her with gentle nostalgia. He expressed appreciation for all of her help in the home and with the children, telling her how grateful he was for her ability and willingness to help, especially with Stella gone and her mother not feeling well. The apparent purpose of the conversation was simply to let her know that her efforts hadn't gone unnoticed, accompanied by a request to keep doing the same so that Eleanore would not overdo and risk her pregnancy. Iris assured him that she had no problem with doing her part, and she didn't consider what she did to be a burden. They joked about her cooking skills. Iris felt certain she was doing all right, as long as Lizzie was beside her, but she could do with a great deal of practice and improvement. But James assured her, in his usual loving way, that she was doing well and she had more of a knack for it than she might believe.

"More of a knack than Mother, is what you mean?" Iris said lightly.

James smiled. "She'll readily admit to it. However, your mother has many gifts that more than compensate."

"Yes, she certainly does," Iris said, wishing as she had many times that it was Eleanore's blood in her veins, and not that of some other woman.

A stretch of silence made Iris wonder if that was all he'd wanted to say, then he cleared his throat quietly, and a subtle tension descended over the room. She knew there was something else.

"I need to inform you of something," he said, and the soberness of his tone captured her full attention. "I'm not telling the other children; they're too young to understand, and it doesn't matter to them."

"Ben?"

"Ben's part in this was made clear to him years ago. There's no need to bring it up again. You see, I changed my will after we adopted him, in order to be certain he was included. And he knows about that. Now that—"

"Wait," she said. "Your *will?* We're talking about *your will?*"

"We are," he said straightly.

"Why?"

"So that you understand my intentions."

"Is there something I don't know about?" Iris felt decidedly panicked at the very thought of losing her father for any reason. She didn't like this conversation at all. "Is there some reason you're suddenly concerned about your will?"

"Not suddenly, Iris. I've had a will since long before you were born. And when changes occur in my life and I feel compelled to make adjustments, I do. A man never knows how long he has. Whenever I leave, I want to know that everything is in order; that it's the way *I* want it to be. I've never spoken to you about it before because . . . well, you were younger, and it didn't seem relevant."

"What makes it relevant now?"

"Now that you're an adult, I want you to know what it says. It's stated clearly, but I wanted you to hear it from me. If the worst happened and both your mother and I were no longer here, the care of the children would be left to you. You're capable of raising them well, and we know that you would."

Iris made an appalled noise and stood abruptly, turning her back to him. "The very thought is unthinkable. I can't believe you would even—"

"Iris, this is not intended to be morbid or difficult. It's simply a matter of good common sense. Of course, everything is stated very clearly regarding the division of my assets, and everyone I care about will be well cared for whenever the good Lord *does* take me, but—"

"I don't care about your assets. The money means nothing without you here or—"

"I'm well aware that my money is of little matter to the things that mean most in this world, but it still takes money to survive, and I'm grateful to know that there is more than sufficient to care for my loved ones. You're missing the point. I simply wanted you to know what the will says; I wanted you to hear it from me so that there's no surprises in the event that something should happen to me or your mother—or both."

Iris forced herself to sit down and take this as matter-of-factly as he was presenting it. "Why now?" she asked.

His eyes flickered in a way that let her know there was something he didn't want to tell her. If he had some sense that his life could be drawing to a close, she wondered if she could bear even hearing such an idea. She was relieved when he answered without hesitation, "I've just felt the need to have the will updated, which brought it to mind, and I felt that you were old enough to know that I have a will, and what it says."

She sensed there was something more he wanted to tell her. When his hesitance made her increasingly nervous, she finally asked, "Is there something else it says that I should be aware of?"

"Yes, but I don't think you're going to like it, so naturally I was hoping to put it off as long as possible." He hesitated again while she wondered if *now* he would tell her that something was wrong with him, or with her mother, or that one of them had been given some spiritual inclination to an event that made this conversation necessary. Her stomach tightened, and her palms became clammy before he finally added, "I've grown to care for Case like a son."

Without thinking, she countered in a voice that attempted to keep the subject light. "If you're trying to tell me that I should marry him so he can officially be a part of the family, you can forget it. I cannot do something that—"

"Whether you marry him is your decision, Iris. And what I do is my decision."

"What are you saying?" she asked, a little breathless as the gist of the conversation began to sink in.

"I've included Case in my will," James said with no apology in his eyes or tone.

Iris was so completely taken off guard—and so furious—that she could hardly draw breath. She thought of a dozen things she wanted to say, all of which would sound utterly disrespectful to her father and make herself sound like a fool. She could only ask, "Why? Why would you do that? Just because he's been here longer than any other hired hand or—"

"It has nothing to do with that, Iris. He's a good man, and this is right. I know it is; simple as that. I just wanted you to know."

"And . . . what if he's not as wonderful as he appears to be?"

"Then I'll be proven a fool for giving him money that he might not get for years yet. This has nothing to do with you, Iris. I just wanted to give you the courtesy of knowing."

Iris stood up, fighting with everything she had to hold back a torrent of emotion, not wanting to cry like a baby over something that shouldn't have mattered to her. But it did. Even if she didn't understand why. "So . . . you're just . . . taking him in . . . like a son . . . and you're making it official. Is that the essence of what I needed to know?"

"Yes, I believe it is."

Iris turned to leave the room, knowing she couldn't maintain her composure many more seconds.

"Where are you going?" her father demanded.

"For a walk," she said and slammed the front door on her way out.

Chapter Nine

FOLLOWING ORDERS

While Case chopped wood, the clouds darkened, then quickly turned to heavy rain that encouraged Case to find tasks that needed doing inside the barn. He was startled by the door opening abruptly, and Jamie, who was very wet, said with some urgency, "Mama sent me to get you. She needs your help."

Case ran into the house and found Eleanore pacing the kitchen while James sat with his head pressed into his hands. He could hear a subtle, familiar wheezing that alerted him to what the problem might be.

"Thank you, Jamie," Eleanore said to him. "I want you to keep an eye on Mariah for a while, please. We need to speak with Case privately."

Jamie quickly obeyed, and Case wondered what James had done that he shouldn't have. He was about to scold him for not asking for help, when Eleanore said in a panicked whisper, "Iris is gone, Case."

"Gone?" he echoed, feeling an immediate panic that completely explained why James was having difficulty breathing.

"She went for a walk. She was upset. She left more than an hour ago . . . and now it's raining so hard, and . . ." her composure failed, "after what happened to David . . ." She couldn't finish, but Case knew what she meant. He'd heard the story of young David running off and getting caught in a sudden storm. The resulting illness had ended in his dying of pneumonia. Case couldn't even imagine the fear

Iris's parents might be feeling right now. "I've insisted that James not go looking for her," Eleanore added, "for obvious reasons, and—"

"I'll find her," Case said and hurried back outside while he wondered if he could. Nothing but divine guidance could lead him to her. He had no idea even where to begin looking.

Case ran to the barn and mounted a stallion bareback; he didn't want to waste time with a saddle. He prayed constantly as he started towards the woods, then felt impressed to go the other direction, toward the bridge. His coat and hat weren't nearly as helpful in keeping the rain off as he would have liked, but he was more concerned with how Iris might have been dressed when she'd left the house for this impulsive walk. His mind began roiling with all the possible things that could have happened to her—or that might result—and he felt sick and scared beyond reason. He forced such thoughts and their accompanying fear away, struggling to focus on faith in the Lord to protect her, and to guide him in finding her. The rain was pounding and the wind fierce as he approached the bridge and crossed it without even wondering if he should go any other direction. He kept pressing on, hesitating here and there until he felt more strongly about going one way as opposed to another. But it was taking far too long, and time made it increasingly difficult to push away doubt and fear.

Case was beginning to think he'd never find her when he saw a hazy image through the rain a short distance ahead. He spoke a soft "thank you" to God and quickened his speed, relieved beyond his own comprehension. He reined the horse in, halting her wavering attempt to move toward home.

"What are you doing?" Iris gasped, startled by his intrusion, but unable to look at him due to the rain pounding on her face.

"I should think it's obvious," he snarled, holding out a hand toward her. She barely glanced at it, then ducked her head down against the rain. "The question is, what are *you* doing?"

Iris attempted to glare at him, but couldn't keep her face turned upward for more than a second. Before she could think of an appropriate retort, he reached his hand further toward her and shouted, "Get on! We'll talk about it later."

Iris could only hesitate for a moment before the stark practicality of the situation made it clear that she had no choice. She lifted her hand, and he gripped her forearm, lifting her onto the horse, with her in front of him. He turned and headed more directly into the rain. She ducked her head, but rain still ran over her face while it pounded mercilessly over her hair. The stallion beneath them proved strong and steady as it pressed willfully through the storm, making fixed progress. She felt disarmed by being so close to Case, and especially with the way he put his arm around her waist to hold her in place while he guided the horse with his other hand. Iris didn't want to admit to her absolute relief about his rescuing her, but she wasn't pleased when he growled close to her ear, "What were you thinking?"

"It wasn't raining when I left."

"No, but there were plenty of clouds and wind." He actually cursed when they were assaulted with a fresh gust of wind.

"So, you're *not* perfect," she said loudly enough to be certain he heard her above the storm.

"Far from it." His voice became more angry, and he tightened his arm around her waist. But she couldn't be sure if the gesture was meant to help protect her, or to assert some indication that he was stronger and in control.

Case chose to avoid any further attempt at conversation when it became too difficult. He wanted to ignore his own reaction to having Iris so near, but he became so consumed with the effect that he was practically oblivious to the storm, horrendous as it was. Initially, he felt her resisting his effort to hold her close in some feeble attempt to block the wind and rain, but gradually she leaned back against his chest, retracting toward him.

When they finally reached the house, Case saw the visible relief of James and Eleanore, who had both been pacing beneath the porch awning. He waved at them and saw them go into the house while he hurried toward the safety of the barn. Once inside, he dismounted and quickly turned to take hold of Iris's waist to help her to her feet. He purposely held her there, forcing her to face him long enough to say, "Do you have any idea how lucky you are that I found you? Next time you go traipsing off in a storm, consider your parents' concerns."

"Like I said," she snapped, "it wasn't raining when I left."

"The storm was coming, and you knew it. After what happened to David, what you just did was thoughtless and cruel."

He saw a flicker of regret in her eyes, and he felt certain the connection had never occurred to her. He wanted her to admit that she *had* been thoughtless, but she only said, "That is between me and my parents."

Iris looked up at Case, finding anger mixed with something unreadable in his eyes that left her uneasy. She wanted to walk away and end this encounter, but she felt powerless to move, as if some invisible magnetic energy kept her feet firmly planted in that spot. Hoping to justify her reasons for not leaving, she struggled for something to say. "It was kind of you to come after me, but you're obviously very angry over the inconvenience I've caused you, Mr. Harrison."

Her formality bit at him, but he ignored it. "I'm angry because your parents were worried."

"Only my parents?"

Case felt more appalled than angry by the question. She might as well have said, *I know you love me and I'm going to taunt you*. The problem was that he *did* love her, and he *had* been worried. He thought of the words in the scriptures, that a soft answer turneth away wrath, and he hoped that it might turn away hers as well as his own.

Iris watched varied emotions pass through Case's eyes and wondered if he felt as frozen and unable to move as she. "Yes, I was worried," he admitted in a gentle voice, his eyes filled with an honesty that left her utterly disarmed when she had been prepared for some sarcastic answer or angry retort. She was surprised at how the confusion and anger left her, and she could only feel as relieved at being home and safe as she was to be facing him. All the thoughts that had churned inside of her, causing her to fume and rage while she'd walked blindly into the storm, had dissipated in her realization that she'd been lost and unable to find her bearings in order to return home. Now, the remaining residue of her negative feelings momentarily dissipated, and she could only feel the moment.

Case saw her soften much more quickly and fully than he'd anticipated. It was the first time she'd looked at him that way since he'd told her the truth about his past and she had banished him from her life. He didn't even think about kissing her; he just did it. He wondered for only a moment if she would respond or slap him. In truth, her response was so immediate and so eager that he felt as if he would melt into the ground. He wrapped her in his arms, kissing her on and on, soaking her into himself as if it might somehow compensate for all these weeks that she had been so cold and inaccessible. He prayed silently while he kissed her, wanting this to be the moment where she came to her senses and realized that they could overcome whatever stood between them. He begged God to soften her heart and allow her to forgive him for his past, and promised his Maker that he would commit his life to making this woman happy if she would only have him. As she took hold of his shoulders and softened further into his arms, Case was amazed at how blissful a kiss could be. He'd never imagined it could be so emotionally and spiritually consuming, while at the same time affecting his every sense. *He loved her so much!*

Case reluctantly eased back enough to look into her eyes, relieved to find them expressing the same awe that he felt. He wanted to tell her how he felt as much as he wanted to hear her say that they could start over. But words felt inadequate, and instead he kissed her again, relishing the experience, wanting to feel this way forever.

Iris forced reason to intrude upon her instincts and consciously realized what she was doing. She wondered when she had lost her mind, and with the evidence of how thoroughly Case was taking advantage of a vulnerable moment, all of her fury rushed back into her like a tornado on a path of destruction.

Case felt her go tense and knew this little oasis of serenity was gone. He tried to tell himself that it had given him some hope to hold onto. Surely there was evidence that her feelings for him were still there, and that with time she could come to terms with whatever was keeping them apart. But hope became difficult to hold onto the moment she pushed him away and stepped back, her eyes ablaze with brittle fury. He saw her intentions in her eyes as she raised her hand to slap him, but he caught her wrist before she could make contact with his face. His own fury deepened, if only to smother the sorrow he felt over her animosity toward him. Still holding her wrist, he said close to her face, "You participated in that kiss every bit as much as I did. So you tell me what it is you hope to accomplish by hitting me. Do you think it will convince me that you hate me? Or will it convince *you?*" She didn't answer, but her eyes betrayed that he'd disarmed her. "Tell me what it is, Miss Barrington, that gives you the right to hurt me. What have I *ever* done to warrant such cruelty? My past is what it is, and I know you don't like it, but I have never done *anything* to deserve your anger *or* your lack of trust."

"That's all a matter of opinion, I suppose," she snapped, and he had no idea what she was talking about.

"Just answer the question."

Again she diverted it. "My father may be too blind to see what's really going on, but *I* can see it, and eventually the truth will come out."

"That's right," he said, moving his face closer to hers, still holding to her wrist. "Eventually the truth will come out, and we'll see who is blind." He lowered his voice to a husky whisper. "Have you ever asked yourself what it is about me that makes you face things about yourself you don't want to look at?" He'd been hoping to make a point, but it only made her eyes more rigid with indignation. Hoping to get some answers before she stormed away, he reiterated what he wanted to know. "You tell me what I ever did to you to make you want to hurt me."

The answer came quickly to Iris's mind, but she hesitated to let it pass through her lips. She countered his gaze, if only to show him that she wasn't intimidated. But the intensity of his eyes made it impossible to ignore words that were sticking strongly in her head. As their honesty became evident, she felt no choice but to let them spew out of her mouth. "You made me love you," she cried, surprised at the emotion that came out along with the truth she'd never been able to admit before. But another truth followed on its heels, and she sobbed to force it out. "And then you betrayed my deepest trust."

Case attempted to take in the full gamut of what she'd just said, but he couldn't. Her admitting to love was somewhat reassuring, but it only made the entire situation all the more poignant and riddled with pain. And for all of his disputing her concept of betrayal, he had to respect her perception of the matter and acknowledge it. He finally found his voice enough to say, "No, Iris, I betrayed you long before I ever loved you; before I ever knew you. And my regret is deeper than I could ever tell you. But I can't change it now. I can only say that . . . I'm truly sorry."

Iris felt completely disarmed by his words, but more so by the way they pierced her so deeply. She consciously attempted to put anger in place to smother any other possible response, but heat burned her throat and moistened her eyes, leaving her to wonder what kind of power this man had over her. How could he provoke such intense emotions in her—both positive and negative—within a matter of moments? Unable to speak or move, she was appalled to realize tears were sliding down her cheeks. Her hope that the rain still on her face might disguise them was dashed when Case let go of her wrist to wipe them away. As he did, all of the conversations and emotions of this day rushed over her, much like the rain she'd recently escaped. She felt so utterly confused and upset that all she could do was turn and run to the sanctuary of the house, fearing Case would come after her and force her to talk to him. Or perhaps fearing more so that he wouldn't.

Iris's parents said little to her when she came in the house. They simply expressed their appreciation that she was all right and ordered her to get into the hot bath that was waiting upstairs. While Iris undressed and soaked in the soothing water, she cried continually. Her head ached from trying to stay quiet enough to not draw attention from anyone who might be in the next room. Her tears finally relented to a solemn shock, not unlike how she'd felt when Stella had died. And she felt equally helpless to change the situation. All she could do was live with it. But by the time she'd finished with her bath and gotten dressed, she knew she *did* have to clarify one point with Case, even if she'd prefer washing every dirty dish for a month rather than facing such a prospect.

Iris dreaded supper when she would have to be in the same room with him while gathering courage to find him alone afterward and say what she needed to say. But Case didn't show up for supper; he'd given Jamie the message to tell the family not to wait for him, that he wasn't feeling well. While they were cleaning up the meal, Eleanore asked Mary Jane to take a plate to Case's room on the chance that he might feel up to eating something. Iris offered to take it instead, hoping she wouldn't regret this as much as she regretted what had happened between them earlier in the barn.

Iris was grateful the rain had stopped as she made her way across the yard to the house where Frederick and Lizzie lived. She went up the stairs on the outside of the house to the attic room where Case had been living since he'd come here last summer. Now summer was almost here again, and she still had no idea what she was doing with her life. At the door she exhaled slowly and knocked.

"It's open," she heard him call, and she stepped into the room. He was standing at the window, looking out. Without turning he said, "What are you doing here?" She wondered how he knew it was her and not someone else. Had he seen her coming from the window? Before she could offer the excuse of bringing his supper, he added, "Did you need to come and get the last word in now that you've stopped crying?"

Her defenses were tempted to the surface, but she couldn't entirely discount such a theory, so she only said, "I've brought some supper."

"Someone else could have brought it. If your mother had asked you to do it and you hadn't wanted to, I'm certain you could have manipulated one of the kids into doing it."

She diverted the topic. "I'd heard you weren't feeling well. Are you—"

"I'm fine," he interrupted. "I didn't want to see you." The declaration held some double meaning in her being in his room now.

Iris set down the tray, knowing she needed to get this over with. "There's something I need to say."

"Then say it."

Iris drew back her shoulders and spouted quickly, "It's over between us, Case." He finally turned to look at her. "I don't want you to interpret what happened today as something to hold onto with the belief that this will be mended between us. It's over. It will never work between us." She exhaled sharply. "There. That's what I needed to say."

"And why, may I ask, will it never work between us?" While she was pondering an answer, he added, "What happened between us today was real, Iris. The way we felt was not some product of our imaginations."

Iris turned her back to him. "Such feelings are not sufficient to base a relationship on."

"We have a great deal to base a relationship on. I could come up with a very long list of reasons why you and I could be happy together, not the least of which is that we love each other. There's only one thing standing in the way. One thing, Iris."

"That's right," she said and turned to face him. "One thing, but it's too big to overlook, and I can't live with it. However attracted I may feel to you, I—"

"Attracted?" He gave a scoffing laugh. "You love me and you know it; you admitted it."

"Then I didn't know what I was saying. And it doesn't matter anyway. However I might feel about you is irrelevant when I can't trust you. I can't have a relationship with a man I can't trust. It's as simple as that."

"So . . ." he motioned with his hand, "you believe I'm going to . . . what? Leave you? Cheat on you? Get drunk? Knock you around?"

"Maybe."

"Oh, Iris, listen to yourself. An intelligent woman cannot be living close to the Spirit and believe something so blindly ignorant. So, based on evidence that I'm completely unclear on, I'm destined to behave in every possible deplorable way and then take your father's money and run. Is that it?"

"Maybe," she said again, and he scoffed more boldly. "Whether it makes sense to you is irrelevant to me. I can't trust you, and therefore I'm not willing to take the risk."

Case turned more fully toward her, and she actually felt afraid of the anger in his eyes. *Would* he hurt her the way his father had hurt his mother? She took a step backwards but found there was nowhere to go in the tiny room with slanted ceilings.

"I cannot believe what I'm hearing," he said in a voice that accentuated his angry expression. "How dare you talk about risk and trust that way, you blind little hypocrite! *You,* who boldly lured my secrets into the open, throwing such words as trust and risk at me to provoke me. I *trusted* you. I *risked* my heart. And what have you done with it? *You* have a great deal to learn about trust and risk, my dear Miss Barrington."

"Just bear this in mind, *Mr. Harrison.* My father trusts you in ways that I will never understand, and if you ever do *anything* to hurt him, or any other member of this family, you will have to answer to me. He may be leaving money to you when he dies, but I intend to see that he lives a very long time, and with any luck he will see the truth before then and do the right thing." She wondered for a moment if she had spilled a secret when she shouldn't have, but it was evident he knew what she was talking about. The thought made her more angry. Not only was her father leaving him money, but he'd told Case that he was.

"Is that what this is about?" Case asked. "Your father's money?"

"What my father does with his money is up to him. My opinion on the matter is irrelevant."

"Not to me, it's not."

"I think you're ingratiating yourself with him to win favor in his eyes, and I think you're doing a very good job of it. He's not easily fooled, you know."

"Or maybe he's not fooled at all," Case said, forcing a level attitude that didn't allow himself to feel the hurt of her accusations—at least not while she was standing there.

"You're impossible!" she snarled and took hold of the doorknob.

"Iris," he said in a softer voice that stopped her, "I would never hurt your father, or anyone else that you love. And I don't want your father's money. Maybe someday you'll trust me enough to believe that."

"There is no someday for us, Case. I can't have a relationship with a man I don't trust."

"Then you're going to spend your life alone, Iris, because you don't trust anyone beyond your own family."

Iris ignored the comment and said, "As I see it, the sooner you go west, the better for all of us." As the words came out of her mouth, she was reminded of a frequent thought and asked, "Why haven't you left, anyway? It's spring now."

"No companies have left yet. But your father asked me to stay."

Iris couldn't counter her father's wishes, but she did say, "If you're staying here, at least have the decency to stay out of my way."

"Glad to," he said as she left, determined to follow her orders. The drama was just too exhausting—and depressing. He watched from the window as she hurried back to the house, praying that she was wrong. He had to believe that there *was* something to hold on to, that it *would* work out between them. He didn't know how it was possible. But he had seen Iris's potential, and his heart believed that eventually she would be able to see it too. Turning to examine the supper she'd brought, he muttered aloud, "Be careful what you pray for, Case. She might end up marrying you, and then what will you do?" He laughed at the thought, if only to keep from crying as he considered the horrible things she'd said to him. But that didn't change the way he felt about her, and he doubted it ever would.

* * * * *

On a warm night late in May, James kissed Iris good night at the door to her room and accepted the usual smile she offered. But he knew it wasn't sincere. She was deeply unhappy, and he was deeply concerned. More than a week had passed since Iris had walked out of the house angry and become lost in that storm. But the storm was still brewing; he could feel it, and he knew something was horribly wrong. He'd prayed and pondered and stewed over his daughter's situation and attitudes, and he'd recognized that there was nothing more to be done. She had to come to terms with this herself. He could continue to pray. He could be available for her if she needed him. And if the Spirit guided him to do or say something, he would follow through. Beyond that, he had to step back and allow her to make her own choices. He only wished he could see any kind of reasoning whatsoever in her behavior.

James entered the bedroom to find Eleanore brushing out her hair. He kissed the side of her throat and told her how he loved her, then he got ready for bed, feeling unusually exhausted. After they had shared the usual bedside prayer, he crawled between the covers and sank quickly into a deep sleep.

James came awake suddenly. With eyes wide open he took in the surrounding silence, the barest hint of light creeping into the room. His mind was empty of any thought beyond wondering what might have awakened him so abruptly from a deep sleep. He wondered if he should feel alarmed, but he felt entirely calm. Then words appeared in his mind with a clarity that was not lessened by the silence in which they were delivered. *It is time, James. Take your family to Zion. Do not delay.*

James felt a constriction in his chest that had nothing to do with his physical ailment. Minutes passed while the silence of the room remained intense and the light of day crept slowly in to illuminate his surroundings. He could only stare toward the ceiling, attempting to accept something he'd waited to hear for more years than he could believe. He'd begun to wonder if it would ever happen, mostly because he couldn't comprehend getting an answer that he'd been praying for since the day he'd been lowered into the waters of baptism. All these years they had been kept apart from the body of the Saints; all this time they'd waited and wondered. Their purpose in Iowa City had been made evident, but their plans to go to Zion were rational and logical. Eleanore was pregnant, and he'd been determined to wait until next year for that reason. His chest tightened further to consider that if they left soon she would undoubtedly give birth on the journey. They could never get to Salt Lake before the baby arrived. But if they waited until it was born, it would be too late in the season to start out.

James got out of bed and quietly paced the room, attempting to accept the message that he had undoubtedly received from the Lord—and the overwhelming ramifications for his family. His spirit felt unnaturally calm, while his mind reeled with a hundred thoughts and fears. He ached to discuss the dramatic change with Eleanore, and the apparent unexpected urgency of their leaving now, as opposed to following their original plans. But at the same time he wanted to delay giving her the news, certain that hearing it would be difficult for her. He knew she would take on the assignment with faith and determination—as she had taken on every challenge in her life. But that didn't necessarily mean she'd be pleased. She'd longed for years, as he had, to live among the Saints, but getting there would not be easy. And now that there were Mormons living in the area, staying in Iowa had not been so difficult. They'd always known it wouldn't be easy to leave their lovely home, where many years of memories and experiences had become a part of their lives. But the blessings of the gospel, and living in Zion, would more than compensate for all they would leave behind. They'd both agreed on this matter long ago, so choosing was not an issue. The only real issue for James was the timing. He reminded himself that thousands of Saints had left their homes with much less planning, and under horrific circumstances. James and his household had been greatly blessed; more blessed than he could possibly assess. Still, the timing of leaving *now* forced him to face fears he'd struggled with for years.

James began mentally planning the exodus of his household. He'd gone over the preparations a thousand times in his mind, and he'd pondered over and over all that he'd heard about the challenges that had been faced by companies going west. All but a few had made it without utter disaster, but the journey was difficult and fraught with uncertainty. Still, he didn't even have to wonder for a moment if there was a choice to be made. He knew the source of the orders he'd been given, and he would not question them now because the timing didn't suit his own concerns. He *would* follow those orders, whatever it took. God had blessed him far too much to even question such a thing now. James only had to wonder if he and Eleanore would both survive the journey.

When James realized Eleanore was coming awake, he sat in a chair near the bed and prayed silently for guidance, strength, and peace. He marveled at how the peace burned inside him. He knew it was right. But the thought of leaving soon was difficult to swallow. He waited for her to come fully awake while he wondered how to tell her. He saw her turn over and look directly at him.

"You're up," she said. "You're dressed." She glanced at the clock. "Did I sleep late?"

"No, I was up early."

"What's wrong?" she asked, sitting up.

"I . . . uh . . . woke up very early . . . very suddenly . . . and—"

Eleanore gasped. "Are the children—"

"Everyone's fine," he said. "I peeked into their rooms a little while ago." He sighed and took a different approach. "You know how . . . years ago . . . I said that I was going to stop asking God if I should take my family to Zion, that He would let me know when the time was right."

"Yes," she drawled with suspicion.

James looked directly at her. "Well, He told me, Ellie. He woke me up and He told me. The impression came to my mind as clearly as any voice speaking it."

Eleanore put a hand over her heart, and tears welled in her eyes. He didn't even have to ask. She'd just been given a witness by the Spirit that what he'd said was true. And she needed that witness; it would be the only thing to carry her through. "When?" she asked.

"Now; as soon as possible."

"What . . . exactly . . . did you hear?"

James repeated it firmly. *"It is time, James. Take your family to Zion. Do not delay."*

Eleanore took a deep breath and said, "Then we'd better start packing."

James moved to the edge of the bed and touched her face, longing for words to tell her how he admired her faith and her strength, and how deeply he loved her. He kissed her and said, "I knew you would say that." He wrapped his arms around her, and she firmly returned his embrace. Then he realized she was crying. He eased back and said, "Talk to me."

"One of my greatest fears has always been losing you . . . the way that Miriam lost Andy." She sniffled and wiped a hand over her face at the mention of their dear friends. "There is no disputing that, given the circumstances of your health, you will be more vulnerable away from home. We have no idea what to expect."

James felt some relief to hear her doubts, which validated his own. Now he was able to admit, "*My* greatest fear has always been the possibility of your having to give birth away from home, without protection from the elements, without the help of a doctor if needed. You're right. We're *all* more vulnerable away from home, and we have no idea what might happen." He sighed loudly. "And here we are. You *will* be giving birth on the journey. We can't wait until after the baby comes, and there's no way we can get there before it does." He put his head down and squeezed his eyes closed. "It's just as Job said, 'The thing which I greatly feared is come upon me.'"

"And so we have no choice but to face our fears." She put her head on his shoulder. "In essence, we both fear the same thing. We're afraid of losing each other." James wrapped her in his arms, and she added, "We have only one choice. We must have faith and trust in the Lord. Our lives are in His hands. They always have been."

"Oh, Ellie." He tightened his embrace. "I pray that God will grant me my greatest wish." He knew she was well aware of what he meant, but he said it anyway. "I pray that you and I will both live to see Zion together, and that we can be sealed for eternity while we are both still living."

"I pray for that too," Eleanore said, unwilling to admit that she prayed equally hard that they could have years together beyond that day. She simply didn't feel ready to let him go, and she doubted that she ever would.

Eleanore knew that at soon as they left this room, nothing would ever be the same. The household would completely shift its focus, and they would very soon be on their way. Before that happened, she took her husband's hand and allowed herself to indulge in nostalgia of all they had shared in this home, the bad and the good. She cried and spoke freely of how hard it would be to leave this beautiful house and all of its memories and the security it offered them. He agreed and cried as well, speaking of his own memories. He got most emotional when he spoke of leaving David's grave behind, and of course, Stella was buried there too. They both agreed that the timing of her death was no coincidence, so that it had not been necessary for her to make this journey.

Eleanore offered a positive note as she mused over what it would be like to be reunited with many friends. Mark and Sally had lived in this very home before James and Eleanore had purchased it. They'd abandoned the home to go to Nauvoo, and from there Sally's letters had become a strength to Eleanore, and they had gained a deep and cherished friendship. Miriam was also very dear to Eleanore. She and her husband, Andy, had been neighbors here in Iowa, and they'd all become very close. Eleanore had shared the gospel with Miriam and her family, and they had lived it together until the family had gone to Nauvoo. Sally and Miriam and their families had been close at one time in Iowa, and they had remained close in Nauvoo, and then at Winter Quarters, where Andy had died of illness. They had all gone together to the Salt Lake Valley with the early companies, and Eleanore missed them terribly. The very idea of being reunited with them eased some of her anxiety. She also spoke of Ralph and his mother, Amanda, who had worked for the Barringtons for many years, and who had become a part of the family. Ralph had gone west with his new bride, Lu, taking his mother along. Ralph and Lu were raising a family in the Salt Lake Valley, and anticipating the opportunity to be with them again felt glorious. Still, the prospect of being with friends again did not alleviate their concerns and fears. But their concerns and fears did not change what they knew they had to do.

They talked and cried until they could hear the sounds of children being awake, and Eleanore knew their reverie was nearing an end. She said firmly to James, "Once we leave this room, I will not look back. I will not indulge in the past."

James nodded stoutly, once again inspired by his wife's faith and determination—and her courage. She wasn't taking this attitude because it was easy; only because she knew it was right. He kissed her and told her how he loved her before he stood to leave the room. Before he reached the door, she said, "I just . . . had an impression that . . . you and I should both get priesthood blessings." Before he could question her reasoning, she added, "You and I are in charge of this household. The others will look to us for strength and answers, and we're both facing potential challenges with our health. I think this is important."

"Of course. You're right." He moved back toward her and touched her face. "Your insight and wisdom have always left me in awe, my dear, sweet wife." He kissed her again. "I'll get Case and Frederick to help us with that right away." He kissed her once more and left the room, determined not to look back.

Chapter Ten

LOOKING AHEAD

Iris and Lizzie worked together to put on breakfast, joking about how good they'd become at working together and maneuvering around each other in the kitchen. Frederick was sitting at the table with his foot up and his crutches nearby. It was typical for him to be wherever Lizzie was working. The doctor had said he could probably remove the splint in a week or so, but it would take longer than that to have the full use of his leg once more. At least he'd long ago stopped having any pain related to the injury.

Case brought fresh milk into the kitchen, talking and laughing with Frederick and Lizzie, and barely speaking a polite "good morning" to Iris. But she was fine with that. She had nothing to offer him but a polite "good morning" in return. Before Case left the kitchen, her father came in, saying, "Case. Good, you're here. I'd like to speak with you in the library, right now if I could." Iris felt inexplicably panicked. The tone of her father's voice suggested some kind of urgency. The oddity of the request heightened her concern.

"Just let me wash up," Case said.

James turned to Frederick. "And you as well, please."

"Of course," Frederick said and reached for his crutches.

Before Iris could ask her father if something was wrong, he simply said, "Priesthood blessings. Nothing to be concerned about."

After the men had left the kitchen, Iris peered into the hall and whispered to Lizzie, "My mother's going in there with them. I wonder if she's having problems with the baby."

"I do hope not," Lizzie said. "But if that were the case, why didn't he just ask *one* of the men to help him. He'd only need both of them if *he* needed a blessing."

"That's true," Iris said after the library door had closed.

"And he said *blessings;* that would mean more than one, wouldn't it?"

"I think you're right," Iris said and wondered what could possibly be going on. She heard Lizzie giggle and asked, "What's so funny?"

"That look on your face. You're almost as curious as that sweet Case."

Iris made a disgruntled noise and got back to work. She didn't want to be compared to Case in any respect, but she didn't at all like hearing him referred to as *sweet.*

* * * * *

Case stood in the doorway of the library, waiting for Frederick to come up the hall more slowly on his crutches. He discreetly observed James take down a little wall hanging that Case had noticed there before: plaster impressions of David's and Iris's hands when they'd been children. He set it on top of a large book that was on the desk. Case recognized that too. The family Bible. He'd seen James read out of it many times. His heart quickened when he heard James say to his wife, "That's it." He looked around the room at the endless rows of books, the fine furnishings and decor. "The rest stays."

Eleanore nodded. James kissed her quickly. Frederick appeared beside Case, and James invited them into the room, closing the door. Without undue explanation, James said, "I wonder if the two of you would help me give my wife a blessing, and then I'd like you to give me one as well."

"Of course," Frederick said at the same time as Case said, "I would be honored."

Case suspected before the blessings began that something had changed, that they were planning to leave. But once the blessings had been given, there was no disputing that course. Through the guidance of the Holy Ghost and the power of the priesthood, these two amazing people were given specific instructions concerning the journey west, and the strength they would be to their family and those around them. They were told of their faithfulness, and how pleased God was for their willingness to do all that was asked of them. And they were each separately promised that they would live to see the desires of their heart. In Eleanore's blessing, that desire was left vague. But with James, he was told that he would live to see Zion with his family, and there be sealed to the woman he loved for time and all eternity.

They were all crying by the time they'd finished, then they all sat in silence for several minutes before James said, "Please don't say anything to the others just yet. We'll meet together as a household later today." He looked directly at Frederick and said, "You've told me many times that you go where I go, that you consider yourself a part of this family. But I'm not just going to assume that's the case now. I need you to make this decision for yourself and your family."

Frederick only smiled. "Nothing's changed, James. I go where you go. We're in this together."

James smiled as well, then turned to Case. "As soon as you get some breakfast, I need you to ride out to Coralville and find out when the next company is leaving. Whether it's tomorrow or next week, we're going with them. So tell whoever's in charge that we'll be there. Don't come back until you can tell me everything I need to know to be ready to go with them, and that everything's arranged."

"Consider it done," Case said and stood. "In fact, I think I'll just skip breakfast."

Before he could open the door, James added, "Case, I assume you're coming with us."

"I go where you go," he said, then forced a chuckle to cover his own emotion. "You need me."

"Yes, I do. And you know you're as good as family, but it needs to be your decision."

"As long as I know you want me around, I'll be around."

Case was surprised when Eleanore stood and crossed the room to face him. She kissed his cheek and murmured with tears in her eyes, "You *are* as good as family, Case. Don't ever forget it."

Case knew what she meant; only Iris would consider him unworthy to be a part of the family. He couldn't speak, so he just nodded. Then Eleanore added, "He *does* need you. And so do I. Watch out for him—

whatever it takes. We need you to help God keep His promise, to be certain that James lives to see Zion. Do you understand what I mean?"

Again Case could only nod, but his effort to hold back his tears faltered when he felt them burn in his eyes. Eleanore seemed to understand by the way she gave him a motherly embrace before he hurried from the room. He took a minute to compose himself before he went into the kitchen and took a couple of freshly cooked pancakes.

"What are you doing?" Iris demanded, and he was almost afraid she'd hit him with the spatula she was holding.

"I need to do an errand for your father. He wouldn't want me to starve." He wrapped the pancakes in a napkin. "Look at it this way; you won't have to tolerate me at breakfast."

Case hurried away before she could retort, or before his emotions could betray him. He could never tell James and Eleanore what their love and acceptance meant to him. And that was coupled with a deep concern regarding the uncertainty of what lay ahead for this family he'd grown to love. Zion felt so far away.

* * * * *

Iris kept busy with her usual chores throughout the morning, trying to ignore the sense that something wasn't right. She'd almost talked herself into believing that everything was just as it should be when her father announced at lunch, "As soon as we've got the kitchen cleaned up, we'll be having a family meeting." His somber demeanor caused Iris's chest to tighten. She wondered if a "family" meeting would exclude Case. As if her father had read her mind, he turned to him and said, "That includes you, Case, of course. This affects all of us."

Iris didn't know if she felt more alarmed by some grave, mysterious issue that would affect them all, or the fact that her father would include Case in that issue. And what bothered her even more was that it was evident Case already knew what was going on. She could see it in his somber expression. He'd been in the library this morning; he'd gone on this undisclosed errand for her father. Combined with the puzzling priesthood blessings this morning, she felt downright terrified and blurted the question, "What's wrong, Papa?"

"Nothing is *wrong*. We'll talk later."

The time it took to finish eating and put the kitchen in order felt far too long. When everyone was finally gathered in the parlor, Iris's nerves were so taut she had difficulty maintaining her composure. The quiet, pensive moods of her parents added to her discomfort.

Once they were seated, her father came straight to the point. "We will be leaving for the Salt Lake Valley in four days." Iris's heart pounded, and her brain raced with questions, but he hurried on. "A wagon company is scheduled to leave then, and we will be going with them."

"No!" Iris protested without even thinking. "We can't leave now. Mother is pregnant, and . . . we—"

"Iris," her father said gently, "your mother and I have discussed this, and we know that this is not how we had planned our departure. We can assure you that the prospect of leaving now, as opposed to later after the baby comes, causes us both a great deal of concern. We can only say that we both absolutely know we need to go now, and we need to have faith that everything will work out according to God's will." Iris watched her father take her mother's hand while they exchanged a wan smile and a concerned gaze.

"But . . . why?" Iris asked, less bold.

"We just know it's right," James Barrington said. "When the Lord tells us to do something, we will do it, no matter what our fears or concerns may be. We've discussed this many times. You all know what to do. Each of you needs to take some time to say good-bye to our home, then take the memories with you and don't look back. Once we drive those wagons out of here, we will only be looking ahead. Is that clear?"

Everyone indicated they understood, except for little Mariah, who was unusually quiet. James explained that he'd previously discussed leaving the house in the care of a man he trusted, the local sheriff who was a good and honest man. When the house sold, this man would send him the money. But it was evident that selling the house was irrelevant. They would leave their home and most of its contents behind and never look back, just as thousands of Saints gone before had done.

The meeting lasted another two hours while they reviewed the preparations they'd made, answered the children's questions, and refined their previous plans to accommodate the present situation. The schedule of the trail was discussed, and individual assignments were made regarding all that would have to be done. There were four wagons to be driven. Frederick was glad that his healing leg would not affect his ability to drive a team. James would drive one, and Ben as well.

Case knew James was going to assign him to drive the fourth team when Iris blurted, "I'll be driving the fourth one."

James said kindly, "I think it would be better if Case—"

"Why? Because I'm a woman? If he weren't here, I'd be driving it. I know how to do it. You know I can handle it."

James sighed. "I know you're capable of doing anything you need to do, Iris, but I'm not sure you have any idea what this is going to entail. It's not like driving the wagon into town. We'll be heavily loaded and we're going over rough terrain. If you—"

"I can do it," Iris insisted.

"Oh, let her do it," Case said with easy nonchalance, knowing he'd never hear the end of it if he usurped her in this task she'd assigned herself. He wondered if Iris doing his work would somehow prove that he wasn't needed. But he focused his thoughts on the larger perspective of the situation. "I'll ride alongside and help where I'm needed."

"All right, then," James said, then he pointed a finger at Iris. "But if anything changes, if I say you let him do it, you let him do it."

Case saw Iris nod, but she glared at him the next moment, silently threatening him not to cross her. He was more than willing to keep his distance. But he wasn't happy about it.

Iris sat on the couch while everyone left the room after the meeting was over. Perhaps if she didn't go out the door, she could more easily accept the news she'd heard since she'd come through it. She became lost in her thoughts until she realized that her father was still there, sitting across from her, looking concerned.

"What's wrong?" he asked.

Not wanting to admit to what bothered her most, she said, "This is real, isn't it."

"It is."

"You're not going to change your mind and decide to stay another year?"

"I'm taking orders from God, Iris. If anyone changes their mind, it will have to be Him."

"So you just . . . woke up this morning . . . and knew it was time?"

"In essence, yes. I shouldn't have to explain such things to you."

"No, of course not."

"Are you worried . . . about the journey?"

"Some, yes. We all are, I believe."

"Of course."

She looked around the room. "It will be hard to leave, even though we all know it's the right thing to do."

"Yes," he said, then a moment later, "You're unhappy about Case going with us."

Iris shot her father a sharp glare. "My opinion on such matters is clearly irrelevant."

"Your opinion won't change what I believe is the right thing to do. That doesn't mean I'm not interested in how you feel."

Iris felt a rush of anger and forced a calm voice that would hopefully disguise it. "Am I the only one who can see that maybe he's not everything he seems to be?" Hearing the tone of the question, she had to admit she'd not done well at concealing her emotions at all.

"No," James countered, "you're the only one who is blind to the fact that he's a kind and decent man. You're the only one who *can't* see that he belongs with us. He *is* going with us, Iris, and if you give him any grief over that, you will have to contend with me. You don't have to trust him, and you don't have to like him, but you *will* respect him, and you *will* be kind. He deserves that, at the very least."

"Yes, Father," Iris said and left the room before she erupted and made a fool of herself.

That night Iris pulled a small wooden chest out from the bottom of her closet. She pressed her hand over the top of it, recalling well when her parents had given it to her some years earlier. They'd acquired one for each member of the household with the admonition to keep anything of any sentimental value inside of it, so that when the time came to leave, they could do so quickly if necessary. Each person could quickly get his or her own little chest, a few clothes and personal items, and be ready. And now the time had come. Iris didn't bother looking at the contents of the box. She only opened it long enough to add a few little items that were scattered around the room, then she closed it securely and left it next to the door. Whatever else she needed could be put into a satchel on the day they would leave. She wanted to think that meant she was ready, but she curled up in her bed and cried at the thought of leaving her home. The examples of faith and courage in her parents, and everyone else for that matter, were somehow lost on her. She didn't want to go, and she felt terrified. She'd heard the stories of what the Saints had encountered crossing the plains of this continent, and she couldn't deny that she enjoyed the luxuries of home. A bathtub and a comfortable bed came to mind. But it would all be left behind. Iris could only hope she'd find some courage—and a lot of it—in the next few days.

* * * * *

Case was amazed at the efficiency and organization with which the preparations came together. Supplies and every needed item were on hand and ready to be loaded. Only one quick trip to town was necessary, but that was mostly to pick up the mail and to let the postmaster know that their mail should be forwarded to the Salt Lake Valley from then on.

Most of the time everyone seemed in good spirits, and they all kept too busy to think about what they were leaving behind, or their concerns for the journey. But there were moments when Case saw evidence of how difficult this was. However, no one complained or expressed any fear, only faith and hope in looking ahead to this great adventure.

Case sensed a change in Iris's mood more than anyone else. He wondered where her thoughts were, and longed to hear her spill them to him. He wanted to hold her in his arms and assure her that everything would be all right, that he would take care of her and do his best to help take care of her family. But she wouldn't even look in his direction, let alone speak to him.

On the evening prior to their leaving, the usual study and prayer in the parlor was anything but usual. During the course of the prayer, every person except Mariah shed tears—including Case. Then they sat together, reminiscing and sharing their testimonies of the gospel, which reinforced their reasons for making this journey. After everyone had gone their separate ways to sleep one last time in this beautiful home, Case sat on the side porch for a long while, pondering the way his life had changed in less than a year. He'd become more accustomed to the new him, and in the process he had become integrated into this amazing family. He had grown to love each and every one of them. He felt their joy and pain, and he would never want to backtrack. Comparing his present life to the life he'd previously lived was like comparing heaven to hell. Even the uncertainty of what was ahead didn't alter that heavenly sensation. Ever since he'd joined the Church, he'd known he would go west. But he'd imagined making the journey alone; with a company, of course, but on his own, with nothing to be concerned about but himself and his meager belongings. To him, being with the Barringtons was evidence of the windows of heaven opening on his behalf. There simply was not room for his heart to hold all the blessings he'd been given. Only when he thought of Iris did he feel regret and sorrow. So he did his best not to think of Iris.

The following day, everyone's personal belongings were packed into the wagons along with the supplies, and some bedding was added, situated mostly in makeshift beds over the top of everything else. Lists were checked, plans reviewed, and the contents of the wagons were assessed one last time.

It was late afternoon when they walked as a family from room to room, silently bidding farewell to their home and savoring the memories. With the house in perfect order, they closed the doors and gathered for prayer on the lawn near the house. After the amen was spoken, James said to the group, "Don't look back. We're leaving now." They all got into their assigned wagons, except for Case, who was riding the horse he'd arrived on ten months earlier, and left their Iowa home behind.

Iris was glad to be driving a team, which meant she was all by herself and no one could see her while tears coursed steadily down her face. She disobeyed her father's edict and looked back only once, wanting to capture the beauty of her home in her memory one last time. She'd spent the majority of her life here, and she didn't want to leave. There had been a time when she'd felt the fire of the gospel burn inside of her, and she had personally longed to be among the

Saints, just as her parents had. But it had been a long time since she'd felt any such thing, and she had to admit that she was only doing this now to be with her family. Perhaps that was the biggest reason she felt so afraid and uncertain. She wanted to have the faith and courage the others had, but she just didn't feel it.

That evening was their first experience of cooking a meal over the fire where they were camped with the rest of the company that was ready to embark the following morning. Iris was grateful that the men all had experience at doing this. Even her father had apparently gotten pretty good at it when he'd made the journey to Winter Quarters and back many years earlier. The stew and biscuits they ate were actually rather good. But Iris felt completely out of sorts, and she was relieved to know that she only had to *help* with meals and see that the children assisted in cleaning dishes after a meal. Frederick and Lizzie were put in charge of the meals, with the understanding that they could ask for assistance from anyone in the family, depending on what needed to be done.

Study and prayer out in the open were an entirely different experience. Iris had vague memories of the journey by wagon from the East Coast to Iowa City. Mostly she remembered that it had been miserable. She wondered how many meals they'd be eating like this, how many prayers, how many nights sleeping in a wagon, how many days of heat and dust and endless miles. As they settled down for the night, she was grateful at least to be able to sleep in the wagon, and Mariah had been assigned as her bed partner, since their mother had difficulty sleeping due to her pregnancy, even under normal circumstances. Iris had offered to watch out for her little sister at night, and she was glad for the companionship of this sweet child, even if she wiggled enough for three children. Mary Jane would also sleep in the wagon with her in the event of bad weather. But tonight she had been intrigued with the idea of sleeping under the stars with the boys. The boys had a wagon to sleep in, but they were currently caught up in the adventurous aspects of this endeavor. She knew they'd worked it out so that Case would sleep in a wagon with them, should the need arise. It would be crowded but adequate, and the boys were thrilled with the idea of having Case be their bunk mate for the journey. But he'd told them he preferred sleeping under the stars, or even under the wagon, unless it rained very badly. And the boys had decided they liked that idea as well.

Iris was grateful to be alone once Mariah had gone to sleep. It was the only time she could cry without drawing anyone else's attention. She hated this already, and she hated the fact that she missed having Case to talk to. Everything felt all wrong, but she didn't know how to make it right.

* * * * *

The first few days of the journey quickly convinced Iris of how much she hated every aspect of this. The unbearable heat was made more aggravating by the dust and the bugs. Oh, how she hated the bugs! She was glad, however, to be driving a team, as opposed to being in charge of keeping the children safe, or simply riding in a wagon or walking alongside the train. There were nearly forty wagons in the company, including the four that had come with her own family, and approximately two hundred people, all under the command of Captain Jesse B. Martin. Iris knew little about him except that he'd been born in West Virginia and had joined the Church in Illinois. He'd gone to Utah in forty-eight, and had later left his family there while he served a mission in England. Iris had overheard her father talking to Captain Martin about their common love of the English countryside and the British people. The captain was now on his way back to Utah and had been put in charge of this company. And the man was only in his early thirties, Iris guessed; somewhere near Case's age.

One of the big challenges in setting out was the difficulty others had in managing the oxen, or in some cases wild steers, that were pulling the wagons. Iris was grateful to be driving well-trained horses. In fact, her family's horses were the only ones in the company.

Iris quickly learned that the company was governed by very strict rules, and that Captain Martin oversaw other captains who were designated to keep track of smaller groups. A captain was assigned to each group of ten, and Iris's father was put in charge of his household, which made it all very convenient and already comfortable for their group of eleven. The company was awakened with a bugle very early each morning, then families would gather for prayer before beginning the day with caring for the animals, having breakfast, and seeing that everything was in order for the day's journey. Then the wagons rolled, and they didn't stop until the bugle sounded in the evening, when everyone kept very busy with dinner, washing, caring again for the teams, and being ready for the next day before they all gathered again for meeting and prayer prior to settling in for the night. The schedule continued even on Sunday, although they did have a meeting that evening, with more hymn singing than usual. Still, Iris felt more like she'd been enlisted into some military regiment as opposed to traveling for the sake of religious beliefs. And she hated it.

On Monday, a week after leaving their beautiful home, they were confronted with heavy rain that delayed their starting out for a couple of hours. The misery of the dust and heat were quickly countered by an equal dose of misery attributable to excessive moisture and the resulting mud. Iris had managed to drive the wagon with little difficulty up to this point, but driving it in mud became an entirely new experience. More than once Case appeared beside her on his horse, asking if she needed any help.

"I'm managing just fine, thank you," she said, trying not to sound terse and defensive, even though that's how she felt.

"Yes, I can see that," he said, smiling even though the circumstances were utterly miserable. "In fact, I've noticed that you manage to do just about everything yourself." He chuckled, and she knew one of his cutting remarks was coming. "And will you have babies and get to the celestial kingdom all by yourself too, Miss Barrington?"

Her astonishment apparently didn't disappoint him when he chuckled again. "You are as rude as you are impertinent, Mr. Harrison."

"You are an excellent example in both regards, Miss Barrington," he said and rode ahead before she could retort. But she felt furious for hours, focusing the energy of her anger on keeping the horses on course, pulling the wagon through the mud. They had to stop more than once to fill mud holes with brush so that the wagons could cross them. Iris let go of her anger to daydream about how she might have spent this day had she been at home. It would have been a perfect day for immersing herself in a good book, watching the rain run down the windows. She thought of the books left behind in the library and started to cry, grateful for the ongoing rain that might disguise her tears should anyone bother to notice.

During one of the stops, Iris got down and went to the wagon ahead to see how her mother was doing. Already the journey had been difficult for her with the pregnancy, and the rain kept the children inside the wagons as opposed to walking beside them. The children moved around to different wagons for variety, and it was difficult to keep track of who was where. She hoped that none of them was making this day harder for their mother. Iris climbed onto the seat next to her father and stuck her head through the opening of the wagon cover right after she'd pulled off her dripping hat. Eleanore was half reclined against a pile of folded blankets, a hand over her well-rounded belly, while Mariah sat close to her, playing with a couple of rag dolls.

"How are you doing?" she asked.

"I'm fine," Eleanore said at the very same moment James said softly, "She's miserable."

"Do you want me to take Mariah with me for a while?" Iris asked.

"No, she's been very good," Eleanore said, smiling at the child. More softly to Iris, she added, "It's good to be with her while I can. After the baby comes it won't be so easy."

"Where are the boys?"

"Ben's got them. He was here a minute ago. They're fine. How are you?"

"I'm fine," Iris lied with the same convincing dignity as her mother. They heard the signal that the wagons were moving, and Iris put her hat back on as she ran to her own wagon and moved her team forward.

The days dragged on with a paradox of grinding, predictable routine intermingled with completely unpredictable events that only slowed their progress and added to Iris's loathing of the experience. Just when she thought the heat and dust would kill her, it would rain in torrents and make her long for heat and dust. One day they didn't move at all due to horrendous rain. Iris enjoyed a day of not moving, but every hour of delay only meant that much longer until they would arrive in the Salt Lake Valley and have this behind them.

Others in the company struggled with lame animals, or animals that wouldn't cooperate. Iris got to know some of the other people traveling in the company, mostly when she followed her father around, since he was very sociable and always tried to be helpful. And of course, Case was rarely far from her father, trying to be helpful to others as well. Iris was vaguely aware at times of dissension between certain people, but she kept her distance, reminding herself that even Mormons weren't perfect. She was certainly a prime example of that. Occasionally they passed through established towns, or had to cross creeks and rivers—an experience that terrified Iris, but made her stoutly determined to do it on her own, if only to prove to Casey Harrison that she could.

Frederick reached a point where he no longer needed his crutches at all, and he was managing to get around fairly well with only a slight limp. The crutches were burned as firewood with a ridiculous amount of celebration over the ritual from the family.

During every aspect of this journey, Casey Harrison was always there. Iris crossed his path far more out here on the prairie than she had back home. She found his presence aggravating for a number of reasons, not the least of which was her complete lack of indifference toward him. She could readily admit that she found him attractive, but she could never trust him, and she doubted that she could ever forgive him. He continued to follow her father around, doing way too much for him, almost mimicking everything about James Barrington. And he seemed closer than ever to Iris's little brothers. They followed him around continually, and there was usually a great deal of laughter that accompanied their time together.

Iris noticed one aspect in which Case made no attempt to mimic her father. Once they were on the trail, James Barrington made no effort to shave, and a beard framed his lower face within days. Iris had seen her father go through stages of being bearded before, and she liked it; she thought it suited him, especially among such rugged surroundings. But Casey Harrison shaved every morning without fail. By the time breakfast was on, he'd appear with his face smooth and his smile brilliant. Occasionally she'd catch a whiff of his shaving lotion as he'd pass by, and her mind would go unwillingly to that day when he'd kissed her in the barn. Her stomach would inevitably flutter, and she'd have to force her thoughts elsewhere to keep from staring at him, which would prove her an utter fool. With some passing of days, Iris had to admit that Case's shaving habit did give her some connection to her father. All through her life—except when her father had worn a beard—she'd almost been able to measure the time of day by the growth on her father's face. By bedtime he'd always had a distinct layer of stubble that had darkened the lower half of his face, and his good-night kisses had pleasantly scratched her cheeks. The hair on Case's face was much lighter, but crossing paths with him several times a day, as she had for months now, Iris had come to notice that the same principle applied. She had to ask herself if she was intrigued simply because it was a comforting reminder of her father and the security he represented for her, or if it was a simple observation of masculinity, intriguing only in the way it separated the nature of men from women. Or were there other reasons entirely that she was preoccupied with silly things like the hair on Casey Harrison's face? She didn't bother thinking too hard about that. It was easier to focus on her own misery as this journey progressed.

One day they passed some men traveling in the other direction from Salt Lake; they brought with them good news of the prosperity of those living in the Valley, which gave a great deal of hope to everyone in the company. But a couple of days later, a child died due to a swift and unspecified illness and was buried near the creek at the end of the day's journey. Iris looked around at her little sister and brothers and prayed that they would all remain safe and healthy. As much as she hated this, she could survive it as long as everyone she loved did the same. A few days after that, a wagon overturned while crossing a creek. All of its contents spilled into the muddy water, along with three children. The baby nearly drowned but was saved. Again Iris felt grateful that, as of yet, her own family had remained free of any illness or mishaps.

They arrived in a town called Florence, which brought on some nostalgia for Ben and also for her father, since it had once been the location of Winter Quarters. Ben's parents had died there, and her father had helped bury them, after which he'd brought Ben home with him. They stayed for a couple of days there, partly due to heavy rain. While they were there, money was raised to purchase a horse for Captain Martin so that he could move quickly up and down the company as it traveled and be able to more easily and effectively keep track of those in his care.

Lost or wandering animals held them up more than once, as did the ongoing unpredictability of the weather. But even more difficult was their encounter with some men who verbally tormented the Saints, swearing at them and hurling threats; they even threatened to kill Captain Martin. Iris found out later that these men had once been members of the Church who had apostatized. Iris felt angry that people would behave in such a way. If they wanted to abandon their beliefs, they certainly had that right, but to turn around and be so cruel to those who believed otherwise was uncalled for. But then, that had been the lot of the Mormons all along—a fact that made Iris begin to wonder why it all had to be so difficult. But she chose not to think too deeply on that either, and instead let her mind wander aimlessly while she drove her team of horses, mile after mile, realizing she'd completely lost track of what day it was, or how long it had been since they'd left their beautiful home. When they set up camp on the banks of the Platte River, her father mentioned that they had been gone a month. To Iris, it felt like much longer than that. She knew they had at least two months of this left to go, and it could be even longer if they kept experiencing delays.

On a particularly difficult day while they endured more delays due to problems with animals wandering or causing destruction, Iris considered her personal situation and wanted to scream or cry—or both. When she was certain no one would miss her, she wandered some distance from camp and sat down in the brush, crying so hard that it hurt. She was startled and embarrassed to feel a hand on her shoulder, but when she looked up to see her mother's compassionate eyes, she only cried harder. Eleanore sat carefully beside Iris and wrapped her in her arms. She spoke soothing words and made comforting noises, taking Iris back to her childhood when this dear, sweet woman had been there to comfort her in ways her own mother never had.

When Iris was finally able to calm down, Eleanore asked gently, "What is it, darling? What's wrong?"

"Everything!" Iris insisted. "Everything is wrong. I hate this. I hate every minute of it. I know I shouldn't complain, and I've tried not to, but I'm just not as brave as you are, and I just *hate* it! I hate

the bugs and the dirt and the heat and the rain and the mud. I just *hate* it!"

Iris felt certain Eleanore would be appalled by her little childish fit, and would quickly put her in her place. But she chuckled softly and touched Iris's face. "I hate it, too."

"But you never complain."

"And neither do you. Being able to vent your feelings to someone you trust is not the same as complaining. I can't help thinking this is funny only because I said almost your exact words to your father not two days ago."

"You did?"

"Oh, yes. Of course, he tells me I'm brave and strong, all the while knowing that I would be a complete mess without him."

"You're not just telling me this to make me feel better, are you?"

"You should know me better than that," Eleanore said. "So, now that we've each had a chance to say how we really feel, we're going to have to accept that we have no choice but to keep moving forward and keep looking ahead. It's the only way we'll make it through this."

Iris sighed and nestled her head on her mother's shoulder. The very idea was depressing, but she felt understood and loved. And with that, she almost believed it was possible to keep going.

Chapter Eleven

RECKONING

Following minutes of silence, Eleanore said to Iris, "What else is troubling you?"

"Other than being in the middle of nowhere and utterly miserable?" Iris asked with sarcasm.

"Other than that," Eleanore said lightly.

"I don't know. I wish I *did* know. I remember a time when I was happy, or at least I think I was. And sometimes I wonder what happened to make me feel this way."

"Are you admitting that you're unhappy?"

"I suppose I am."

"Don't expect me to be surprised," Eleanore said. "Your father and I have been very much aware of your unhappiness for a long time."

"So you talk about me," Iris said, pretending to sound offended, if only to keep the mood light.

"We talk about all of our children. We have that right. You've certainly had some events in your life that have been disappointing, but in my opinion, there's something more—something that made those events hurt you more deeply than perhaps they should have."

Iris recounted the conversation thus far and wondered how it had come to this. She'd avoided talking to anyone in any such way for so long that doing so now felt strange and a little frightening. Her mother offered a clue to what the difference might be when she added, "We've been praying for you, Iris, very much, for a very long time. We want you to be happy."

A little unnerved by the sensitivity of the subject, she countered her mother's remark by saying glibly, "When we get to Salt Lake I'll be happy."

Eleanore immediately retorted, "Will you really? As happy as you were before we left?" Iris sighed but felt no desire to answer. But unlike in the past, she felt some desire to discover the truth beneath her mother's questions. She didn't want to go on feeling this way. Not knowing what to say, she was relieved when Eleanore added, "There's no disputing that this journey is difficult, Iris. I've been thinking a great deal of how our going to Zion feels symbolic of our journey through life. And perhaps God wants us to see it that way. The scriptures are full of symbols and meaning in the experiences of the people. If we want to return to live with our Father in Heaven—and we do—then we must prove ourselves faithful no matter what ill fate might befall us. Your father and I have gotten through many trials by remembering that it's the blessings of the next life that matter more than the difficulties of this one. Therefore, doing as God wants us to do is most important, above all else. I have no trouble admitting that this is not what I would like to be doing, but I am able to get up every morning and keep doing it because I know beyond any doubt that it's right, that it's what God wants me to do." She put a fist to her chest, and her eyes took on a distinct sparkle. "It is my testimony of the truthfulness of this gospel that carries me through these difficult days, Iris. Without it, how would we ever survive the disappointments of life, whether they be out here in the middle of nowhere, or living in a lovely home with every comfort provided? Wherever we may be, and whatever might happen, my knowledge of God's presence in our lives is the constancy that keeps me going. By living close to the Spirit, that comfort is always present, even if it's not always easy to feel. I know, Iris, because I remember so well how the fire of the gospel burned in your spirit. I remember your enthusiasm to be baptized, and your conviction to living righteously."

"But I made mistakes, and—"

"We all make mistakes. We must put the past in the past and leave it behind. In that way too, this journey is symbolic. When our sins are repented of and forgiven, they need to be left behind, and we must focus only on moving forward, not looking back. You're a good woman, Iris, and the answers are inside of you. As you pray for those answers, they will come. I know they will."

Iris had nothing to say. It was difficult to admit even to herself how much she *hadn't* been praying—for a very long time. How could she admit it aloud? She couldn't remember the last time she could say that she'd really felt the Spirit close in her life. And perhaps that was the greatest source of her unhappiness. Suddenly overwhelmed with far too much to think about, she was relieved when the boys came looking for them and they headed back to camp. Before they arrived, Eleanore said, "You know where to find us if you need to talk."

"Thank you," Iris said and hugged her tightly.

For days Iris pondered her mother's words while she drove over endless miles of tedious landscape that passed by far too slowly. She began praying with more purpose, both morning and night, and many times during the days while her thoughts wandered and she tried to make sense of them. She felt as weary of the journey as she did of feeling this way about her life. For years now she'd felt unhappy, ever since Miles had betrayed her trust in every possible way. She'd loved him, and she'd believed he loved her. But why had the event affected her so deeply? Why had she not felt truly happy since? Asking herself silent questions, she was startled to hear a silent answer in her mind. *You were happy with Case.*

Iris slammed a figurative door in the face of such an idea and forced her thoughts elsewhere throughout the remaining hours of the day. But that night as she knelt in prayer, the idea came back to her. She crawled into bed with her prayer unfinished while her mind couldn't get past the idea enough to think of anything else. *Had* she been happy with Case? But he had betrayed her just as Miles had. Hadn't he? Or was it different? If it *was* different, why couldn't she see those differences and let go of her ill feelings in regard to both of them?

When questions regarding Case became too painful and confusing, Iris focused her attention instead on coming to terms with feelings inside herself that had nothing to do with him. She asked forgiveness for her often-deplorable behavior, her cynical attitude, and for neglecting the things in her life that she should have been doing to remain close to the Spirit. She was surprised at how quickly a sense of peace and comfort surrounded her, like a warm blanket in a storm. For the first time in years she knew the gospel was true. It was real, and God was there. That in itself made the prospect of continuing this journey feel easier already. But she knew she had a long way to go to understand the full depth of the confusion going on inside of her. And she had no intention of ever needing to reckon with her feelings regarding Casey Harrison.

Iris's newly rediscovered faith was tested when disaster happened within the company. While the captain was dealing with some kind of disagreement between a couple of men, some cattle were startled and started to run—with wagons attached. What followed was utterly horrifying. Wagons were severely damaged, and many people were injured. But worst of all, two people were killed. After the animals were brought under control and the wounded had been cared for, Captain Martin called a special meeting where he made it clear that these events were the chastening hand of the Lord. He spoke of division and rebellion in the camp, and called the people to repentance. He said firmly that he would not move from that spot unless the people would covenant before God to abide by the captain's counsel from that moment until they reached their destination. Iris listened to his words and felt them pierce her heart. She had no awareness of what might have been going on with others in camp, and she didn't want to know. But she was brought to an appalling awareness of how much her own ill feelings had adversely affected her entire family. Her prayers were being heard and answered. The Lord was guiding her to an understanding of the reasons for her unhappiness, and she didn't like what she was seeing. And it was even more difficult knowing that she needed to rectify the problem. She found some hope as Captain Martin promised the company that if they kept this covenant, they would move forward in peace and safety without any further difficulties due to animals stampeding or running off. And Iris believed him. She could feel the power of God with this man, and knew he had been commissioned to lead these people to Zion. And she felt that she would find the same comfort and peace if she committed herself to making some changes. She just wasn't certain how to go about it.

That night after the dead had been buried and the wagons had been mended, there was a marked peacefulness in the camp that softened the grief of losing two people that day. Iris hadn't known them personally, but it wasn't difficult to find empathy for those who had lost loved ones. For the first time in many days, she thought of David and missed him deeply. What might it have been like if he were still alive? How might his being among the family now have affected each of their lives? They were pointless questions, but she couldn't help wondering.

A few days beyond the tragedy, they encountered some Indians, though not for the first time. However, Iris hadn't gotten a very good look at them previously. Their dress and manner were fascinating to her, and she remained at a reasonable distance, discreetly observing Captain Martin and some other gentlemen buying things from them and offering them gifts. Iris had heard it said throughout the company that most of the time the Indians were friendly with the Mormons. They were both a people who had been senselessly driven by the government, and there seemed to be a common respect between them.

Challenges continued during the journey, but Iris began to feel more at home with other people in the company; some were especially friendly and helpful. She was grateful they had plenty to eat, although the monotony of their diet was getting old. Throughout the days she snacked on biscuits and dried fruit, daydreaming about the lovely meals they'd enjoyed at home, especially when Stella or Amanda had been doing the cooking. She was always relieved when the men were able to find wild game, and rabbit or venison added pleasant variety to their menus.

The flies and mosquitoes were horribly annoying, and the weather continued to plague them, whether it was heat or rain. But Iris couldn't deny a different feeling among the company. Apparently Captain Martin's edict had been taken to heart by many people other than her.

On the morning of the twenty-fourth of July, mention was made of it being the ten-year anniversary of the original company of Saints arriving in the Salt Lake Valley. After traveling eight miles and crossing Rattlesnake Creek, the company stopped on the banks of the Platte River. Iris could see trees on the other side and realized how much she'd come to miss trees. It had been a long time since she'd seen one at all. After two hours they set out again, and hours later Iris's mind was wandering through a recently familiar stream of unanswered questions regarding her own life and what she'd done to make it this way. She didn't feel any closer to the answers, but she did feel more determined to find them, as opposed to simply avoiding the questions. She hoped that indicated some measure of progress.

Iris was startled when Case jumped onto the wagon beside her, seemingly out of nowhere. His urgency made her heart pound as he took the reins out of her hands, saying, "Let me take this. Your mother needs you. Hurry."

"She's in labor?" Iris asked as Case stopped the wagon long enough for her to jump down.

"Yes," he said. "Lizzie's with her, and they have what they need, but you know the train won't stop for this. Lizzie can't do it alone."

Iris nodded and ran to the wagon ahead. They'd all gotten fairly adept at getting in and out of wagons while they plodded slowly along. But she heard her mother groaning in pain and hesitated a long moment, wondering how she could possibly be of any help if she felt this terrified. They'd discussed the plan many times, and they were as prepared as they could possibly be. Lizzie had helped Eleanore through this before, but Iris had always been as far away as possible when her mother had given birth. There had been other women there to help her. Now, both Lizzie and Eleanore had insisted that Iris's help would be needed to ensure that all went well. And while they'd been prepared for this for quite some time now, it had come earlier than expected, and Iris didn't feel ready. She heard her mother groan again, and she took a deep breath, uttering a quick, silent prayer as she climbed into the wagon to find Lizzie on her knees, holding Eleanore's hand while she writhed in pain.

"Oh," Eleanore said and reached out her other hand to Iris, "you're here."

"Tell me what to do," Iris said.

"Just . . . be with me," Eleanore muttered. "It's not time yet, but . . . oh!"

She became consumed with pain, and Lizzie explained quietly, "The contractions come and go and get closer together as they get stronger."

Iris nodded. She'd known that, but she'd forgotten.

As the pain eased off, Eleanore asked, "How long until we stop?"

"I have no idea," Iris said. "I lost track."

Iris knew her mother had been walking far more than riding in the wagon ever since they'd left Iowa City. As often as the weather would allow, she'd far preferred walking over the bumpy, uncomfortable ride. While Iris hadn't personally experienced pregnancy, she'd observed her mother's difficulty in walking at all during the final weeks. If that was preferable to riding, then riding had to be pretty bad. And now Iris couldn't even comprehend how that sensation had to be compounding the pain Eleanore was in—pain that Iris couldn't even fathom.

"That's what I told her," Lizzie said. Then to Eleanore, "It will be fine. Whatever happens, we'll get through it. You mustn't worry."

Eleanore nodded, and another contraction came on. The pains continued, becoming stronger and closer together. The bumpiness of the wagon didn't help, and Iris wanted to scream that they needed to stop until they got through this. But she knew they wouldn't, and the family was required to stay with the company. Occasionally, Iris's father would inquire over the progress from where he was driving the wagon. With the cover tied open, he was far more aware of his wife's suffering than he was of guiding the horses that were well accustomed to following the wagon in front of them. It was evident that James didn't feel nearly as calm as he was putting on, but Lizzie just kept telling him that everything was fine.

When the pain suddenly became more intense and dramatic, Lizzie began to frantically make preparations for the birth, with everything already within handy access there in the wagon. She instructed Iris to simply stay close to her mother and offer comfort and encouragement. Iris met her father's eyes several times, seeing her own alarm mirrored there, and when he started reassuring *her* that this was normal, she wondered what good she was doing in being there at all.

They all heaved a tremendous sigh of relief when the bugle sounded to bring the company to a halt for the evening. James brought the wagon to a stop and climbed in to sit behind his wife, holding her in his arms so that she could lean against his chest. It was evident he'd helped her through this before and he knew what to do. About twenty minutes later, Eleanore gave birth to a perfect baby girl. For Iris, it was the most frightening and wonderful thing she'd ever witnessed. Once the ordeal was over, Iris stepped down from the wagon with a basin full of blood-stained rags, grateful to realize they were stopped near a stream of running water. Her feet barely touched the ground before Case appeared directly in front of her, looking distraught.

"Is she all right?" he demanded quietly.

"Yes," Iris said.

"I heard the baby cry, but . . ." His words faded.

"It's a girl," Iris said, wondering if he'd been out here pacing since the wagons had stopped.

"Oh." He let out a delighted little laugh. "That's wonderful."

"Yes, it is," Iris said and moved around him. Suddenly on the verge of tears, she had no desire to spill them to Case. But he followed her. She swallowed hard and forced a steady voice with the hope of sending him elsewhere. "Are the children—"

"Mary Jane took them for a walk."

"We could use some hot water to clean—"

"It's already on the fire heating, and I unharnessed the horses. Frederick's feeding them."

Iris squatted down by the stream, wondering why he seemed so intent on remaining close to her. She wanted him to go away so she could have a good cry with some privacy.

"Can I help?" he asked.

"No," she said and focused on rinsing out the rags. The horror and wonder of the ordeal ran through her mind again, and the tears became harder to hold back.

"Are you all right?" he asked, and she wanted to yell at him, to tell him to leave her in peace. But his question brought the full torrent rushing out, and she hung her head as the tears spilled. "Iris?" he drawled, and she shook her head as she stood and turned away from him, leaving the basin of rags at her feet. "Iris?" he asked again, more softly, and she felt his hands on her shoulders. She felt too overcome and brimming with emotion to protest. Instead she turned and melted into his once-comfortable embrace and wept without restraint. He stroked her hair and whispered soothing words while she held to his shoulders and cried the way she'd wanted to from the first moment of witnessing her mother's labor. When she finally calmed down, she felt reluctant to let him go, but foolish for indulging in something that would surely lead him to believe that she might have changed her mind about her feelings for him. She wondered how to clarify that without turning this moment into one of contention. As if he knew her better than she knew herself, he said gently, "Don't worry, Iris. I'm not expecting this to change anything between us. But I'm happy to be the shoulder you cry on any time you need one."

Case felt her relax in his embrace and press the side of her face against his chest. He savored the moment, unable to count how many weeks it had been since he'd held her so close. In his heart he'd never been able to stop believing that she would soften and they could be together. But most days he just tried not to think about it when her continual distance from him was so discouraging. For whatever reason, she had ended up here now, and he was going to enjoy it while it lasted. And perhaps she might sense how much he loved her, even if he would never dare say it.

"May I ask why you're so upset? Everything's all right, isn't it?"

"Everything's fine," she said. "It was just so . . . horrible. I never imagined."

"Does this mean you're never going to have any babies?"

Without thinking, Iris looked up at him as she clarified firmly, "But it was so wonderful." The conversation combined with the silent intensity of his eyes made her heart pound. She took a step back, certain it was more her knowing how he felt than anything else that made the moment awkward. Not wanting to sound defensive or impolite, she quickly said, "Thank you," and returned to her task.

She heaved a deep sigh of relief when he walked away, saying over his shoulder, "Any time."

Throughout the evening, Iris stayed close to her mother and the newly born Olivia Barrington. Her father also stayed close, expressing great relief to have it over with and to see Eleanore doing so well. He told Iris that it was the easiest time she'd ever had giving birth, and that they'd been greatly blessed. Iris tried to comprehend what the other experiences must have been like if this had been the easiest.

Seeing her parents with her new baby sister, Iris felt a tangible ache swell inside herself that she'd not acknowledged in a very long time. She was lonely. She wanted a man like her father; she wanted to have children of her own. Wondering if it would ever be possible, she was prone to escape for another fit of crying, grateful to have no one follow her this time.

The following days were difficult for Eleanore. Iris saw much evidence of her mother's courage, and she never heard her complain. But she was in pain, as any woman would be recovering from childbirth. And it was difficult to stay clean and care for an infant under the circumstances. While Iris drove the wagon for long hours, she pondered how witnessing Olivia's birth had affected her. That lonely ache in her was becoming more prominent, reminding her that she wasn't getting any younger. She wondered if she might meet a fine man in the Salt Lake Valley who would meet all of her criteria, a man she could trust and love, and who would love her back. But as she prayed and sincerely asked for answers to her ongoing dilemmas, it occurred to her that until she sorted out all of the confusion and heartache within herself, *no* man could make her happy. And unless she wanted to live this way for the rest of her life, it was high time she did something about it.

That evening after the children were settled down for the night and the camp became quiet, Iris found her father sitting near the dying embers of the fire.

"Can we talk?" she asked, sitting beside him on the ground.

"Of course," he said and immediately put his arm around her. "You've seemed especially thoughtful lately. I've been wondering what's on your mind."

"I suppose all those hours driving have given me a lot of time to think."

"Yes, I would agree with that. So what have you been thinking about?"

"A lot of things, but . . . after being there when the baby was born, I . . . well, that's given me even more to think about . . . and I'm having trouble putting it all together in my head, but . . . I do want to say . . . how grateful I am that you married the governess. She's an amazing woman, and I'm glad you made her my mother."

She heard her father sigh. "Marrying her is the best thing I ever did," he said. "I wonder where you and I would be without her."

"I wouldn't want to even think about that."

"No, nor would I."

Iris hesitated to voice her next thought, but it wouldn't leave. "I often wish it was her blood in my veins. I've come to realize that I'm likely far too much like my blood mother, and I don't like it."

James moved abruptly in order to see Iris's face in the fire's glow. "What on earth are you saying, Iris?"

She felt taken aback, wondering why he would be so alarmed—or surprised. "I'm saying that I think I'm very much like her. I don't want to be, but . . . perhaps that's just the way life is, and—"

"How exactly do you believe that you're like her?"

"I look like her, for one thing, and—"

"Yes, you inherited your mother's beauty, Iris. I used to see her in you all the time. I don't anymore; I only see you. And this conversation has nothing to do with physical resemblance, does it."

"No, I suppose it doesn't. I just . . . remember how . . . unkind she was; how cynical. Maybe that's why I am the way I am." She sensed him wanting to protest and hurried to finish expressing the full extent of the thoughts that had haunted her for years, before she lost momentum. "And she was immoral."

Iris saw her father's eyes go wide with astonishment. He turned so that he was facing her directly. She sensed him measuring his words carefully while her heart pounded. She was surprised, now that the words were out in the open, how long and how deeply she had believed them, even though she'd never been able to admit it. She waited for her father to speak, certain he would wisely tell her that there were some things in life we just inherit and we have to live with them. He took hold of her chin and looked directly into her eyes. "Your mother *was* unkind and cynical, Iris. And she *was* immoral. But those things have nothing to do with you."

"They *do,"* she said, her voice cracking. "I *am* unkind and cynical. I can see that now. I've been praying and trying to understand, because I don't want to feel this way. But maybe it's just who I am. Maybe it's just my disposition to be so—"

"Stop right there. There is only one possible source of such thoughts and feelings, Iris. Satan is whispering these things to you, planting them in your head to feed your self-doubt and your anger. And it's working, isn't it. I'm not going to tell you that you haven't struggled with your attitude about life and . . . certain people, but . . . that doesn't mean it's some predetermined part of your character. Your mother made *choices* on how to respond to the circumstances of her life, and you have the free agency to do the same. And unless there's something you haven't told me about—something that's happened since you were sixteen, then I'm wondering why you're concerned about immorality."

"There's nothing I haven't told you," she said, "but . . . what I did then was . . ."

"A mistake, Iris. It was wiped clean a long time ago. Have you been holding onto guilt over that all this time?" Iris couldn't answer. "Why would you think this way? Help me understand."

Iris prayed silently that she could find the answer to the question, instinctively knowing that she could never come to terms with these feelings if she didn't. Emotion bubbled out of her as the words appeared clearly in her mind. Her father took her face into his hands, making it clear that he would not let go until she answered his question. Iris gasped for breath in the midst of her sobbing and just said it. "She . . . called me . . . a . . . wicked child." She heard her father suck in his breath with astonishment. "And . . . the servants . . . they said that I . . . was like her."

Iris saw tears trickle down her father's face as he tightened his hold on hers. "No, Iris," he murmured with conviction. "It's not true; it was *never* true! You're hurting and scared and confused. But you have *never* been wicked. She chose to live the life she lived, Iris. And you have chosen to embrace the gospel and live righteously. We all make mistakes; we all struggle. Then we need to move on. Do you hear what I'm saying?"

Iris nodded and allowed his message and conviction to seep into her heart. She crumbled into his arms and cried like a child. Warmth and comfort crept into her, the same as it always had. He'd always been there for her; he'd been her strength and her wisdom, and he'd always loved her perfectly, even when she'd struggled and made mistakes.

When her tears quieted, Iris remained where she was, never wanting to be without her father's comforting embrace. She was surprised when he asked, "Does this have anything to do with Case?"

She didn't want to answer the question, but considered it carefully. "I don't know. Why?"

"Well . . . if you want me to be completely honest, then—"

"Of course I do."

"You haven't always responded well to my being honest over certain things."

"I'm sorry about that." She sniffled. "I never meant to be so difficult. And I never understood why I was. I guess I'm trying to understand now."

"And that's a good thing."

"So, please . . . be honest with me, Papa."

"Truthfully, I've never seen you cynical or unkind toward anyone but . . ."

"Case?"

"Him and the half dozen other men who came before him, somewhere between Case and Miles."

"They were all idiots," she said in a light tone that she hoped wouldn't make her sound quite so unkind and cynical.

"I'll admit they had some problems, some more than others. But maybe after the way Miles betrayed your trust, you put your expectations a little too high, thinking it might be safer that way."

"Maybe," she had to concede.

"And do you suppose you became so accustomed to seeing men as idiots, that when Case showed up you just . . ." Iris lifted her head to look at her father, but she didn't know what to say. She wasn't pleased when he asked, "What is it you have against Case?"

"I don't trust him," she insisted, settling her head back on her father's shoulder, if only to avoid looking at him while the conversation was sensitive.

"Do you have something to base this on?"

"Yes, actually. But I don't want to talk about that yet."

"Yet or ever?"

"I don't know."

"If you're trying to figure out what's going on inside yourself, eventually you're going to have to come to terms with what happened between the two of you. I'm not saying you have to marry him, but I *do* think you have to forgive him for whatever he did to hurt you. And as long as we're being perfectly honest, I think you owe him an apology."

Iris took a deep breath and had to admit, "I'm sure you're right." She committed silently to work on that, realizing that she didn't have to trust him in order to let go of her ill feelings.

"There's something else I need to say. I'm not going to tell you whether or not he's the right man for you; only you can know that. But I will tell you that hiding behind a broken heart will not only hurt your, it will hurt everyone who loves you."

Iris's heart quickened at the evidence of his sincerity. He was speaking from experience. "What are you saying?" she asked in a whisper.

James Barrington looked at the ground and withdrew his arm from around her in order to interlace his fingers. "It's something I've felt I should share with you for a long time now, but at the same time I haven't wanted to. And I knew the moment needed to be right. Sometimes we just aren't ready to hear certain things." He looked at her, his eyes penetrating. "You're a woman now, Iris. You need to know there was a time when I let fear and pride keep me from giving my heart. I was terrified of having it broken again. You know the truth about your mother, but what you might not realize is how I held on to the way she'd hurt me, and without even realizing it, I used it as an excuse to shut my heart away. If that's what you're doing, Iris, you need to let go and move on. It's important for you to know that your father not only survived a broken heart, he found happiness beyond it that he'd never imagined possible. There was a time when I had resigned myself to never love again, certain my heart would never recover. When I proposed to your mother—Eleanore—I told her I could never love her; love wasn't part of the deal, I said."

"You *said* that . . . to a woman you were proposing to?"

"I did," he said, sounding embarrassed. "But I was lying to myself even more than I was lying to her. I'd proposed a very practical arrangement. It was a marriage of convenience, Iris. But I believe I loved her all along; I was simply too proud to admit it. I kept my heart from her for a very long time because I was afraid." He took her hand. "I don't want you to make that mistake, Iris. Don't hold your heart back from someone who deserves it because someone who didn't caused you pain."

"Are you saying you think Case deserves my heart, Papa?" she asked, certain inside herself that he didn't. There was far more to her issues with Case than she could ever put into words.

"I think he's a good man. Only you can know if he's the right man to give your heart to. But whether or not he is, it's time to let go of the past and move forward."

"And how do I do that?" she asked, tightening her hold on his hand. "How did *you* do it?"

"It's all about forgiveness. First I had to forgive her, but I realized it was easier to do that than it was to forgive myself."

"Forgive yourself . . . for what?"

Iris wondered if her father had done something in his younger years that he might have difficulty admitting to, but he said firmly, "For loving her, believing in her; for trusting her. I had to forgive myself for being fool enough to *let* her break my heart. And perhaps it was even more difficult to forgive myself for choosing her to be a mother to you and David."

Iris was overtaken by unexpected tears and couldn't deny that his words struck something deep inside her.

"I had to give it to God, Iris," he went on. "All of it. And when I did that, I discovered that my heart wasn't nearly so broken as I thought it was. Your mother, your *real* mother, had healed it, and I hadn't even realized."

While her father wiped away her tears, Iris asked, "Why have you never told me this before?"

"You weren't ready to hear it." He pressed a hand over her face. "I sense something changing in you; softening."

Iris looked down. "I suppose it is. This journey has forced me to ask myself what I'm doing out here, and what I expect to happen once this journey's over. I don't have all the answers, but I think I'm getting closer."

"That's good, then," James said and put an arm around her again.

"Maybe," she said lightly in an effort to ease the somber mood, "my expectations are high for a reason. If I compare all men to my father, they will surely fall short."

He chuckled humbly. "That's because you don't see me the way my wife sees me. I think you'd do well to keep me off of any pedestals, precious."

"I'll just keep you right here," she said and wrapped her arms around him, praying that he would live a very long time. She couldn't imagine ever living without him.

Chapter Twelve

BREATHLESS

It took Iris a few days to reckon with all the things her father had said. She prayed fervently and began studying the scriptures in a personal way that she'd completely gotten out of the habit of doing. Now that she could feel the presence of the Spirit coming back into her life, she wondered how she had managed to live without it all this time. She found that she *was* able to forgive herself for the mistakes she'd made, and to give whatever might be left of her burdens related to the past and her mother to the Savior. She worked on more fully forgiving Miles for his betrayal, and on forgiving the other idiots who had followed in his wake, vying for her affection in ridiculous ways. When she felt confident that all of those things were in order, there was only one issue left. But it was a big one. It took another few days to fully let everything settle into her spirit, and to get up the courage to do what needed to be done.

Before breakfast Iris found Case feeding the horses. She knew he'd be there and that he'd be alone, and she wanted to get it over with before the exodus proceeded once again.

"Hello," she said, and he looked up, then characteristically looked behind himself as if he were certain she couldn't be talking to him.

"Hello." He smiled. "Did you need something?"

"I've come to apologize. Try not to gloat about it."

Her attempt at humor was lost when he said firmly, "Of course not." His astonishment was clearly evident.

"Of course not," she repeated, looking down. "You wouldn't; I know that." She drew the courage to look at him again and get this over with. "But there's no excuse for the way I've treated you at times, and I've behaved very badly. I ask your forgiveness."

"Of course," he said so quickly it startled her.

"Don't you need to think about it?"

"No."

"So, you'll just . . . wipe away all of my crimes against you . . . just like that?"

"Yes. Yes, I will. Isn't that the Christian thing to do?"

She let out a stilted laugh to cover her own guilt over the analogy. "Yes, it *would* be the Christian thing to do, but it's apparent you're a much better Christian than I am."

"Perhaps you're too hard on yourself, Iris."

"And perhaps I need to examine my motives a little more closely. But that's none of your concern. Thank you for accepting my apology. I will do my best to behave more appropriately in the future."

Case's relief turned to panic when it became evident she was leaving. "Wait a minute," he said. "That's it?"

"Was my apology not adequate?"

"More than adequate," he said. "But . . . you're just going to ignore what's happened between us?"

He saw a subtle quivering of her chin while her eyes avoided his. "I believe it's better that way."

"Better for you . . . or for me?"

"For both of us."

"And on what exactly are you basing *this* assumption?"

She looked at him firmly then. "You deserve better than what I can give you, Case. My lack of trust may not be appropriate, but being able to admit it doesn't instantly make it go away. I'm not completely sure why it's there, but—"

"Then figure it out," he said, and she looked astonished. "If something's holding you back, you need to figure it out and fix it so you can get on with your life."

Iris didn't want to admit to him that she was working on exactly that. Knowing she still had a long way to go, she said, "You make it sound so easy."

"It's *not* easy, but it's possible." He closed the space between them and took her shoulders into his hands. "Don't let it come between us, Iris."

Iris looked into his eyes and wanted him to kiss her, but she turned away and forced her thoughts elsewhere. "It already has," she said and moved away. "Forgive me for any grief I may have caused you," she added quickly and walked away.

Case was so stunned that he could hardly breathe. He considered her apology a huge step, but her ongoing lack of trust threatened to break his heart open a little further. Knowing he could do nothing about it, he simply prayed that her heart would be softened even more, and that with time she would come to realize that he would never hurt her.

* * * * *

James wondered if he would ever get used to such afternoon heat. He daydreamed about the cool air of England while he kept the reins steady, but such thoughts only enhanced his misery, made worse by a dryness in the air that seemed to be growing steadily, so unlike the humid heat of Iowa. James's preoccupation with the heat lessened as his chest began to tighten. It had been so long since it had happened that he'd almost forgotten how uncomfortable—and disconcerting—it could be. He tried to relax and breathe deeply while he kept the horses on track, but it gradually worsened as the sun moved across the sky. He began counting minutes, wondering how long before they would stop to make camp for the night. He habitually turned to peek between the canvas flaps at Eleanore resting with the baby. Once when she was awake, she looked up at him and asked, "Are you all right?"

He wondered if it showed in his face. He'd committed to being completely honest about his health issues, but he knew if he told her the whole truth at the moment she would fly into a panic, and he didn't want an uproar to upset the entire company when there was nothing to be done about it anyway. He settled for saying, "It's hot and dusty, and I'm tired." All true.

"How soon until we stop for the night?"

"Not soon enough," he said. Also true. "How are *you?*" he asked.

"I'm fine," she said and seemed to mean it. He was grateful for that. She smiled down at the baby, and he did too. Then he closed the flap and focused on the road, if only to avoid any further conversation that might incriminate him.

James tried not to panic when the constriction increased and he could hear himself wheezing. He prayed fervently to be able to keep breathing until they got to Zion, then he prayed that he could keep breathing until they stopped for the night, as opposed to keeling over dead with the reins in his hand. The discomfort gradually became painful, and the wheezing more audible. The fear of losing consciousness pressed him to the determination to get some help. While he was wondering how to go about it without alarming Eleanore, the bugle sounded and the company came to a halt. He closed his eyes and muttered a raspy, "Thank you, God." He echoed the thought silently when Case appeared beside him on horseback. His smile and whatever thought he might have had on his mind instantly faded with one glance at James.

"What's wrong?" Case demanded.

James hoped Eleanore wouldn't overhear as he barely managed to say, "I . . . can't breathe. Help me . . . down."

Case dismounted, determined to remain calm and rational in spite of his consuming fear. He'd never seen James look so bad. His face was pallid, and his lips were almost blue. He leaned heavily on Case as he stepped carefully down from the wagon, only to collapse to his knees.

"How long have you been like this?" Case demanded.

"Hours," James sputtered, feeling panic tighten his chest further, now that he could share the burden. He lowered his head and could barely spit out his deepest wish. "Please, God, don't let me die. I'm not ready to die."

"You're forgetting what God already told you," Case said, and James looked up at him. "It's not time yet."

James nodded, and Case resisted the urge to scold him for not soliciting some help sooner. Instead he took hold of James's shoulders, kneeling on the ground to face him. "Come on, breathe," he encouraged gently, looking into his eyes. "Take it slow. Just breathe."

James attempted to follow Case's lead and take slow, even breaths as much as it was possible. He felt his panic subside only a little, then he heard Iris say, "What's wrong?"

James gasped for breath—and reason—as it became evident there was no hiding his condition from his daughter any longer. Case echoed his thoughts when he said, "I think your secret is out, old man."

"What secret?" Iris insisted with a panic in her voice that spurred James to a complete inability to draw breath.

Case saw James go ashen as the wheezing became louder but more shallow. "Whoa! Take it easy, James." He attempted to sound calm, even light, while lowering him back onto the ground. "Breathe with me, my friend. Just breathe."

"What's wrong with him?" Iris practically shrieked.

James turned helpless eyes toward his daughter. His view of her face hovering somewhere above him began to go splotchy. He heard Case answer in a panicked voice, "He can't breathe. Get Frederick—now! We need to give him a blessing. Now! And get your mother."

Iris ran to do as she'd been told, heaving for breath herself. Knots tightened her stomach, and her thudding heart pumped fear through her every vein even while her mind was trying to assess the image of her father struggling to breathe and looking half dead. And it was obvious that this was not something new, and it was certainly not something that seemed surprising to Case. *Your secret is out,* he'd said. What did that mean? She forced her mind to the moment and found Frederick just beginning to unharness his horses.

"Come quickly," she said. "It's my father. He needs a blessing . . . right now."

Frederick was running before she finished the sentence. Iris followed him, pausing only long enough to stick her head into the wagon cover where she knew her mother would be. "Mother," she said, and Eleanore lifted her head, her eyes heavy with sleep, which explained her obliviousness to the commotion going on outside. "Something's wrong with Father," she said. "You must come quickly. Let me help you."

Eleanore took hold of Iris's hand to step carefully down from the wagon, while she murmured under her breath. "Not now. Not yet."

Iris bit her tongue to keep from screaming. Another clue that she'd been purposely kept ignorant of something that others had been aware of for a long time. And the implication was clear. Not *now?* Not *yet?* Was her father dying and she'd been given no clue, no warning? Relief engulfed her to see Case and Frederick on their knees beside where her father was lying, the vial of precious oil in Frederick's hand. Then she got a good look at her father's face at the same moment her mother knelt next to him.

"Heaven help us," Eleanore murmured, her voice trembling. She took his face into her hands, and he looked up at her with glazed eyes while he barely drew in enough breath to remain conscious. His skin had taken on a bluish hue, and the sound of his breathing inspired terror in Iris's heart. She didn't know where the children were, but she hoped they would stay away and not see their father like this. She put her complete focus on the power of the priesthood at their disposal. She couldn't comprehend anything else being able to save him.

"Don't you leave me, James!" Eleanore cried.

"He'll be fine," Case muttered and placed his hands on James's head.

Eleanore eased back to allow the men the space they needed to give the blessing. She took James's hand, and Iris noted how tightly they held to each other, as if it were the only thing holding him to this side of the veil.

Case attempted to focus only on being receptive to the Spirit, rather than being distracted by the urgency of James's struggle to breathe and the fear and panic of the women hovering nearby. While he listened to Frederick speaking the majority of the blessing, he felt a calm peace within himself that validated what James had been told in a previous blessing—that he *would* live to see Zion with his family, and to be sealed to his wife for eternity. Case felt a thrilling warmth consume him briefly as the miracle of the gospel on the earth and the power of the priesthood being used momentarily filled his soul. His mind became deeply impressed with the great nobility in God's eyes of this man being blessed, this man who had become such a hero to him. And then, as unexpected and abrupt as a flash of lightning, a series of brief images appeared in Case's mind, seemingly all at once, yet separate, illustrating very clearly the solution to keeping James well. At the very moment the impression came to him, he heard Frederick take a sharp breath, then pause, then declare that James would be well through the remainder of the journey provided he did everything the Spirit guided him to do to protect him from the substance in the air that was presently causing this affliction. He was plainly told that this trial was for the purpose of making it clear to James, and to those who loved him, that the Lord was present with them in their journey, and that only through the hand of the Lord would he remain living. James was commanded to breathe and promised the sustenance of life. Then the amen was spoken.

Before Case opened his eyes, he noticed an absence of the raspy wheezing that had been so terrifying. If not for the words he'd just heard uttered, he might have expected to open his eyes and find James dead. As it was, he found him looking a little dazed, but breathing normally, with color coming back to his face. Case let out a little laugh of relief and saw James's lips returning to their normal shade of pink.

"Oh, thank you, Father," he heard Eleanore mutter before she pressed her face to James's shoulder and wept. He heard Iris crying and looked up to see her kneeling nearby, her hand pressed over her mouth. He felt tears slide down his own cheeks as he turned to see Eleanore lift her head and take her husband's face into her hands. "I love you," she murmured. "I love you so much. Please don't leave me."

"I'm all right now," James said and touched her face in return. "I love you too."

Eleanore sobbed with laughter, and Case could well imagine that, to her, just hearing him speak at all was a miracle. James glanced at Case, then at Frederick, muttering a quiet, "Thank you." Then his eyes focused on Iris, his concern evident. He reached a hand toward her, and she put trembling fingers into his.

Iris glanced quickly at her mother, then at Case and Frederick, then back to her father, saying with a hint of anger, "Why am I the only one here who was surprised that you couldn't breathe?"

"He didn't want you to worry," Eleanore explained.

"Worry?" Iris echoed, coming to her feet.

James moved to sit up, and Frederick helped him. "Iris, sweetheart," James said, "you must understand that—"

"I can't talk about it right now," she said and hurried away.

"I'll talk to her," Case said and nearly stood, but Eleanore put a hand on his arm.

"Perhaps you should give her a little time first," she said.

Case nodded, and Frederick said, "I saw in my mind what we need to do, James, to keep you well."

"I saw it, too," Case said, forcing his preoccupation away from his concern for Iris. He then listened in awe as Frederick repeated exactly what Case had seen in his own mind. He spoke as clearly as any well-educated doctor might have about the asthma and its two main causes for impaired breathing. One was exertion; the other was something in the air that created an adverse reaction. In order for James to be protected, he needed to remain inside the covered wagon and leave it only when absolutely necessary. When he *did* go out, he needed to tie a bandanna over his nose and mouth, the same way he did when there was trail dust in the air. Keeping the scarf wet would also help. Case interjected that in his mind it was as if the canvas covering of the wagon had almost glowed, as if it would serve as a protection from anything that would prevent James from being able to breathe, no matter who or what went in and out. Frederick smiled and said he'd seen exactly the same thing.

"It's a miracle," Eleanore declared.

"More than one, I think," Frederick said. "Also, I had the impression that at every opportunity, James, you should immerse yourself completely in water to wash away whatever substance is on your hair and clothing."

Case admitted that he'd seen that, as well, and he marveled that between the two of them they were able to recall the details of the instructions, and also to validate that they had come from a divine source. James glanced around and said, "How far are we from the river?"

"It's close," Frederick said. "We'll go after supper."

Frederick and Case helped James into the wagon, while he showed no apparent challenge whatsoever in breathing. Frederick left to make certain Lizzie was watching out for the children, and James said to Case, "Thank you."

Case smiled. "Just keep breathing, old man."

"Apparently I'll be fine."

"As long as you aren't too proud to stay down and do what you're told," Eleanore said.

James gave her a comical scowl, then said to Case, "Would you please find Iris? Try to explain, and . . . tell her to come and talk to me."

"I will," Case said. "Do you need anything right now?"

"No," James said. "Frederick and Lizzie will take care of the children. You keep an eye on Iris."

Case nodded and went looking for her. He found her ambling slowly through a patch of sagebrush, not terribly far from where the company was setting up camp. He felt inclined to give her a little more time and helped Frederick unharness the wagons and give feed and water to the horses. Lizzie had a fire built and had the children helping her with supper. Frederick went to check on James and Eleanore. Case took a deep breath, said a quick prayer, and walked slowly toward where Iris was hovering nearby. The sun was almost out of sight when he came up beside her. She glanced toward him, her face tear stained, then she turned her back to him and wrapped her arms tightly around herself.

"I need to be alone," she said.

"Your father asked me to check on you."

"I'm fine, as you can see."

"I can see that you're safe, but I don't think that was his concern."

Iris sighed, resigning herself to this conversation. She knew it was inevitable but had hoped to postpone it. Her thoughts were still swirling with facts and implications and the emotional trauma of seeing her father almost die. And then there was the undeniable miracle she'd witnessed that had restored the breath of life. The evidence of God's hand in the situation was the only thing that gave her any peace at all. If not for that, she knew she would be fuming and utterly terrified—one likely a result of the other. But she forced herself to take a deep breath, certain there was some metaphor in the need to do so that was meant to teach her something profound. She turned to look at Casey Harrison, standing there with the setting sun at his back, which left his features darkened by shadows. As she took a moment to separate her flurry of thoughts into categories, she had to consider what this meant in relation to him. It was difficult to know what to say. But she had to say something.

"You always do what my father asks of you." It wasn't a question.

"Yes," he said. "Yes, I do."

"So, you walk all the way out here to check on me at his request, knowing full well that I might be angry enough to slap your face." He only looked down, and she added, "But you do it anyway—only because he asks you to."

"Not *only* because of that."

"Then why?"

"I share his concern," Case admitted. "You can't help but feel shocked by what just happened."

"But you're not."

"Not as much as you are, I admit."

Iris let out a sardonic chuckle. "You knew. You knew something was wrong with him."

"Yes," he said again. "Yes, I did."

"But he asked you not to tell me."

"That's right."

Iris was overcome by fresh tears as she forced the truth out of her mouth. "So you . . . you've been protecting him . . . all this time; protecting me . . . and the boys . . . from worrying. You let me think . . . horrible things about you . . . and say . . . horrible things to you . . . but you wouldn't go back . . . on what he asked you to do."

Case couldn't figure if she was angry or just upset. Either way, he simply said, "Would you have wanted me to?"

"No," she said firmly, and he felt some relief. "I don't agree with his keeping it from me, but I understand it." Silence fell between them and became awkward until she added, "How long have you known?"

"From the start," he said, and she looked astonished, but not angry. "He didn't choose to tell me, Iris. I found him in the barn, barely able to breathe. He told me then that it was probably best I'd figured it out, because he needed me to help him make his life appear as normal as possible. He was adamant that he wouldn't have his children worried and afraid. And then Frederick broke his leg."

Iris shook her head as the events of the last year came back to her with greater significance than she'd ever imagined. She said the obvious. "He never would have been able to manage without you; or at least he never would have been able to keep it a secret."

"That's right."

Iris looked hard at him while the last sliver of the sun disappeared behind the distant horizon and his face became visible. She attempted to digest how what she had just learned changed everything she had believed about him. And she was pleasantly surprised at how easily it settled into her. There was something she needed to say, and knowing it would be difficult, she figured it was best to just say it and get it over with. She swallowed carefully and forced the words off her tongue. "Forgive me."

"For what?" he asked, and she felt certain he wanted to be sure her apology was accurate—and sincere. And she couldn't blame him.

"For being so judgmental; for the awful way I treated you, for the things I said."

"We already had this conversation, Iris."

"Maybe we need to have it again. Everything is different now."

"Is it?" he asked, and she nodded.

"Forgive me," she repeated.

He quickly said, "I already have. I've told you this before. I forgave you a long time ago."

"Just like that?" In spite of their previous conversation, she couldn't believe it. Her new perspective made the entire issue different. "I hadn't even *asked.*"

"I don't think that's required. I never *liked* your attitude toward me, and I'll admit I had some trouble dealing with it, but it was never my right to judge your reasons for being that way, or to hold it against you. That's between you and the Lord, Iris. What's between you and me starts over right now."

Iris couldn't believe what she was hearing—and seeing. The sincerity of his words was echoed by the intensity of his eyes. "Just like that?" she asked again, feeling her chin quiver.

"Just like that," he said and took a step closer. "Only if that's what you want, of course."

Case looked into her moist eyes and considered the enormity of the moment. But there was more to this situation than she fully realized, and there was far more between them than simply the issue regarding her father's health. He felt certain her mind was too focused on what had happened today to recall that her reasons for not trusting him went far deeper than this. But he knew it would come up again. They were making progress, but they had a long way to go, and he wasn't going to get ahead of himself only to be knocked back down. He also refused to have anything undone between them. He'd learned how to carefully protect his heart from her distrusting attitudes; he wouldn't be fully opening it until he had solid evidence that he could trust *her.*

Sticking to the present situation, he felt the need to say, "I too must ask your forgiveness."

"Why?"

"For being stubborn," he said readily and took a deep breath, wondering if her softness toward him would fade with this confession. "Before we left Iowa . . . that day we were arguing in the barn, and your father walked in."

"I remember."

"He overheard what was said." Iris cringed at the thought of how cruel she'd been that day. She looked away and waited for Case to continue. "He wanted to tell you the truth. He didn't want there to be such ill feelings between us simply because of poor communication. I told him I didn't want you to know. So, I guess that means your being left ignorant was *my* decision beyond that point."

"I see," Iris said, resisting the habitual urge to get angry or defensive. She thought of her father's words regarding free agency. If Iris's mother had chosen to be unkind and cynical, Iris could certainly choose to be otherwise. But it wasn't easy. Especially when she was hearing something that left her so uneasy. Wanting to understand this more fully, she simply asked, "Why?" He looked confused, so she clarified, "Why didn't you want me to know?"

"Are you asking me to be completely honest here, Iris? Because that hasn't always turned out well."

"Of course I want you to be honest," she insisted.

"Are you sure? You've apologized for your behavior, but I wonder if you've fully looked at your behavior. If I answer the question honestly, are you going to throw it back at me and storm away angry? Or are you willing to really listen to what I have to say and try to understand why I made this decision?"

Iris swallowed carefully. With all of her prayer and efforts to understand her own unhappiness and come to terms with it, she had never predicted a moment like this. But she could hardly expect God to answer her prayers if she couldn't humbly listen to what this man had to say, a man she had been apologizing to only minutes earlier. If she behaved badly, then she would be proving to Case—and to

God—that her apology had been insincere. She thought of scriptures she had read recently that had helped her understand the difference between pride and humility. She wanted to be a humble person, but she didn't always feel that way. Maybe she *did* have some of her mother in her, if such things as attitudes and behaviors could be inherited. But maybe that didn't matter. It was up to her to choose a life different from her mother's, whether it was easy or not. It took her half a minute to know that she could honestly tell Case that she wanted him to be honest, and another half a minute to gather the courage to hear whatever he might have to say and be open to it. She willed herself to put away all defensiveness and pride, and to hear him with an open heart—and an open spirit. The image of her father nearly dying came into her mind, reminding her that petty grievances didn't seem nearly so important in the eternal perspective of this life. She swallowed carefully and looked directly at him. "Yes," she said, "I want you to be honest." Tears came as she felt compelled to admit, "I'm trying to be a better person, Case. Be patient with me."

"Fair enough," he said with no hesitation and an unmistakable gentleness in his eyes. She considered the possibility that some men might have taken advantage of such an opportunity to get back at a woman who had been so unkind. But she sensed only concern and compassion from him. He cleared his throat softly and said, "I didn't want your father to tell you, because that was only one part of the problems between us. I told him it wasn't about poor communication. It was about judgment and prejudice." Iris took a sharp breath, feeling as if she'd been slapped. But she held her tongue and prayed again for humility. "I told him that if you couldn't learn to see me for who I really am, then anything else was irrelevant. The issue of your father's health was only one of the things that had come up that day. Erasing one item wasn't going to eliminate the rest. If you recall, you'd also accused me of flirting with your mother and turning your brothers against you." Iris hung her head and squeezed her eyes closed as a burning pain gathered in her chest and forehead. "And I was well aware then, as I am now, that even if you didn't believe I had some kind of hideous motives in the present, you'd still made it clear that you were unwilling to let go of my past." She heard him take a sustaining breath, as if saying what he'd said had been difficult. "So, letting you know the truth about his health would only have made you worry—which he didn't want—and it would not have solved the problems between us. And for what it's worth, I don't believe these things you're struggling with make you a bad person, Iris. I have no right to judge what you're feeling or thinking, because I can't possibly understand. I think you're confused and scared, and I just happened to get in the way. There, that's what I needed to say."

Iris felt so close to completely crumbling that she wondered how she could even speak. She prayed for the presence of mind to do so, and managed to utter, "I feel like such a fool."

"There's no need for that, Iris. You've apologized; it's forgiven. It's in the past. You need to come to terms with it and leave it there. And as you have pointed out, you don't have to trust me to forgive me. I would prefer that you trust me as well, but that's going to have to be up to you. I beg you to forgive *me,* for anything and everything I've done to hurt you—whether intentional or otherwise—because I don't want you to carry such a burden, Iris. Give it to the Lord and find peace so that you can be happy." He chuckled softly. "That's something I think we can both agree on, that you should be happy."

Iris felt too stunned to speak, and so overcome she could barely breathe. She wanted to be alone, but didn't know how to ask. She was reminded of his perceptive nature when he said, "I'll give you some time to yourself, if that's what you want." She nodded. "Your father wants you to come and talk to him. I'll tell him you'll be there in a while." She nodded again, fearing that to even utter a syllable would unleash the temptation to sob uncontrollably. He walked one direction and she walked the other, farther away from camp so that she *could* cry and attempt to vent even a degree of this burning pain. Her regrets oozed through her, brutally reminding her of all she'd said and done that had caused grief for herself and others. And Case had gotten the worst of it. She *did* feel like a fool. And yet he was so gracious about the whole thing, willing to just wipe it all away and start over.

Iris miraculously found a tree—likely the only one in many miles—where she was able to conceal herself from anyone's view and cry while she prayed fervently and attempted to come to terms with everything that Case had said, and the reality that her father had a life-threatening illness. She finally found enough strength and composure to head back to camp, motivated mostly by her desire to not cause her father to worry. But she knew she had a long way to go in coming to terms with everything that had just transpired.

Chapter Thirteen

TRUST

Iris returned to camp to find supper over and cleaned up. Lizzie told her she could reheat something for her, but Iris thanked her and declined, feeling the need to begin a fast, for a number of reasons. She found her mother sitting outside, reading with the boys.

"How are you feeling?" Iris asked her, noting she still looked a little pale since giving birth, though she was getting around some.

"I'm fine," she said. "How are you?"

"I didn't give birth in that wagon," Iris said lightly, not wanting attention drawn to her fragile emotional state. "For that reason, I'm great."

"I'm fine," Eleanore repeated. "Your father wants to see you." She nodded toward the wagon. "Mariah's asleep in there with him, so don't be too loud. She didn't get a nap today, so I think she's down for the night."

Iris nodded and went quietly into the wagon where she found her father lying down but staring upward, with Mariah asleep on one side of him and Olivia on the other. "Ah," he said when he saw her, "now I have my three little girls all together."

"I'm not very little anymore, Papa," she said.

"No, but . . ." he glanced at Mariah, then at Olivia, "I can still remember what you were like. I always loved to hold you when you were sleeping, until you got too big to hold. I'd sneak into your room and take you out of your bed just to hold you."

"And when I got too big?"

"I'd sneak into your room and sit beside you, watching you."

"And when did you stop doing that?"

"Who said I'd stopped?" he asked, and she realized he was serious. "I'm usually the last one awake around here, and I have to peek in on all of you and make certain you're where you're supposed to be, just so I know that everything's all right. I love to watch you and Mariah sleeping side by side. You're both so precious."

Iris sat beside him and he sat up, taking her hand into his. "How are you?" she asked.

"I'm fine, as you can see."

"For the moment."

"Yes, for the moment," he said, looking down. "Iris, I . . . I'm sorry I didn't tell you. I knew you would worry. And until today, as long as I didn't exert myself, I was fine. I'm still not certain what happened today. But maybe it's good that you know."

Iris forced herself to ask the question that terrified her the most. "Is this . . . going to kill you?"

He looked at her straightly. "I don't know. But I've had to accept the possibility that it's likely. God promised me in a blessing that I would live to see Zion with my family. Beyond that . . ." He shrugged but didn't finish the sentence.

Iris wrapped her arms around him and put her head on his shoulder, holding to him desperately. "I can't bear to lose you, Papa. I can't!"

He held her close and stroked her hair. "My time on this earth is in God's hands, Iris. No matter how badly I want to stay, it's not up to me."

Iris took advantage of the silence to just revel in his presence. She could hear his heart beating, feel the rise and fall of his chest with each breath. After what she'd witnessed today, it was a miracle. But she wondered how long the miracle would last. She'd longed every hour of every day since leaving Iowa City for this journey to be over. Now she wondered if the end of the journey would bring the end of her father's life, and she wanted to stay out here on this miserable prairie forever.

James broke the silence by saying, "I'm sure you realize now that Case knew about this."

"Yes, I know."

"I must apologize for the misunderstanding it caused between the two of you."

"It doesn't matter," she said. "There was much more to it than that, Papa. That's all in the past."

"But you still don't trust him?"

"I don't know," she admitted tearfully. "Right now I don't know anything. I just . . . need some time . . . to think."

"Of course."

Iris's mind whirled through more minutes of silence, until she asked, "Do *you* trust him?"

"I do." He drew back and took Iris's shoulders into his hands. "I need you to understand something, precious. I don't trust human beings blindly. I consider myself a cautious man, and I've had a great deal of life's experiences that have taught me that some people simply are not trustworthy. I think we should believe the best of people until they give us evidence otherwise, and it's still possible to trust someone and be cautious until you've had the opportunity to truly know them. We all trusted Miles. He didn't give us any reason not to. But he was working very hard at deceiving us, and he did a good job of it. We all learned something from that, and we were all hurt. I admit that my experience with Miles has made me more cautious. But it taught me something very important. All the time you were seeing Miles, I sensed unrest in you, and I felt concerned. Looking back, I realized that I'd never bothered to ask God about this man. Did you?"

"Not specifically, I suppose."

"I felt good about Case the moment I looked into his eyes; I felt good about giving him a job and making him feel welcome. But that very first night I prayed specifically to know Case's heart. Within a few days, I got my answer. In fact, I got more of an answer than I'd ever anticipated. I knew beyond any doubt that he was not only trustworthy, but that he had been sent to me for a purpose. I didn't know then, and I'm not sure now, if that purpose has anything specifically to do with you. That's for you to decide. But I know firmly that Case was meant to be my son as much as Ben was. He had been denied the blessing of a good family, and he was being rewarded for his faithfulness by being brought into this one. In return, I knew that he would richly bless our household, and that we would all be irrevocably connected."

"And you've known that from the start?"

"Yes."

"Why didn't you say something?"

"It was a sacred experience for me, Iris. I believe that such things should only be shared when and how the Spirit prompts us. The time wasn't right."

"It is now?"

"Apparently."

"Have you told Case?"

"No, not yet. When the time is right, I will."

"So," Iris sniffled and wiped tears off her face, "why do you think it might be right to tell me now?"

"Because I know you're struggling to come to terms with some difficult things in your life, and you were just given one more thing to contend with. I know that your relationship with Case is complicated at best. I'm not telling you that you should trust him based on my word, any more than I would tell you to believe the Church is true based on what I or anyone else might say. You have to get the answers for yourself, Iris. I *am* telling you that you have a right to those answers. It might be difficult for you to trust Case, based on your life's experiences and issues that stand between the two of you. But God knows his heart, and He knows yours. If you can't trust Case, at least trust in the Lord. You must trust in Him above all else, Iris. Before you can ever fully open your heart to any human being and be completely happy and at peace, you must first trust in Him . . . to heal your wounds and your pain, to forgive your mistakes. Through Him, all things are made right, whether they make complete sense to us or not."

Iris let that settle in before she asked, "So, you really believe it's possible for me to put all of the past behind me and completely start over?"

"I know it's possible, Iris. That is the very definition of redemption. If you know within yourself that Jesus is the Christ, then you must believe that through Him, all things are possible."

They talked about less serious matters for a while longer, then she asked how his breathing problems had come to light, and what had been done. She wanted to know everything he knew about this threat against his health. He told her that he'd told the boys about it earlier while she'd been away from camp. Now that James would be mostly confined to the interior of the wagon, it could no longer be kept a secret. He told Iris they had taken it rather well, but they likely had no idea of the possible severity of his condition. He asked her to be mindful of their moods or concerns, and to let him know if any of them might need his personal attention in regard to any matter that he might not be aware of under the circumstances. He told her how he loved her, and what a good woman she was, and Iris returned to her own wagon to sleep, carrying Mariah in her arms, wanting with all her heart to believe all of the things her father had told her.

By candlelight, Iris took out her Book of Mormon to read, surprised when it fell open to First Nephi, chapter ten, when Nephi told the angel that he desired to behold the things which his father had seen, and he declared that he believed all the words of his father.

Iris felt as stunned by what she was reading as by the fact that she could not have possibly been led here by coincidence. Tears and a rush of goosebumps confirmed what seemed evident. God was indeed mindful of her, and the things her father had said *were* true. *Everything* he had said. She prayed until she slept, and she woke up praying, determined to find that complete peace and happiness her father had spoken of.

At breakfast it became evident that Case would be driving the wagon that James had been driving. "Unless you want to drive that one," Case said to Iris with no hint of humor or sarcasm. "Maybe you'd prefer being closer to your parents."

Iris answered with equal sincerity. "I think they're in better hands with you. If I tip a wagon over, I don't want it to be the one with the sick people and babies in it."

"You're doing just fine," Frederick said to her. "In fact, I think you're doing amazingly well at keeping everything steady with the terrain we've had to cover."

"I would agree with that," Case said, and Iris almost felt embarrassed.

"Now that we need Case to drive your father's wagon," Frederick went on, "it's a good thing we have you driving as well. What would we have done?"

"I could drive it!" Jamie volunteered.

"I'm sure you could." Frederick chuckled. "But we have some of the most difficult trail yet to cross."

"We do?" Iris asked, alarmed.

"We'll be just fine," Frederick said and left to attend to the animals.

"Yes. Yes, we will," Case said, winking at Iris before he followed after him.

For days Iris prayed, studied, and pondered as she never had before in her life. The wagon train moved on, facing challenges and overcoming them. Iris fasted, then ate a meal, then fasted again, pleading with the Lord to give her a new start, a second chance, and to purge anything inside of her that kept her from feeling free of her burdens and to help her find that inner happiness she had seen in others, most especially her father and his sweet Eleanore, who had been such a perfect mother to Iris. She might have some other woman's blood in her veins, but she had a lifetime of Eleanore's example of being Christlike and faithful.

One morning Iris woke up and realized she felt happy. It hadn't come to her all at once in some grand flash or bolt of lightning. She just felt better. She found no ill feelings inside of her, toward herself or others, and she felt capable of doing anything that might be required of her. The remainder of the journey to the Salt Lake Valley didn't seem so ominous with the realization that they would be gathered with the Saints. It was Zion! And she felt deeply grateful to be part of a family that had embraced such beliefs and was willing to sacrifice so much to live them. Before the day began, Iris crept into the wagon where her parents were just coming awake. She snuggled between them as she had many times during her childhood, and she tearfully told them all she was feeling, and all she had learned. They cried with her, sharing her joy as much as they had shared every aspect of her sorrows, far more than she had ever been aware of. She asked their forgiveness for any grief she might have caused them because of her difficult attitudes. And like Case, they assured her that it had all been forgiven long ago; they only wanted her to be happy.

As the day progressed, Iris knew there was only one thing standing in her way to feeling completely at peace. Once again, she needed to speak to Case. She dreaded it, but she longed to have it behind her. She wasn't certain what path the conversation might take; she was merely allowing herself to be open to the Spirit and listen to what it told her. But she did have a sense that it wasn't going to be brief.

Iris waited until supper was over and all of the evening tasks had been completed. She told her parents she intended to talk to Case, and that it might take some time; she didn't want them becoming alarmed if they weren't around. They both smiled and wished her well. Iris found Case teasing the boys in the midst of making them clean their teeth before bed. She watched them for a minute, then said, "I wonder if we could talk . . . privately."

He smiled. "Of course." Then to Jamie. "You make sure your brothers do what they're supposed to do, then go tell your parents that you're all ready for bed." Jamie nodded, and Case motioned with his arm while saying to Iris, "We could walk this way through some lovely sagebrush, or we could go that way through some lovely sagebrush."

"Sagebrush is fine," she said. "I think I'm getting used to it."

She started walking away from camp, which was the only way to have complete privacy. He walked beside her for several minutes and said nothing. It was evident he expected her to do the talking, since she'd initiated the conversation.

"First of all," she said, "I want to thank you again for all you've done for my father; for the whole family, but especially for him."

"I love your father, Iris. I've never known a finer man. I wonder every day why he would be so good to me."

Iris looked down. "Oh, I wouldn't wonder that." He didn't comment, and she added, "When I think of how much you've done for him, I really don't know what to say."

"You don't have to say anything. It's no sacrifice to help your father. He's done more for me than I could ever do for him if he lived to be a hundred."

Iris felt a painful tightening in her chest and had to say, "But he won't, will he."

"No, I don't think he will."

Fearing she would start wailing like a child, Iris moved the conversation along. "I just want to make it clear that I'm grateful for your efforts on his behalf."

Case responded to the pounding of his heart by turning to look at this woman as if he'd never seen her before. Preferring to take this head-on, he said, "Careful, Iris. That sounded like a compliment."

"Did it?" she asked, still focused on the ground. "I'm certain it's long past due. Which, I suppose, brings me to my next point. I know we've gone through all of the apologies and forgiveness already. My purpose is not to hash through all of that again. But for myself, I feel the need to clarify some things. I really don't know how this conversation is supposed to go. I only know that I felt like I needed to talk to you, and perhaps talking through my feelings will help me understand them better. I hope you'll bear with me."

"Of course."

"I've been very . . . suspicious, and . . . I've judged you unfairly. The problem is not with you, Case, it's me."

"I'm sure there are reasons for that, Iris," he said gently when she wouldn't have blamed him for gloating over her confession. "We could talk about that, you know."

"I'm not sure I *want* to talk about it."

"Have you ever talked to *anyone* about it?"

"My parents know."

"They know, but have you talked to them about it? I mean . . . really *talked* about it?" Her silence confirmed the truth. He added, "I don't know how you could ever get over something so painful while it rolls around in your head and never goes away."

Iris considered the accuracy of his words. Until that moment, she had believed that the part Miles had played in her life was behind her. But it suddenly didn't feel that way, and she wondered if Case sensed something that she hadn't been able to define. Perhaps, for all her efforts, there was still residue left inside of her that she needed to get out. She wondered if she was capable of talking about it in such depth when she'd held it so close to her heart all these years. For a moment she felt certain she could never speak about it, especially to Case. Then it occurred to her that she was having this conversation because she trusted him. She'd been praying for peace, for the means to move on with her life. Was this the answer to her prayers, staring her in the face? She resigned herself quickly to saying the words, and didn't give herself time to think about them before they fell off her tongue. "I believe I mentioned this briefly before, but . . ." She couldn't remember what she'd told him and figured she should just say what she needed to, even if she were repeating herself. "He told me he loved me; said I was the only one. He wasn't a member, but he told me he was reading the Book of Mormon, that he wanted to be baptized; he just needed some time. We were close for many months. He kept talking about marriage, but nothing ever changed. I grew to love him. I believed he was the one. Then my parents saw him with another woman. Months after that I learned there were many women. And then I found out some girl in town was . . . pregnant with his baby. He'd tried once to have his way with me, but I'd made it clear where I stood on such things, and I had every reason to believe he respected that. I figured he didn't know any better because he hadn't been raised the way I'd been raised. We loved each other, and it was certainly tempting. Then it became evident that what had happened with her happened long after it had almost happened with me, but right at the time when he'd been regularly declaring his love and devotion to me. When all of this came to light, I went to his home and confronted him, even though I hadn't seen him for months. There was no apparent regret. He said it wasn't that serious because he didn't love her, he loved me. He said it would never happen again, and he begged me to take him back. He said he'd not seen me for months because my father had threatened him to keep his distance, but he still loved me. How could I believe him? He admitted that the Church really wasn't for him; he'd just been humoring me. He didn't put it exactly like that, but that's what he meant. And he couldn't believe that I was refusing to take him back over something so . . . petty. That's what he said; he said it was petty." She wrapped her shawl more tightly around her. "I've wondered a hundred times what might have happened to me if I hadn't held to what I'd been taught, or if I didn't have the gospel in my life. Would I have ended up pregnant too? Would he have married me, sentenced me to a miserable life? Or would he have abandoned me like he did the other one?"

"So, you can be grateful you *do* have the gospel, that you *do* know better."

"Yes, I am grateful, but . . . that doesn't change the fact that . . ." Sorrow finally crept in to join her words, and she found it impossible to speak.

"That you loved him?" Case guessed, and she nodded, pressing a hand over her mouth. She turned her back to him, and he added, "You don't have to hide your tears from me, Iris. He broke your heart, and you have a right to cry over that."

"Maybe I do," she said, making no further effort to conceal her emotion. "But . . . I don't have the right to pass it around. I've spent years holding the pain so close to my heart that . . . I've surely . . . hurt others and . . ." She sobbed and took a moment to compose herself. "I've been cruel to you, and . . . I've been unfair, and . . ."

"Iris," he took hold of her shoulders, "I understand, perhaps more than you could ever know. I understand what it's like to hold pain close to your heart, oblivious to the damage that's wreaking havoc on yourself and anyone who gets in your way. Your response to how he hurt you is so minor compared to the horrible things I did. If *I* can make peace with myself, then surely you can do the same."

Iris absorbed his words with some measure of comfort, then a thought materialized in her mind so suddenly that her heart pounded in response. *He's speaking from experience, Iris. He needs to share his burdens with you as surely as you need to share yours with him.* She didn't even have to wonder over the source of such an impression. It was emblazoned clearly into her mind as well as her spirit. She reasoned that Case *had* shared his burdens with her. Hadn't he? He'd told her about the horrors of his childhood and the horrible things he'd done while he'd been drinking too much and trying to forget. She'd judged him cruelly over his confessions and could see now that she had no hope of putting her own past behind her if she was unwilling to allow Case to do the same. The gravity of their sins and the intentions behind them were not for either of them to judge. Such matters were in God's hands.

Iris turned abruptly to look into his eyes while an irrational compassion rose inside of her on his behalf. What would make a man like Casey Harrison behave so deplorably? She could sense as surely as if she were being taught by some divine source the path of self-destruction he'd been on when he'd encountered the gospel and it had changed his life. What had happened to drive him to make such choices? Her heart pounded anew as she fully accepted that God expected her to ask him, and to get an answer. She prayed that she could be accepting and compassionate, that he could trust her in spite of how she'd broken his trust in the past. She sought for the words with which to begin, and they came to her.

"Tell me how you understand," she said gently.

He shrugged, but she sensed a subtle uneasiness that she might not have noticed if the Spirit had not alerted her to a deeper problem. "You know all of this, Iris."

"Tell me again. So much is different now. Please tell me again."

He chuckled tensely. "You know this story, Iris. My dad used to get drunk and beat me, so when I was old enough, I started getting drunk to try to forget. It's easy now to see how ludicrous that is, but pain has a way of blurring our perceptions." He looked at her more intensely. "The gospel changed me, Iris. It taught me how to forgive, and how to give my pain away. It taught me that there's not much in this life we can't get through and still be happy."

"Is that why you're always smiling?"

He chuckled. "Am I?"

"Oh, yes!"

"I *am* happy, Iris. God has blessed me tremendously. There's no reason to go back to the past."

"Maybe there is," she said, then felt compelled to borrow his words. "Have you ever really talked about it? I mean . . . *really* talked about it? I don't know how you could ever get over something so painful while it rolls around in your head and never goes away."

Case felt immediately breathless. How could she have known there were secrets buried deep in his heart when he'd worked so hard to keep them locked away there? He'd believed that they were best left untouched and unspoken, and he'd buried them so deeply that he'd convinced himself they were truly in the past. Then the memories rushed vividly into his mind, and the fear and horror accompanying them surrounded his heart. A tangible pain gathered in his chest, and he put a hand there while he stared at Iris, wishing he hadn't just given her irrefutable evidence that she was right. He turned his back to her, struggling to breathe, wondering how their conversation had come to *this.*

"Talk to me," she urged gently from behind him.

"Why?" he snapped, wishing it hadn't sounded so harsh. His tone in and of itself proved him guilty.

"If you don't, then coaxing *my* confessions out of *me* would indicate that you're not the man you profess to be. And you wouldn't want me to believe that, not after we've come so far."

Case pressed both hands to his chest, but the pain only intensified. Fighting for a reason—any reason—to skirt around this, he said, "Call me a hypocrite if you like, Iris. There are things in my past that need to stay there."

"And you will be able to leave them there more easily once you've shared them."

"How can I?" he asked and heard his voice quaver. He felt certain he was one step away from sobbing uncontrollably. "How can I . . . tell you things that . . . will surely make you think less of me, when . . . the last time I told you such things . . ." He couldn't finish without tempting tears too close to the surface.

"I turned on you and used it against you, I know. And I'm sorry for that. It was never my right to judge those things, Case. I was wrong."

"Are you saying you've forgiven me for that?" He needed to be absolutely certain they were talking about the same thing. "The other women?"

"Yes," she said firmly. He squeezed his eyes closed, and tears came, but they were warm, soothing tears that somewhat eased the pain burning inside of him. He'd longed for months to hear such words from her, not daring to believe that it was possible. He'd wished and hoped for such a moment, believing that if she could only forgive him of his past, they could share a future that was bright and secure. He'd never imagined that the moment he'd dreamed of could be interlaced into a conversation such as this. He wanted to run and hide and never face her again.

"Talk to me," she added. "Share your burdens with me. Then we'll be even."

"Even?" he echoed, his tone scoffing. "Oh, Iris, I could never hope to be even with a woman like you. What I have done and seen in my lifetime leaves me unworthy to even be in your presence."

"Now you *are* being a hypocrite. You've told me the past no longer matters. If we give our burdens to the Savior, then you and I stand on equal ground."

Case wanted to believe that; in his heart he *did* believe it. But he'd never imagined having to face this as a necessary part of proving such belief. "I don't think I can say it, Iris."

"Yes you can. You need to."

"How do you know that?"

"I just know," she said, and he turned to look at her, searching for evidence of the meaning beneath her words. As if she knew his thoughts, she added, her eyes glistening with tears, "The Lord would not tell me that you needed to share your burdens if He didn't know it was necessary."

Case took a sharp breath and felt the truth of her words settle into him, easing his anxiety. She touched his face with soothing fingers as she added, "Prove to me that you've forgiven me for the way that I hurt you, Case. Prove to me that you trust me, that you believe I would never hurt you again, no matter what you tell me. Talk to me, Case." She offered a wan smile, and tears spilled down her cheeks. "Share your burden with me, and we will give it to the Savior—together. And then we will never speak of it again. But we will always know that wherever life takes us, we were able to help each other become better people, and to truly let go of the past and leave it behind us." She lowered her voice to a whisper. "Tell me." When he hesitated still, she added, "I don't need to hear details. Just . . . say what you need to say."

Case prayed silently and was surprised at how quickly he felt a personal confirmation that she was being guided by the Spirit, and that this was important for him. In the breadth of a second he gained an understanding of how this might adversely affect his future at some unforeseen moment if he didn't contend with it now and give it fully to his Savior. Feeling strength from that very Source, he took a deep breath and just said it, surprised at how even his voice came. "He killed her."

Iris felt stunned, wondering what she'd expected. It certainly wasn't this. "Who?" she asked, relying on the ongoing influence of the Spirit to guide this conversation until she knew it was done.

"My father . . . killed my mother." His voice became less steady, then his knees became weak and he sat abruptly on the ground. Iris sat to face him and took his hand into hers, silently encouraging him to continue. "He beat her to death. My brothers and I saw it. We were hiding so he wouldn't come after us. He didn't know we were there."

Iris watched the glazed distance in his eyes, saw his chin quiver and the muscles of his face go rigid. Her heart thumped painfully as she tried to imagine something so horrible, and realized that she couldn't. She could never have empathy for witnessing such an event. But she could have compassion. She touched his face with her free hand, and he put his over it, as if holding it there might give him strength. He closed his eyes, and his voice trembled as he went on. "When it was over, when we knew she was dead, my brother went crazy. It all happened so fast that . . . my other brother and I had no idea what was happening until it was over. The two of us watched him take the gun from over the fireplace, and he shot our father. I remember seeing them both dead on the floor. And I felt grateful more than anything. I was grateful my mother was free of her pain. My only exposure to religion had been her quiet teachings on the matter, and they were few. But she'd taught me of heaven and hell. I knew she was in heaven, and she would never live in fear again. And I hoped my father was in hell. I was grateful my brother had killed him, so I wouldn't be tempted to. But then . . . we had to deal with what had happened, and fast. Half an hour later we were all gone. We packed some things and left, and we never went back." He hung his head and made an anguished noise, and Iris knew there was more to come. "The three of us stayed together until . . . my brother . . . the one who had killed him . . . took his own life. He'd never been able to live with it. That's when I started drinking. You know the rest."

When Case realized he'd actually uttered all of that aloud, he felt a little startled. He took in his surroundings in the little remaining light of day and felt as if he'd been gone for a few minutes, but now he was back. Tears trickled down his face, and he looked up to see Iris crying as well. But there was nothing but compassion and concern in her eyes. She *had* changed. And now she knew everything he'd always been afraid to tell her—or anyone. He was surprised when she asked, "Have you forgiven him?"

"Who?"

"Your father?"

"Yes," he said so quickly that it surprised even himself. He knew the answer deeply and firmly. "When I was baptized," he explained, "I felt them with me; my brother and my parents. I could never explain how I knew; I just knew they were there. And I knew they were all right. I learned more from that experience about the nature of heaven than I ever could have by reading the scriptures, although things I've read since have verified what I learned. My father behaved that way because generations before him had done the same. He didn't know any better. My brother was a victim of that, the same as my mother. But they were all learning and progressing. I knew it then. I know it now. And I will see them again one day."

Iris smiled and pressed her hand more tightly to his face. "Now, don't you feel better?"

"Yes, actually, I do."

Iris knew that the purpose of this conversation was complete, and that they both needed time to digest all they'd learned and felt. In order to alleviate the somber residue in the air, she said lightly, "Aren't you glad that we can trust each other with such confessions?"

"Are you saying that you trust me?"

"I should think that's evident." She squeezed his hand, then stood up and walked away, sensing that he needed some time alone. She prayed for him as she walked back to camp, and she thanked her Father in Heaven for allowing her to be part of such a moment of healing for this good man. She did not know what might lay ahead for them. But for now, she felt completely at peace, and she prayed that Case did too. He was a good man, and he deserved to be happy.

* * * * *

Over the next few days, Iris kept her typical distance from Case, but she made an effort to treat him like one of the family, instead of trying to pretend he didn't exist. Occasionally they shared a smile or a glance that held some meaning concerning the secrets they'd shared, but she left him to sort out his feelings while she was doing the same. Given all that had happened, she found herself discreetly observing him through new eyes. She saw him giving piggyback rides to the children until he was exhausted and dripping with sweat. She saw him carry water for her mother, and during the time they were not moving, he never went long without checking on her father to see that he had all he needed. She saw him nudge Benjamin to do things to help his parents so they wouldn't have to ask. He was often reminding the younger children to do what had been asked of them. And he always did it with kindness—and usually with a smile. She asked herself the same old questions, even though she already knew the answers. But perhaps she needed to become completely comfortable with them. Was he doing this for ulterior motives? Was he pretending to be a nice guy to make himself a part of the family? He was already part of the family. He didn't need her or anybody else to make that happen. And she had to give some credit to her parents. They would not have tolerated someone being this heavily involved with their children for so long if they had any doubts about his character. Her parents were discerning people who followed the Spirit in their lives, and they were sharp. They clearly loved and respected Casey Harrison. And why wouldn't they? As far as pretending went, no man could pretend to be anything different than what he was for this long. She'd seen him frustrated, angry, and completely worn out. But never once had he behaved unseemly. All the evidence tallied; she couldn't find a single reason to be afraid of trusting such a man. Which only left one problem. And she would be a fool to let pride keep her from admitting that she'd been wrong about the only thing left standing between them.

Chapter Fourteen

ZION

After the day's usual traversing of dusty miles had ended, Iris found Case alone with the horses, giving them water. Just seeing him quickened her heart, and it was difficult not to let go of a giddy laugh. She'd thought of a dozen ways to tell him, to open the conversation, to repair the bridge that had been broken between them. But now that she was here, words felt trite and not nearly powerful enough to let him know how she felt. She stood a few feet away until he became aware of her presence and turned toward her.

"Hello," he said with a smile and a distinct sparkle in his eyes. He was happy to see her. If she believed his feelings for her had changed, she would never be able to take this step. As it was, she had no problem closing the distance between them and lifting her lips to his. She felt his surprise quickly melt into a warm response that had once been so familiar to her. She pressed her hands over his shoulders, and he wrapped her in his arms, kissing her with a fervor that brought tears to her eyes.

"Iris," he murmured when their kiss had ended, but he kept her firmly in his embrace. "You know how I feel about you."

"Do I?"

His eyes sparkled with subtle humor. "You're going to make me say it, aren't you."

She felt no humor at all as she replied, "If you don't say it, how can I believe it?"

He put a hand on her face, touching one cheek, then the other. "And how do I know that if I say it, you won't throw it back at me and use it against me?"

Iris smiled and touched his face in return, exploring the stubble there that indicated the day was almost over. "You're just going to have to trust me."

"Oh, well," he drawled with light sarcasm. "I said I'd forgiven you. I didn't say I trusted you."

"So, what would make you trust me?"

"The truth," he said firmly. "I've seen the truth in your eyes for months now." He lowered his voice. "But how can I believe it if you don't say it?"

"So, I'll say it." She drew a deep breath and was surprised at how easily the confession rolled out of her. "I love you, Casey Harrison."

Case was entirely unprepared for how her words impacted him. A thousand times since anger and distrust had come between them, he'd imagined her saying it with such conviction, but he'd not anticipated his own emotional response. He put a hand over his eyes to hide the tears, then moved it over his heart as if he could hide the way it burned in his chest. "Wow," he said and sniffled, rubbing his eyes with his fingers in an attempt to force the tears back. "I think you really mean that."

"I really do," she said. "I was just . . . afraid, and . . . for that too . . . I'm sorry."

Case took in her words, her eyes, the change in her countenance. He was struck with a memory and felt compelled to share it. "Remember that day in the library?" he said. "When you fell?"

"Of course I do." It seemed like another lifetime to Iris; it *was* another lifetime.

"You asked me later what I'd come to talk to you about."

"That's when you first asked me to marry you," she said with a smile.

"Yes, but . . . what I also wanted to tell you . . . was that I loved you."

Iris felt stunned. "You barely knew me; we didn't even like each other."

"I know. But I knew we were supposed to be together."

"You knew?"

He touched her face. "Yes. Yes, I knew. But there have been many times since that I had trouble believing it could be possible." He smiled, then chuckled. "I love you too, Iris," he murmured and kissed her again. "I believe I loved you before this world was ever created." He spoke with his lips close to hers. "And I will love you for all eternity." He kissed her once more.

Iris looked into his eyes and nearly expected a marriage proposal, but they were interrupted by the boys coming in search of him. He smiled and winked at her, saying, "May I count on a walk after these crazy monkeys are in bed?"

"I'll be looking forward to it," she said and went to see if her parents needed anything.

Later that evening, after supper was cleaned up, everyone was surprised to find James sitting down by the fire. Eleanore began to scold him, but he said, "I feel the need to talk to my family. I asked the Lord to make that possible. I won't stay out long, I promise." He asked everyone to sit down so that he could share the thoughts he'd been having before they had prayer. Iris discreetly eased close to Case and held his hand while they listened to her father share a firm testimony of the truth and light of the gospel, and his gratitude for all he had been blessed with. Iris felt deeply touched by what he was saying, but she hoped it wasn't being spurred by some preparation to leave his family. She ignored that possibility and focused only on his marvelous wisdom and insight as he spoke of the different pieces of information he'd gathered from others who had come from Salt Lake since spring; some that he'd spoken with back in Iowa, some in passing through the course of their journey. He talked of the two handcart companies who had set out the previous summer, how he'd helped those people and had come to know many of them. He talked of the disaster that had befallen them, of the lives lost and the sacrifices made. He expressed gratitude that their own journey had not been fraught with such intense challenges, and that his family had remained healthy and safe. He specifically spoke of his thankfulness for Eleanore doing so well in bringing Olivia into the world, and to see her feeling better every day.

James then became mildly emotional as he said, "Captain Martin tells me that we will be crossing the Sweetwater River tomorrow. I've heard more than once a story regarding those handcart companies and this river, and I now feel strongly compelled to share it. My thoughts have been with it for hours, and of the meaning I believe it has for all of us. Perhaps it's a story that will be passed down for many generations and have meaning for all who share our beliefs for decades to come."

He told the story of the rescue parties that Brigham Young had sent out for the companies once he'd gotten word of their plight. But even with the help they'd been given, the people were so physically weary and emotionally overwrought that when they reached the banks of the river on a cold November day, many broke down and simply couldn't cross. Some young men in the rescue parties carried many of the Saints over the river. James couldn't speak for several long moments while he struggled to gain his composure. He then bore personal witness to the times in his life when he likely wouldn't have been able to keep going if not for God sending someone into his life to carry him through. He spoke individually to each person there, telling them how their lives had touched his own, how they had inspired and strengthened him. Then he asked them to all remember as they crossed the Sweetwater the following day those people in their lives that God had sent to carry them through the difficult times. He finished by bearing testimony of the Savior, then he asked Frederick to offer a prayer. By the time the prayer was finished, James was having difficulty breathing, and he asked Case and Frederick to help him back to the wagon.

Iris felt the spirit and impact of her father's words remain with her as she helped her mother with the baby, then got Mariah ready for bed. She was glad to see that her father seemed fine now that he was back in the sanctuary of the wagon's cover that somehow miraculously kept him protected. When everyone was down for the night, Iris told Mary Jane she would be coming to bed a little later, and asked her to watch out for Mariah. She found Case standing near the dying fire, staring into its few remaining embers. She slipped her hand into his and said, "You owe me a walk."

"So I do," he said with a smile that quickened her heart. But he stood where he was as he expressed how touched he felt by everything her father had said. Iris agreed with him, and together they marveled at what a great man he was, and how blessed they were to know him.

While they talked, Iris found it difficult to believe how perfectly comfortable she felt with Case, but it was easy to see, looking back, that even through their arguments and bantering, they had grown accustomed to each other, and had come to know each other well. She was deeply grateful for that level of comfort as she wrapped her arms tightly around him and settled her head against his chest. Thoughts of her father brought to mind the state of his health, and she had to speak her most prevalent thought. "He's going to die, isn't he."

Iris felt Case sigh as he tightened his embrace. He pressed a kiss into her hair. "I don't know, Iris. He was told he would live to see Zion with his family. Beyond that, I don't think the Lord's making any promises." He pressed a hand into her hair, holding her more tightly. "He's the finest man I've ever known. I don't see how anyone who knows him can bear to live without him."

"Case," she said, breaking the silence of deep thought, "if my father's time on this earth is nearly done . . . if it's inevitable that it's his time to go . . . then wouldn't it be pointless to pray that he will live?"

"Of course we must accept God's will above all else," he said, "but I still think we should ask. And maybe we'll be blessed with a miracle." He kissed the top of her head. "It certainly can't hurt to ask."

Iris looked up at him. "You're just like him, you know."

"Am I?" He chuckled. "I think that's the nicest thing anyone has ever said to me."

"Well, it's true. You're both stubborn and proud, and . . ." her voice quivered, "overflowing with integrity and . . . goodness, and . . . you're both completely . . ." It took her several seconds to work through her emotions enough to finish with a word she'd never believed she would attribute to Casey Harrison. But now that she'd come to see it, she could see that it fit him perfectly. "Completely trustworthy," she finally said.

Case was so stunned he could hardly breathe. Even though he now had much evidence that she trusted him, he'd not quite come to believe it. Aside from the sensation giving him a momentary empathy for James's condition, he felt consumed with the realization that he could actually allow himself to accept how he felt about her, and that it was all right to feel it. He could only smile and kiss her, realizing he felt completely exhausted at the same moment as he sensed that she felt the same. He walked her to her wagon and kissed her again while he silently thanked God for more miracles in his life than he could count.

* * * * *

The night crept on while Iris lay wide awake, still unable to perceive the wonder of all the good that had happened in her life in so short a time. She felt at peace with herself and completely happy at the prospect of sharing her life with Case. Her love for Case—and his for her—filled every crevice of her being with hope and joy. Thoughts of his kiss made her heart quicken and her stomach quiver. She could see the future spreading out before them, living it together, as naturally as knowing the sun would continue to rise each morning. Then her thoughts would shift to her father, and every morsel of joy became immediately counterbalanced with equally unfathomable dread. The future felt perfectly right with Case in it, and entirely wrong without her father there at every turn. James Barrington was the most solid, unmoving aspect of her life. She found strength in the gospel, and nothing could compare to her testimony of its truths. Her mother was her best friend, and she'd be lost without her. Every member of her family was precious to her, and losing any one of them would be devastating and unthinkable. But her father had been there from the start. There was a life Iris had lived long before this one, a childhood long before Eleanore had become the governess and eventually her stepmother, a world where James Barrington had been her guiding force and her one true star. Long before the gospel had come into her life, Iris had been able to look to her father and find answers to questions that had made no sense to her. He had compensated for her own mother's lack of love and her deplorable behavior. He had taught her truth and integrity. He had remained steady through every storm. And now she had to face the possibility that the remainder of his life was being measured in weeks, perhaps days. How could it be? What would she do without him? An endless flow of tears accompanied the questions most prominent in her mind. And the answer appeared readily. Casey Harrison. He could never replace her father in her life, but he could hold her steady when she might otherwise fall. If anyone could carry her through life's difficulties and hold her together, it would be Case. In fact, he already had. His very presence was evidence of God being mindful of her—and her family. That reminder in itself gave her some glimmer of peace. Case would be a strength to all of the family, and he had already proven he was capable of doing so. He could never replace the man James Barrington was, but he could help fill the void.

Iris curled deeper into the bed and felt Mariah shift in her sleep, making her usual funny little noises as she did. She was grateful for the perspective in her mind and the comfort in her spirit. But neither could eradicate the fact that her father was dying. And for all of her knowing that they could be together again in the next life, she couldn't imagine how much she was going to miss him in this one. She'd always taken for granted that he would be involved in her life for years to come, that he would be the strength to her children that he'd been to her. It was easy to imagine him being a grandfather, and to envision the joy he would find in his posterity. Now she wondered if she truly had to accept that such a vision would never come to pass in this life.

Iris heard noises outside and became alert. She'd learned long ago that there was no good in becoming alarmed. Then the pace of her heartbeat responded to hearing her name whispered.

"Iris," Case repeated, "are you awake?"

"Yes," she whispered back, glad to note that both Mariah's and Mary Jane's breathing remained even. "What are you doing?"

"I need to talk to you," he said. "Can you come out here?"

"I'm coming," she answered, grateful for the hundredth time since this journey began to be sleeping in her clothes.

Iris slithered out of the wagon and found a strong hand there to help her step down. The moment her feet touched the ground, she was in his arms, consumed by his kiss. "I couldn't sleep," he muttered. "I had to see you." He kissed her again. "I didn't wake you, did I?"

"No," she said, hearing a dreaminess in her own voice that almost made her laugh. "I couldn't sleep either." Thoughts of her father fled completely while she urged Case to kiss her again.

"That's good," he said, then chuckled. "I didn't *want* to wake you, but I probably would have anyway." He kissed her still again.

"Oh, Case," she murmured against his lips, "I can't believe this is happening to me."

"I know exactly how you feel. That's why I need to talk to you."

"And it couldn't wait until morning?" She laughed softly. "Not that I'm complaining."

"No, it couldn't wait until morning. Once morning comes we'll be on the move again, and we can't wait another day."

"What do you mean?"

"Marry me, Iris," he muttered with fervency. "I love you. I know this is right. I don't want to wait any longer."

Iris laughed through her tears and lifted her lips to his before she muttered in return, "Of course I'll marry you. The sooner the better."

Case chuckled and kissed her again. The miracles just kept flowing.

* * * * *

The following morning, Case was up earlier than usual, watching for any sign that James might be awake while he went about his usual chores. Once Eleanore came out of the wagon, Case called to James, "Hey, old man, are you awake?"

"Yes," James drawled. "What do you need?"

Case pushed the cover of the wagon aside and said, "I need to ask you a question."

"I'm listening," James said with a sparkle of humor in his eyes that made Case wonder if he knew what was coming.

"I need to ask for your daughter's hand, sir. I want to marry her . . . right away . . . if it's all right with you."

James chuckled and said, "I think that's the stupidest question you've ever asked me." He smiled, but his eyes were firm and resolute. "If she'll have you, I'll kiss your feet."

"No," Case chuckled, "I think that *I* will kiss *yours.*"

He discussed his plans briefly with James, then hurried to find Captain Martin. He was able to make the arrangements so quickly and easily that he felt sure God had known for quite some time that it needed to happen on this day.

Before the wagons started to roll, Case found Iris and kissed her before he said, "We're getting married today."

"Today?" she echoed and laughed.

"If that's all right."

She kissed him again. "Oh, it's more than all right," she said, then they had to part to get to the wagons.

While Iris drove, she couldn't keep from laughing spontaneously every so often, and occasionally she wept. She was overcome with more awe and elation than she had ever felt. She was especially amazed to feel so thoroughly happy out in the middle of nowhere, sticky with dust and sweat, and baking under the summer sun. The only deterrent to her happiness came with concern over her father's health, but even the prospect of losing him didn't seem quite so unbearable, now that she had Case to stand beside her, no matter what the future might bring. She certainly didn't *want* to live without her father, and prayed that he might be spared. But for the first time since she'd learned of his physical ailment, she believed that she could actually survive losing him, if his time on this earth was indeed drawing to a close.

The wagons stopped while some repairs were done farther ahead in the company. Not thirty seconds after they came to a halt, Case was helping her down with his hands at her waist, and then he was kissing her, as if she were water and he'd had nothing to drink through these many hours in the hot sun.

"Oh, I love you!" he muttered, and she laughed softly before he kissed her again.

"I love you, too," she whispered and kissed him still again.

They forced themselves apart to see that all was in order, and before they started again, Iris found Eleanore next to her on the seat, with a pillow to sit on.

"Hello, Mother," Iris said.

Eleanore smiled. "I hear we're having a wedding later today."

"That's what I hear," Iris said and laughed softly.

"You're obviously happy."

"I am," Iris said with fervor. "Now that I've stopped being such a fool, I'm more happy than I'd ever thought possible."

"I know that kind of happiness," Eleanore said, "although I didn't feel it until long after I'd actually married your father. But when those feelings finally came to life in me, it was surely one of the most heavenly feelings possible on this earth."

"I'm certain you're right."

They were silent a few minutes before Eleanore said, "The present circumstances are not very conducive to a pleasant honeymoon."

Iris took in the implication and felt a little embarrassed, while at the same time tingling with anticipation. Keeping her thoughts in the moment, Iris felt certain her mother had a distinct purpose for this conversation. They had long ago discussed the sensitivities regarding the intimate relationship between a man and a woman, and the profound importance of keeping such intimacy within the bonds of marriage. Iris wondered if her mother would repeat any of that now, but it seemed she was either gathering her words or waiting for Iris to comment. Iris opted for a question, "Where did you spend *your* honeymoon?"

"We didn't have one," Eleanore said, but not without a little smile. "At least, we didn't travel anywhere. We remained at home since we were very busy making preparations to go to America. But we *were* living in the manor house, with every possible luxury. Now, you're getting married in the middle of . . . this." She motioned with her hand to the wide expanse of hot and dusty plains.

"It's all right," Iris said. "When you love someone, just being together can make all of *this,*" she mimicked with light sarcasm, motioning the same way with her hand, "almost tolerable."

"That's definitely true," Eleanore said. "And you're finally admitting that you love him; that's good."

It took a moment for Iris to grasp the implication. "How long have you known?"

"What? That you love him?" Iris nodded, and Eleanore smiled. "I've suspected for . . . well, before we left home; I don't know exactly."

Iris sighed. "I feel like such a fool."

"There's no need for that. You've come to terms with your feelings now. The past doesn't matter. Your father and I are both very happy for you. Case is a good man; he'll take good care of you."

"Yes, I'm certain he will."

There was silence for a few moments before Eleanore said, "I'm certain you know enough to be prepared for marriage." Iris knew she was speaking of intimacy again. "But if you have any questions, you know that you can ask me anything."

"Yes, I know . . . and I'm grateful for that." Iris wondered if she *did* have questions, and if so, how she might actually put them into words. Memories of previous conversations with her mother over sensitive topics left her confident that she *could* ask anything and get a fair, straightforward answer without any embarrassment or shame.

Eleanore added gently, "The most important thing to remember is that no greater happiness can be found in this world than in the righteous, intimate relationship between a man and a woman. The more that time passes and you become more comfortable with each other, the more you will find great joy and a marvelous sanctuary from the struggles of life in all that you share with your husband."

Iris measured her mother's words with her feelings for Case and felt deep peace, along with a tremor of anticipation. The two of them talked for a long while about marriage and other things while Iris gained a new level of appreciation for her relationship with this fine woman. She thanked God for the day her father had brought Eleanore into their family, and then she thanked Him for putting Case there, as well.

* * * * *

Case and Iris were married on the bank of the Sweetwater River, with everyone in the company present. After their vows had been finalized with a kiss, he lifted her into his arms and carried her across the river. Iris felt it was appropriate that he would; he'd many times carried her through the difficulties of her life.

The remainder of the company crossed the river while they sang together, then the wagons were rolling again, pressing on toward Zion. A brother in the company offered to drive one of their wagons for the remainder of the day so that Case and Iris could at least sit together on their wedding day.

"You're very good at that," Iris said to her new husband, nodding to the reins in his hands.

"And you've come a long way to actually let me drive," he said and chuckled.

Iris smiled at him and declared firmly, "A woman should be able to admit that there are some things much better done by a man, and there are many things best shared with an eternal companion."

"Hear, hear," Case said and kissed her.

That evening during supper, Case and Iris endured some gentle teasing about the change in sleeping arrangements. Ben would be watching out for the boys, and Mariah would be in Lizzie's care, so that Case and Iris could share a wagon. They took the teasing all in stride and joked about the luxurious honeymoon suite and the beautiful surroundings that would contribute to any romantic vacation.

When it came time to settle down for the night, Iris felt more nervous than she'd anticipated. But Case just held her in his arms for a long while, talking of his happiness and the life they would share together. When being close to him seemed the most natural thing in the world, the rest was easy and more wondrous than she ever could have imagined. For one tiny moment, Iris wondered about the women in Case's past, but she pushed that thought away. He'd repented, and he'd been forgiven, and such things had no place in the life they shared together.

The journey from that point became easier for Iris. The days were as long and tedious as they had been since leaving Iowa City, and Iris would have preferred to be with Case every minute. But they were each needed to drive separate wagons, and she always had the end of the day to look forward to, when they could be together. She'd never imagined that she could be so happy, and certainly not in such surroundings. Case's presence in her life hadn't changed the hardship of the journey, but it had made the journey worth enduring.

After stopping in Fort Bridger for supplies, the company embarked on the final—and perhaps most difficult—stretch of the journey. The mountains that had to be crossed in order to reach the Salt Lake Valley were ominous and even frightening. But Iris rejoiced in the realization that they were almost there, and the journey was nearly behind them. And while they traversed those final days, her spirit came to understand that Zion wasn't just a place, it was an attitude, a way of living. It was holding the light of Christ in one's heart and making Him the center of all things. She had found Zion with her family long ago, and with her husband more recently. Zion was firm in her heart long before they finally emerged from Emigration Canyon to see the valley spreading out before them, glowing in the sun.

* * * * *

James refused to remain inside the wagon as they finally descended into the Salt Lake Valley. He held the reins himself for the first time in weeks, while Eleanore sat at his side, both silently in awe. He knew she shared his disbelief that they had finally arrived, that they would, at last, be given the great privilege to live among the Saints. The years that had passed while this had been their utmost desire felt eternal to James, and yet in a strange way, now that they were here, the time didn't seem so long. In the eternal perspective, the wait hardly felt significant.

James had to wipe an occasional tear as the wagon company entered the city, and the welcome they received was beyond anything he'd ever imagined. And he knew that Eleanore was weeping. The thriving sense of the community reminded him of being in Nauvoo many years earlier. They'd not been there for long, and at the time, James had been resistant to accepting the gospel. But his memories of Nauvoo were clear and strong; they'd hovered in his mind all these many years, offering him some measure of a prototype for what it might be like when they were finally able to live in Zion. And now they were here. He couldn't believe it! His chest burned with inexpressible joy.

Following their arrival in the city, it didn't take long to find the two homes, side by side, where Sally and Miriam lived. As the four wagons belonging to the Barrington household came to a stop in front of the houses, both women ran out of their front doors, squealing with laughter, as if they'd both happened to be near a window and had become aware of the grand arrival at the very same moment. Eleanore jumped down from the wagon and was quickly smothered by her friends. The three women gripped each other in a tiny circle, laughing and weeping beyond the ability to speak. Members of Sally's and Miriam's families followed them to the street while the occupants of the wagons all got out and gradually became a part of the reunion. Embraces and handshakes went around in abundance amidst exclamations of how much children had grown and people had changed. And introductions were made for those who had never met. Miriam had been gone before many of James's and Eleanore's children had been born. Mark and Sally had never met anyone in the family but James, Eleanore, and Frederick. And Iris was pleased to introduce her husband to all of them.

Somewhere in the midst of all the excitement and chatter, James felt his chest constricting. He immediately took hold of Case's arm, since he happened to be standing the closest. Their eyes barely met before Case said, "Eleanore, we need to get your husband inside."

Eleanore turned toward them with panicked eyes, but James had come far beyond embarrassment over this problem. He was too afraid of having to leave his family to care how much they fussed and fretted over the problem.

"Are you all right?" Eleanore asked, taking hold of his shoulders. He could only shake his head.

"What's wrong?" Sally demanded, and Case gave her—and everyone else within earshot—a brief and accurate explanation of the problem.

"We need to get him inside and get him clean," Case insisted as if he knew these people as well as anyone.

With due efficiency, James was taken into Sally's home, where he was quickly able to bathe, even though the water wasn't very warm. Wearing clean clothes borrowed from Mark, he hoped that whatever he'd been breathing that was the greatest source of the problem would be washed away. He felt mildly better for a short while, but the difficulty in breathing didn't relent. While everyone else was busy, divided between Sally's and Miriam's households, bathing and catching up, James lay on top of the patchwork quilt spread over a bed that was more comfortable than he'd enjoyed in months. But he didn't feel comfortable at all. He closed his eyes and prayed earnestly, at the same time willing himself to take deep, even breaths. But he couldn't fill his lungs; his breaths felt shallow and strained, and the subtle wheezing sound he made thundered in his own ears, sounding an alarm regarding the urgency of the matter.

When Eleanore came to check on him for the third time in an hour, his panic increased to see her expression.

"What?" he demanded, his voice unusually raspy.

"James," she muttered and went to her knees beside the bed, holding his hand tightly. She said nothing more, but the tears in her frightened eyes explained everything.

"We need to be sealed," James said.

Eleanore nodded and attempted to accept the implication. It had been her greatest wish for many years to be sealed to her husband, so that they could be together for all eternity. But now that this day had come, her joy was tethered with sorrow and fear. Her husband had been promised that he would live to be sealed. But after that? Was the end truly drawing close for him? Would she be left to endure many years alone in this life until they could be reunited? Her thoughts were made worse by the stark evidence on James's face that the situation was grave. His skin and lips had an unnatural color, and the sound made by his breathing left her terrified. She gripped his hand tightly with both of hers, as if doing so might hold him to this world. The expectancy in his eyes reminded her that she needed to respond to his plea. "I know," she said. "Mark has gone to arrange it. He's certain that President Young will see us right away when he learns of the situation." Eleanore wiped tears with one hand while keeping hold of his with the other. Then she saw tears run from the corners of her husband's eyes into his hair, and she wiped those away as well.

"Everything will be all right," he said with a forced smile. "We're here, Eleanore. We did it. We've come to Zion, and we're together." He brought her hand to his lips and kissed it, repeating, "Everything will be all right."

Eleanore nodded stoutly, wanting to believe him. In the eternal nature of things, it surely would be. But at the moment, she could only try to comprehend how she might survive without him. The very idea was so painful she had to push it away. Instead she sat on the edge of the bed and bent over to kiss him, trying to ignore all of the physical evidence that indicated his life was being measured in hours.

Case and Iris came through the open door, and Eleanore turned toward them, making no effort to hide her tears. Eleanore knew they shared her concern and understood her emotion when they got a good look at James. Their shock was evident.

"Papa," Iris said, moving to the other side of him. She sat on the bed and took his other hand. "Please don't leave us," she cried.

"It's not up to me, Iris," James whispered.

"We need to give him a blessing," Case said and left the room, returning in seconds with Frederick at his side. Eleanore silently prayed that her husband might be given some miraculous promise of being healed, while at the same time she had to concede that her prayers could not override God's will.

In the blessing, James was told that his Heavenly Father was pleased with his faithfulness, and that his posterity would be richly blessed for many generations because of it. He was promised the blessings of eternity with his loved ones, and told that his breathing would improve in order for him to do what was needed. Eleanore was grateful to hear that he would hold on, but *how long* he might do so was vague. After the amen was spoken, James did look a little better, and his breathing was not so strained. Mark returned to tell them that President Young would see them in his office the following morning. Eleanore wanted to shout and say that it was too soon. If the prophet were not able to see them for a few days, or a week, then perhaps her husband's life would be extended and she would be able to share a few more moments with him.

Throughout the evening, Eleanore forced her thoughts away from her fears of the future, and instead soaked in the glorious joy of the present. Ralph, Lu, and Amanda were summoned from their nearby home, and Eleanore wept again to embrace her dear friends whom she'd missed so much. James became teary as well when he saw them. They were like family, and now they were together again. Everyone gathered for a lovely supper that tasted all the better after months of what they'd been able to cook on campfires as they crossed the plains. There were so many people that most of them had to eat outside, but the joy in these reunions filled the air, both inside and out. James remained in bed, and Eleanore stayed close to him most of the time, while others came and went from the room, talking and laughing and behaving as if nothing in the world was wrong. Little Olivia was passed around and fussed over with a great deal of joy from everyone.

After they were all settled for the night and the baby was sleeping, Eleanore lay close to her husband's side, her hand on his chest, conscious of it moving up and down with each breath, reassuring her that he was alive. They spoke quietly of their joy in finally being among the Saints after so many years, then James drifted to sleep, and Eleanore wept silently, praying with all her soul that her husband might be spared. And if it were truly his time to go, she prayed that she might be strengthened enough to endure his absence and help her family through such an unfathomable loss.

Eleanore woke twice in the night to the baby's cry, then went back to sleep when Olivia did, having first assured herself that James was breathing. As noisy as his breathing had become, it wasn't difficult to tell. She came awake to sunlight filling the room, and Olivia still sleeping. Hearing no sound at all, her heart pounded to consider the possibility that James might have died in the night. She turned over abruptly, but found him absent. Her panic took on a different color as she wondered what foolishness he might be indulging in that could worsen his condition. Eleanore pulled on a robe and hurried into the hall. The upstairs was quiet and empty, and she realized she'd slept late. A burst of laughter in the distance lured her down the stairs to find its source. She entered the kitchen to see it crowded with friends and members of her own family. She first noticed Case sitting on a chair with Iris on his lap, and she was struck with how thoroughly happy they looked. Hearing her husband's voice, she turned to see him sitting across the table from Case and Iris, looking as healthy as he had the day she'd met him. Her startled gasp stopped the conversation, and everyone turned to look at her. She ignored everything and everyone but James. As she crossed the room, he came to his feet with no struggle. A little sob escaped her lips as she pressed her hands to his face and took note of his healthy color and effortless breathing.

"You're all right?" she asked.

He chuckled and kissed her quickly. "I've never felt better."

Eleanore laughed, then cried, wrapping her arms tightly around him, not caring what the others might think of her emotion.

"It's a miracle," she heard Case say.

"We've had a lot of those," Iris added.

Eleanore laughed again as the children all crowded around them, bombarding them with a circle of hugs.

"Yes, we certainly have," James said, looking into her eyes. He smiled and added, "Welcome to Zion, Mrs. Barrington."

Epilogue

The Jesse B. Martin Company arrived in the Salt Lake Valley on September 12, 1857. The following day, James and Eleanore Barrington were sealed for all eternity in the office of President Brigham Young. Frederick and Elizabeth Higgins were also sealed, as well as Casey and Iris Harrison.

Two days later, according to the prophet's specific instructions, the family began a journey south, over the point of the mountain, to a beautiful community nestled in the mountains. President Young had recently changed the name of this lovely town from Mountainville to Alpine, because of the majesty of the peaks that were reminiscent of the Swiss Alps.

James had no difficulty with his breathing or any other matters of health throughout the course of their journey, or while they worked together to build their homes in this place where they intended to stay and live out their lives among the Saints. According to a promise given to James and Eleanore at the time of their sealing, they would grow old together there, and find great joy in their posterity.

AUTHOR'S SUGGESTIONS FOR READERS GROUP DISCUSSION

1. Knowing the eventual outcome, what feelings are evoked in the reader when James is concerned for the members of the handcart companies that left in July of 1856?

2. How does Casey's life, before and after his baptism, illustrate the miracle of the gospel?

3. What do you feel was the greatest contributing factor to Iris's antagonism?

4. What can we learn from Iris's attitude toward Casey about Christ-like acceptance and forgiveness?

5. Although the Barrington family has wealth and financial security, what do we see concerning where their hearts are as they prepare to go west?

6. How can we apply in our lives today the faith that caused James to immediately do as the Lord told him when he received the personal revelation to take his family to the Salt Lake Valley?

7. Concerning the spiritual changes Iris underwent, what can we learn about eliminating pride from our own lives, and the importance of remaining close to the Spirit?

8. How does the journey west for the Saints symbolize our journey through life?

ABOUT THE AUTHOR

Anita Stansfield, the LDS market's number-one best-selling romance novelist, is a prolific and imaginative writer. Her novels have captivated and moved hundreds of thousands of readers, and she is a popular speaker for women's groups and in literary circles. She and her husband, Vince, are the parents of five children and grandparents of one and live in Alpine, Utah.